MOONSTONE
Beach

LINDA SEED

MOONSTONE Beach

Linda Seed

MOONSTONE BEACH. Copyright © 2015 by Linda Seed.

The author is available for book signings, book club discussions, conferences, and other appearances.

Linda Seed may be contacted via email at lindaseed24@gmail.com or on Facebook at www.facebook.com/LindaSeedAuthor.

Front cover photo by Soloviova Liudmyla.
Back cover photo by miramiska.
Cover design by Kari March.

ISBN-13: 978-1518-6289-17
ISBN-10: 1-5186-2891-5
First Trade Paperback Printing: October 2015

For John
Now and always

Chapter One

"Well, look what the cat dragged in."

Althea Morgan, sales assistant at Swept Away, peered with disdain at Kate Bennet, the bookstore's owner, as Kate hurried into the store. "I expected you at nine. And here it is … " She checked her watch. " … Almost *nine forty-two*." The woman had her fists planted on her impossibly narrow hips, and her lips were pursed, causing unsightly lines to form around her mouth. "We've had a rush, and I had to get orders ready to ship, and I didn't know *when* you were going to come in, so I had to tell Mr. Belmont that I … "

"Althea." Kate had barely gotten in the door, and she was still balancing a stack of books and her purse in her arms.

"Now, I know it's probably not my business, but … "

"*Althea.*"

"I'm just saying, it wouldn't hurt you to *call* … "

"ALTHEA!"

The older woman looked at Kate as though she'd suddenly been awakened from a nap during the REM cycle. She blinked several times, her brightly lipsticked mouth slack.

"I'm sorry I'm late, but I had some things to attend to. It was inconsiderate of me, you're right. I apologize." Kate smiled in what she hoped was a winning way. She teetered over to the counter on heels that were too high, and put down her things with a sigh of relief.

Althea, who would not reveal her age but was probably somewhere in her late sixties, patted her dark-dyed helmet of hair and straightened the flowy turquoise silk jacket she was wearing over white capris and a white tank. "Well. It just seems to me that as the *owner*, you should try to set some sort of *example* ...."

"You're right. I'm sorry," Kate said again.

"I just ..."

"Did Elliot call? I was expecting to hear from him about our quarterly taxes." In fact, Kate hadn't expected to hear from her accountant, but she hoped that an abrupt change of subject would derail Althea's criticisms. Once Althea got going, it was difficult to stop her by direct means.

"He might have. I've just been so *busy* trying to do everything alone, I didn't even have time to check the phone messages," Althea fussed.

Kate waited until Althea turned away, then rolled her eyes. Kate's friends who ran the shops on either side of her had urged her to stop placating Althea and fire the ill-tempered old bat—show her who ran the place once and for all—but the truth was that Kate couldn't bring herself to do it. Althea knew books. She often knew what Kate needed done before Kate knew it herself. But most importantly, Althea had been hired by Kate's mother, back when Lydia Bennet had built the business from nothing more than a dream. Lydia was gone now, but the spirit of what she had made here remained. So, Althea stayed, and Kate soothed and apologized.

"Those shoes probably slow you down," Althea said, pointing a heavily lacquered fingernail toward Kate's feet. "They are lovely, though."

Kate stuck out one foot and turned it this way and that, displaying it for Althea's approval. "They are, aren't they? I'm not the best with three-inch spikes, but they were half price. I think I just need practice."

Althea's lips pursed tightly. "Just make sure you don't break an ankle while you're practicing. With you in a cast, you wouldn't be able to do *anything* around here. Though, I can't see how that would be much different ... "

Kate pretended not to hear that last insult. She carried her books and her bag into the tiny back room, which was stacked with rare volumes, remainders, and damaged books that needed to be returned or repaired. She took a deep breath and inhaled the scent of old pages mixed with the briny smell of the ocean. It was an aroma that always made her happy.

This will never get old.

She ran a hand through her shoulder-length dark hair to smooth it and emerged into the front room of the store. The shop was small, with floor-to-ceiling bookshelves crammed with every possible genre: mystery, romance, literary novels, biography, history, and more. The hardwood floors and dark wood shelves created the sense that you'd gone back in time, to a library in an English country house that had seen better days but was, nonetheless, much loved. One middle-aged man in Bermuda shorts, a tank top, and wide leather sandals was browsing through the James Pattersons. Other than that, the place was empty except for Jane Austen, the Swept Away cat. This was what Althea called a rush?

"Good morning," Kate said warmly to the guy in the Bermudas. "Welcome to Swept Away. Is there anything I can help you find?"

"Oh, no thanks, I'm just browsing," he said.

"Of course," Kate answered. "Used mystery and crime paperbacks are buy one get one free all this week."

The guy brightened. "Hey! Thanks."

He selected four books for a total of $4.75 plus tax. Kate finished the sale, put the books into a bag, and wished the guy a lovely time in Cambria.

He was barely out the door before it burst open again, the bell attached to the top jingling in panic. A stunning woman with long, blond hair piled into a messy bun on the top of her head exploded into the room, her arms flying.

"Kate! You're here! What took you so long? Red alert! Red alert!"

Kate's eyebrows shot up. "Really?"

Lacy Jordan rushed behind the counter, grabbed Kate's arm, and yanked her toward the door. "Would I lie to you about a red alert?"

"Well, no. Where? Where?"

"In my shop! Hurry!"

Lacy was still wearing the coffee-stained apron she sported while serving customers at the espresso place next door. Her sneakers, with faded jeans and a tight white T-shirt, allowed her more freedom of movement than Kate had in her heels and pencil skirt.

"Oh, come on!" Lacy urged. "Why would you wear those shoes when you know there might be a red alert?"

"I guess I wasn't thinking," Kate said.

"I guess not!"

Kate click-clacked as quickly as she could across the sidewalk and past a pair of milling tourists, until Lacy thrust her by the arm through the door of Jitters, the coffee bar where her friend worked. The force with which Lacy propelled her through the door caused Kate to teeter on the heels before finally righting herself.

"Where?" she whispered, out of breath.

"Left rear corner."

Kate looked around the room until her eyes rested on the man sitting at a small, round café table, sipping something from a white ceramic cup.

"Oh," she breathed.

"Yeah."

It was him, all right. The first spotting had been three days earlier, at the wine tasting bar run by Rose Watkins, the third of their foursome of friends. The guy, a cross between David Beckham and Chris Hemsworth, was such a ticking bomb of sex appeal that Rose had immediately and surreptitiously called all of them over from their respective places of business to come in and get a look at him. After some discussion, they'd decided that he would be the perfect practice man for Kate, who—two years post-divorce—had recently decided she was ready to start dating again. Flirting was the first step, and who better to flirt with than a guy who could be a Calvin Klein underwear model?

The "red alert" system had been created to deal with any future sightings—not only so Kate could polish up skills that had suffered from disuse, but also so the other women could get another chance to bask in his glory.

"Did you call Rose and Gen?" Kate was whispering out of the side of her mouth, all systems in stealth mode, though Mr. Beautiful likely couldn't hear them from where he sat.

"Gen's not at the gallery, and Rose is stuck doing a tasting for a big group." She sighed. "He's all ours."

"Wow." They stood together, thinking. "Well, I'm just gonna start with a stroll to the ladies' room. Just a little fly-by. Get a better look," Kate said.

Lacy clapped her on the back companionably. "Good plan."

Kate took a deep breath and squared her shoulders. "Wish me luck. I'm going in."

She did one or two cleansing breaths and then started to walk casually toward the back of the shop. Just a woman on her way to the restroom. Nothing unusual going on here at all. The trick was to look at him while pretending not to look at him. He was facing away from her now, so the stealthy looking probably would work best on the way back.

As she passed, he was looking down at a newspaper that was folded next to his coffee mug. Black T-shirt stretched across a muscular back. Three-day scruff of beard. Black hair still wet. From a shower? From a dip at the beach? From surfing? Oh, surfing. She pictured him in a skin-tight wetsuit, hair dripping with ocean water. Yum.

It was this train of thought Kate was following—just as she was passing Mr. Beautiful's table—when the heel of her left shoe went into a groove of the fashionably rough-hewn wood floor, causing her to pitch forward. She pinwheeled her arms desperately to regain her balance, but it wasn't enough to keep her from colliding with the floor with a loud *whump*.

She was still lying there, trying to figure out how best to get up and maintain her dignity—though it was obviously too late for that—when she looked up and saw Mr. Beautiful looming over her.

"Are you okay?" He offered her a hand, but his eyes were drifting lower. She looked down and realized that her skirt had ridden up in the fall, exposing about three-fourths of her thighs.

"Um, yeah. Everything still works, I think." She blushed furiously. She slapped at her skirt to put it back into place as she took his hand and got to her feet. "Thanks."

"You'd better have a seat. Take a minute to regroup." He pulled out a seat at his table and ushered her into it. "I'm Zach." He offered her the hand she'd only moments ago released.

"Kate." They shook. His grip was firm, his palm cool and smooth. "Hey, look. I should go. I don't want to interrupt you in the middle of your ..." She waved her hand vaguely. "Your cappuccino and your newspaper and ..." More vague waving. "... And whatever it was you were doing."

He nodded sagely. "Cappuccino and newspaper do require a lot of concentration." One corner of his mouth quirked up in a sexy smile.

"Well." She blushed again. She could feel the red wave of her embarrassment start at her neck and move up toward her hairline.

"Can I buy you a coffee?" he offered.

"Oh. I ..." Before she could answer, Lacy called over from behind the counter.

"I've got your regular going, Kate! Soy latte, extra foam. Coming up!"

That woman could eavesdrop from the next town during a thunderstorm.

"Well, I guess that settles it," he said. "You sure you didn't hurt yourself? That was quite a fall."

"I'm sure," she said. "Just embarrassed. I'm such an idiot. It's these shoes. They're torture devices."

He peered down at her shoes—fire engine red pumps with pointed toes and stiletto heels—and let out a long whistle. "I've got to think they're worth the trouble," he said.

"Well, that's the hope, anyway." She crossed her legs and watched him watch them. "Are you in town visiting?"

He nodded, taking a sip of his cappuccino. He licked a bit of foam from his upper lip, and Kate felt her own mouth go dry. "Yeah. Just taking a little vacation. I'm staying at a B&B on the beach. The Central Coast is beautiful this time of year."

"It's beautiful any time of year."

Lacy came over with Kate's latte. She set the drink on the table and shot Kate a wink before hurrying away.

"Cambria was my wife's favorite place."

Wife? Was? She tried to figure out how to ask. "Is she …"

"We're divorced."

"Ah. Me too." Kate felt relieved that she hadn't stumbled onto a grieving widower. It would be a shame if she'd crashed into the hardwood only to have to console him while he cried and showed her pictures of the wedding.

No sooner had she thought it than he pulled a phone from his back pocket and scrolled through his photos before showing one to Kate. "Here she is. This is Sherry." His voice sounded wistful as he offered the phone to Kate.

"Wow." The woman in the photo was supermodel gorgeous, with long, silky black hair, eyes the color of espresso, and flawless skin the shade of warm caramel. Kate would not have been surprised to see a tiara and a sash. "She's beautiful."

"Yeah." He took the phone back and replaced it in his pocket. "We spent our honeymoon here."

"In Cambria?"

"In the same B&B."

Kate looked at him blankly. "Oh. And you came here because …"

"I guess I just wanted to feel close to her again." A tear came to his eye, and he brushed it away.

This encounter was so clearly going nowhere that Kate tried to think of a graceful way to excuse herself. With exquisite timing, Althea came bursting through the doorway of the café.

"Kate!" the older woman boomed, her face red, looking pissed-off.

"Oops. I'm so sorry, I have to get going," she told Mr. Beautiful, whom she now thought of as Mr. Sad and Beautiful. "I have to get back to work. I work next door. At the bookshop. I mean, I own it. The bookshop. I … Um. Bye. It was really nice to meet you."

She grabbed her latte cup and click-clicked with tiny little steps (all her pencil skirt would allow) toward the door. "I'm coming, Althea. Bye, Lacy! I'll see you later!"

Lacy shot her a questioning look, a *why are you leaving without a wedding date or at least a phone number* kind of glare. Kate put her thumb and pinkie to her face in the universal gesture of *call me*. Then she followed Althea out the door.

"Why, first you're late, and then you rush out the door in some kind of 'red alert' nonsense," the older woman was going on. "Sometimes it's like you don't take your work seriously at all, Katherine. I mean, it's beyond me. Your mother would never …"

Kate let her go on, barely listening.

Her cell phone was ringing on the bookstore's counter before Kate was even all the way inside.

"What happened? Why did you leave?"

Kate could hear espresso machines whirring and milk steamers hissing in the background.

"Yeah, that one's not gonna work out," Kate said.

"Why not? Is he too good looking? Is that it? Is the splendor of his beauty too much for your eyes?"

"He's mourning his wife."

"Oh. Yikes. Dead?"

"Divorced. He's here to relive their honeymoon. Alone. He showed me her picture."

Lacy was silent for a moment. "Yeah, that's not going any-where."

"No." With the phone to her ear, Kate started leafing through a pile of paperwork Althea had thrust in front of her. With dismay she noted that it was mostly bills.

"It's too bad," Lacy mused. "That pratfall of yours was pure genius. Part Julia Roberts, part Lucille Ball. I'm in awe. I'm so proud. I'm like a proud mama."

"I'd like to say I did it on purpose, but …"

"What?" Lacy called out. "What? I can't hear you over the espresso machine! I can't acknowledge a single thing you just said! I have to go! Bye, hon!"

Chapter Two

The next morning, Kate woke to the sound of someone rummaging around in her kitchen, banging cabinet doors and sifting through the silverware drawer. Groggy, she looked at the clock. Six thirty-two. Pale sunlight filtered through the white linen curtains above the bed. She rolled over and tried to go back to sleep, but then she started to smell coffee, which made it impossible. Damn it.

Squinty-eyed, she emerged from the bedroom to find Genevieve Porter pouring herself a mug of black coffee in Kate's tiny kitchen.

"You run out again?" She rubbed her eyes and yawned.

"Yeah. I hope you don't mind. You always have better coffee than I do, anyway."

"Mi casa es … something. It's too early for foreign languages." Kate took a thick ceramic mug from the cupboard above the coffee pot and poured herself a cup. She added cream and an obscene amount of sugar. That first sip tasted like sweet salvation.

"Ah, God. I want to be mad at you for waking me up at six-something-ridiculous, but you made me coffee. So there's that."

Genevieve, who rented the tiny downstairs apartment on the first floor of Kate's house, owned the Porter Gallery, a small storefront on Main Street that offered fine art as well as the seascape watercolors and ceramic tchotchkes the tourists loved. She was five-foot-two, with fiery red, curly hair that put one in mind of Merida, the Disney princess from *Brave*. Gen and Kate were, in some ways, opposites. While Gen worked out every day without fail, Kate had a vast and impressive array of excuses to avoid the gym. Where Gen was completely at home in a sheath dress and three-inch heels, Kate—as her encounter with Zach had proved—could barely manage in anything but flats. Gen was kale and egg-white omelets; Kate was Froot Loops and Pop-Tarts. Somehow, the contrasts had allowed them to complement each other in a way that had cemented their friendship from the day they'd met.

Gen was already dressed in spandex shorts and a pink, racer-back athletic top, running shoes on her feet, her mass of unruly hair coaxed into a more subdued ponytail. "Come for a run with me?" she said, batting her eyes at Kate over the rim of her cup.

"You've got to be on crack."

"Well, no. But the runner's high is pretty good."

"Get your happy, sunshiny, athletic self out of here before I beat you with a broom."

Gen cocked her head to the side, appraising Kate. "So that's no, then?"

"Shoo!"

When Gen was gone, Kate took her coffee mug out onto the back deck and sighed as she plopped into an Adirondack chair. The house, though old, small, and in a state of mild disrepair, had one of the best views in Cambria. It sat halfway up a hill that rose above the shoreline, giving the back deck a 180-degree view of the Pacific Ocean. Morning was the best time to enjoy the view, with the sun rising gently in the east. In the afternoon, it would be glaring down on her, prompting her to reach for a sun hat, sunglasses, and, ideally, a large umbrella. Right now, though, it was perfect; in June, the air was cool but not cold even this early in the morning. She could relax in her plaid pajama pants and T-shirt without the need for a sweat-shirt or a blanket to keep her comfortable.

As she sipped the strong, sweet brew, she heard sea lions barking from where they perched on the rocks below. Seagulls soared overhead. And on the grassy patch one story below, just outside Gen's back door, a doe grazed, its legs long and grace-ful. Kate kept quiet so she wouldn't disturb it.

This had to be paradise, and if it wasn't, she couldn't ima-gine anywhere better. Maybe if she'd been raised here, maybe if she'd grown up in this town on the Central California coast, gone to school here, rode her bicycle on the winding, hilly roads day after day, she might have become so familiar with its beauty that she'd have stopped seeing it. As it was, though, she was thankful every day to find herself here, despite the influx of tourists that disrupted the quiet every summer, despite the struggle of keeping the bookstore running, despite the little things that kept going wrong with the house—the roof that needed repair, the persistent ant problem, the plumbing that made a kind of singing noise when you turned on the water. All of that was insignificant compared with waking up to this.

Kate had inherited the house—and the business—from her mother about five years before. Lydia Bennet had been a housewife for most of her adulthood, but when Kate's father had left her for another woman ten years ago, when Kate was twenty-two, Lydia had taken it as a second chance at making a life of her own. She'd sold their house in Los Angeles, bought this place, and opened the bookstore. Lydia had hired Althea soon afterward.

Because Kate had been busy attending UCLA and then launching her own career teaching college-level English, she'd never lived in Cambria until her mother had died of ovarian cancer. Kate had come up here to feel closer to her mother, to grieve, to heal. Then she'd fallen in love with the place and had never gotten around to leaving.

She went inside for another cup of coffee and checked the clock. She didn't want to be late to the shop again and risk the wrath of Althea. The shop didn't open until ten a.m. on weekdays, but she'd agreed to come in early to meet with Althea to discuss their plans for the annual Cambria Art Walk.

The Art Walk name was misleading; the event had started out, many years ago, as a way for the town to highlight the many local artists who showed their work in Cambria's galleries. Tourists and locals were encouraged to go from gallery to gallery on a warm summer evening, taking in culture and sampling hors d'oeuvres and local wines. Over the years, the event had expanded as more and more local businesses had wanted in on the action. Now, it was more of an open house that ran all up and down Main Street on one night each July. No longer was it limited to art galleries. These days, pretty much everybody—the boutiques, the coffee houses, the souvenir shops, the restaurants, and, of course, the bookstore— offered something special to visitors on the night of the Art Walk. The events and attractions included everything from live music to ceramics demonstrations to food and craft booths set up on the sidewalks. Last year, the toy store down the street had hosted a juggling show that had been a favorite among families with children.

Althea insisted that Swept Away's usual offering—a book reading and signing, with free coffee and cookies—was the correct, and most dignified, way to go. After all, what else would a bookstore do but a reading? It made sense, Kate had to admit, but she couldn't help cringing when she remembered what had happened last year. The local author they'd brought in had been so epically boring, so inept a public speaker, that people had started walking out during the reading. To avoid embarrassing the author—a genuinely nice person and a very talented writer—Kate and Althea had rushed around on the street, finding their friends and using bribes, guilt, and quid-pro-quo promises to fill the modest number of folding chairs they'd set out in the shop. Their efforts had ultimately failed, and the author had slinked away with a crushed ego, pathetic sales, and a bakery box full of leftover cookies that had been purchased for a crowd that hadn't come.

This year, Kate wanted to do something different, something exciting. Unfortunately, she had no idea what it might be. She thought about it as she crunched on a bowl of Frosted Flakes at her kitchen table. She was halfway through the bowl when Gen, sweaty and breathless, poked her head in the front door.

"You should have come, Kate. It's awesome out here."

"Yeah. But why waste all that awesomeness with … you know, panting and sweating."

Gen looked at Kate's breakfast and scrunched up her nose. "You really need to do something about your nutrition."

"Hey," Kate said, changing the subject. "What's the gallery going to do for Art Walk?"

Gen came in and plopped down across from Kate at the table. "Don't know yet. We've got a pretty good show lined up—a local abstract expressionist I'm really excited about—but we need something … else. Something more."

Kate sighed. "I'm having that same problem. Althea wants boring. I don't want to do boring. We tried that last year."

"Ugh," Gen said. "I remember. The pain is still fresh." Her expression brightened suddenly. "Speaking of pain, I hear you ate the floor over at Jitters yesterday in front of Mr. Beautiful." She wiggled her eyebrows.

Kate grimaced. "Word travels fast."

"It does. I also heard that he invited you to have a coffee with him."

Kate got up to take her cereal bowl to the sink. "Did you also hear that he's like a lovesick puppy over his ex-wife?"

Gen slumped a little in her chair. "I heard that. Are you sure, though? I mean, maybe you misinterpreted things."

"He showed me her picture and cried."

Gen opened her mouth to say something, closed it, and looked at Kate. "I have literally no way to spin that to make it sound okay."

Kate waved an arm dismissively. "It doesn't matter. I could never be with a guy that good-looking anyway. I'd constantly feel all sad and frumpy in comparison."

Gen looked at her with sympathy. "You're not sad and frumpy."

"No. I don't think I am. But I would *feel* that way if I were dating a male supermodel. I'd look like me, like the Kate you're used to seeing, but I'd feel like that elf from Harry Potter. What's his name?"

"Dobby," Gen supplied.

"Right. I'd feel like Dobby."

"Yeah. I get it." Gen sighed. "I could probably manage it, myself."

Kate grinned. "Hey, go for it. Next time we have a red alert, you can be the one to go sprawling all over the floor, see what happens."

"I'll have some knee and elbow pads ready, just in case." Gen frowned. "Wait. That sounds kinky."

"It really does."

Kate looked at the clock, said, "Oh, crap," shooed Gen out, and hurried in to get showered and ready for work. She considered her wardrobe options, wistfully looked at her single pair of high-heeled shoes, remembered the humiliation of the day before, and chose flats instead.

"Althea, we can't just do a book signing. Last year was awful. Do I have to remind you what it was like having to practically abduct people from the street and force them into the shop? I was doing favors for *months* to pay people back."

Kate and Althea were sitting in the leather club chairs positioned in one corner of the store to give customers somewhere comfortable to read. The seating area was between the biographies and the military histories, just to the left of the diet books. It was an hour before opening, and Kate was holding a yellow legal pad on her lap, pen poised, ready to take notes should they come up with any brilliant ideas for the Art Walk. Which they hadn't yet.

"Yes, but book signings are what bookstores *do*," Althea insisted, not unreasonably. "We just need to get a better author this time."

"That's where we went wrong," Kate mused. "Todd Lansing *is* a good author. He's just not a good speaker. Which we didn't know."

"Well, we do now." Althea shook her head sadly at the memory.

"I'll say."

The legal pad was still blank, its long, yellow pages mocking her.

They both turned at the rap on the front door. Kate peeked through the glass and saw Rose Watkins standing there with a square white plate in her hand. Kate opened the door, and Rose rushed in, already talking.

"You've got to try these. You too, Althea. Tell me what you think, and don't hold back. If these are crap, I've got to know now. Only six weeks until Art Walk! I'm doing a wine and small plate pairing, and these are supposed to go with the merlot, but jeez, I'm not sure. They might go better with a pinot noir, but Jackson says, no, go with the merlot. Here. Eat, eat!"

Rose thrust the plate at them. The manager of De-Vine, the shop two doors down that offered wine tasting along with gourmet food items and various wine-related novelties, Rose was an unusual fit for the small-town atmosphere of Cambria. With her chin-length, purple hair, her nose and eyebrow piercings, and the rose tattoo that just peeked out above the neckline of her black T-shirt, she'd have been more at home in L.A. or New York City. The owner at De-Vine, an elderly woman who favored pink Lacoste polo shirts and pastel pleated slacks, had balked at first when Rose had applied for the job. But when she'd realized how much Rose really did know about wine—that Rose could tell the difference between a Napa cabernet sauvignon and one from Bordeaux simply by aroma—she'd decided that Rose's unconventional appearance was worth getting used to.

Kate peered at the plate and saw two ovals of bruschetta topped with a thin slice of Italian sausage and fennel. She reached out for one, and Rose yanked the plate back.

"Wait! Don't eat that! Just ... wait!" She put the plate on a side table and ran out the door and down the street toward the wine shop. Less than two minutes later she was back with two wine glasses in her hand, each bearing an ounce of deep red liquid.

She backed through the door because each hand held a glass, then spun and faced Kate and Althea. "The wine! You've got to have it with the wine, obviously, or how will you know if Jackson is right about the pairing? Now, I'm not going to tell you which wine is which. Just try the wine and the app together." She stopped, presumably for air.

Kate took a bite of bruschetta, followed by a sip from one of the glasses. Then, at Rose's insistence, she took another bite, then a sip from the other glass.

Rose looked at her expectantly. "Well? Which one do you like better?"

Kate wasn't sure she liked either one better than the other—they were both delicious—so she pointed at the glass on the right. "That one." Rose pumped a fist in the air in triumph.

"Okay. Althea, it's your turn."

Althea pursed her lips. "I'm sorry, dear. I don't take wine." She said it in the same tone one might say, *I don't shoot heroin.*

Althea reached out for the remaining piece of bruschetta, but Rose slapped her hand away. "You can't have it if you're not going to try it with the wine. Sorry."

She picked up the plate and the two wine glasses and headed back out the door. "Thanks, Kate!"

Kate took a deep breath, locked the front door behind Rose, picked up her legal pad again, and turned to Althea, ready to regroup and resume brainstorming ideas for the Art Walk. She had just managed to utter the words, "So, which authors … " when Jackson Graham tried to barrel his way through the door of the bookstore, found it locked, and pounded on the glass.

Althea opened the door, and Jackson charged in with Rose close behind him. His face was red, and the white apron he wore around his waist was lightly smeared with some kind of sauce. "Who's the idiot who wanted to pair the bruschetta with the pinot noir?"

Kate opened her mouth to speak, closed it, and then said, eloquently, "Uh ... " She was rendered speechless by her conflicting emotions. On one hand, she was intimidated by his obvious anger and disdain. On the other, she was immobilized by how absolutely steaming-hot sexy he was when he was mad. Which was most of the time.

"I guess ... well ... I suppose I'm the idiot," she said, raising her hand as though she were in second grade, waiting for the teacher to call on her but knowing she hadn't done her homework.

"She's not an idiot. She's right," Rose said.

He took one step back. "Oh." He ran a hand through his wavy, chestnut hair. "Well, look, I didn't mean ... but, really. The *pinot*?"

Jackson was head chef at Neptune, Cambria's most upscale restaurant. Apparently, he was helping Rose create a tasting menu for the Art Walk event. Kate had known Jackson since he'd moved to town three years before—known him in a *wave to each other on the street, give my regards to your aunt* kind of way. She might have gotten to know him better, but she was so often flustered by the man's tempest-like moods. The way he was looking at her now was hard to interpret. Was he personally offended by her choice of wine, or was he suffering from an annoying rash?

"I don't know anything about food and wine, except ... you know, I eat. And sometimes drink. Rose told me to pick one, so I picked one."

He planted his hands on his hips. "Well, you picked the *wrong* one."

She smiled at him sweetly. "Well, Rose seemed to think I chose correctly, and she *is* the prodigy."

"I am," Rose said helpfully.

He pointed a finger at Kate. "Just because she knows wine doesn't mean she … Why the hell am I arguing about this with you?" He stomped out of the store. Kate could practically see the steam rising from his ears. Rose winked at Kate and followed him.

"Well, he was certainly worked up," Kate told Althea after he'd left.

"Temperamental," Althea observed, her lips pressed into a judgmental line. "But the man *is* a genius with seafood and field greens."

Chapter Three

"I can't believe I called her an idiot." Later that night, Jackson sat at the bar at Ted's with Daniel Reed, a local glass artist who had been his friend since Jackson had moved to Cambria three years earlier. Ted's, a somewhat rundown saloon that offered pool, darts, and occasional live music on the weekends, was well off of Main Street, so its clientele was mostly locals rather than the tourists who took over the town every summer. Jackson found tourists to be a necessary annoyance. They paid the bills, but that didn't mean he had to hang out with them during his down time.

Now, Jackson took a deep drink from his beer bottle and ran a hand through his hair. "'Idiot.' That's what I said. *I'm* the idiot. Obviously."

Daniel nodded his head. "Can't argue with that. At the very least, your skills with women could use some improvement."

Jackson groaned. "Look. It's not like I'm *pining* for her or anything."

"Right. You're not pining."

"Of course not."

"And since you're not pining, I'm sure she's got nothing to do with the fact that you haven't dated anyone seriously in three years."

He looked up at Daniel, surprised. "That's not ... I've dated. I've dated *a lot.*"

"Sure, but it's been quantity, not quality." Daniel looked at Jackson with amusement in his hazel eyes. "You haven't been serious about anyone in three years. Hmm. That's about when you met her, isn't it?"

"Shut up."

"I'm just saying."

"And I'm just saying you should shut your pie hole."

Daniel raised his beer bottle to Jackson in mock salute. "Those people skills, right there, are the ones that are going to win you that woman's heart, mark my words."

Jackson groaned again, and put his head on the bar. "I'm screwed, aren't I?"

"Yep. And not in a good way."

They sat in companionable silence for a while, Daniel drinking, Jackson wallowing in misery.

"What I don't get," Daniel said finally, "is why you haven't made your move yet. You're single. She's single. You've had plenty of opportunity. Looks-wise, you're not completely repellent to women, probably. You're gainfully employed. What's the holdup?"

Jackson lifted his head from the bar and took a drink from his Widmer Hefeweizen, which was almost gone. "She wasn't single when I met her. She was married. And then she was going through a divorce, and I'm not stupid enough to get in the middle of *that*. And then …"

"And then you were so used to adoring her from afar that you didn't know how to change the dynamic."

He shrugged. "I guess."

"And then there's the other thing," Daniel said.

"What other thing?"

"The thing where you're an ill-tempered pain in the ass, and when women figure that out, they tend to run away like their hair's on fire."

"They don't always run away."

"The smart ones do. The ones whose daddies treated them right, taught them to expect better."

Daniel's assessment was so on-target it took Jackson's breath away. It also made him feel more hopeless than ever.

"Well, if I'm such an asshole, maybe I'd be doing her a favor to just forget the whole thing." Suddenly, he really needed another beer. He signaled for one from the bartender.

"Or, there's another alternative," Daniel offered.

"What's that?"

"Just stop being an asshole."

Jackson sighed deeply. "Yeah. Like that's gonna happen."

"There's another wrinkle." Daniel waited expectantly for Jackson to ask.

"Yeah? And what might that be?" He had to raise his voice to be heard over the music being played over the sound system and the loud, drunken chatter of the two guys at the pool table.

"I was over at the gallery yesterday and I heard Gen on the phone talking to Lacy over at Jitters. Seems Kate has decided she's ready to dip a toe back into the dating pool. The girls—Lacy, Gen, and Rose—have been trying to set her up with some guy staying over at the B&B on Washington Street. She had coffee with him." Daniel's eyebrows went up and down.

Jackson glared at him. "From your face, I'd guess 'having coffee' is a euphemism. Please tell me it was real coffee and not … you know. Metaphorical coffee."

Daniel barked out a laugh. "It was real coffee. The good news is, I don't think it went all that well. The bad news is, this guy's apparently some kind of Greek god or Speedo model or something."

Jackson should have been comforted that it hadn't gone well, but he was unaccountably irritable, as though he had a layer of sand under his skin that no amount of scratching would relieve.

"Well, why the hell are they trying to fix her up with *him*? If the guy's at the B&B, he's not local, so it's not going to go anywhere."

Daniel shrugged. "I think that's part of the appeal."

"What do you mean?"

"Well ..." He gestured with his beer bottle. "It makes sense when you think about it. Maybe she's ready for *something*, but she's not ready for a relationship. So she goes out with the guy, has some fun, he moves on, and now she's back in the game."

"Well, shit." He didn't want to think about her being *back in the game,* unless he was one of the players.

"Yep." Daniel picked up his beer bottle and clinked it against Jackson's, which sat, ignored, on the bar. "Seems to me she's not going to be the spinster book lady for much longer. Whatever you're gonna do, I'd say you'd better go ahead and do it."

Two days after the Jitters incident, one day after Jackson and Daniel deconstructed said incident at Ted's, Zach—the gorgeous hunk of man with the helpless longing for his ex-wife—came into Kate's bookstore. It was midafternoon, Althea had gone home for the day, and Kate had her head bent over a stack of invoices and an Excel spreadsheet when the bell on the front door started jingling merrily. At first, she didn't look up.

"Welcome to Swept Away," she said automatically, her eyes still on her calculations. "Romance is half off. Please let me know if there's anything I can help you find."

His voice was deep and sensuous when he answered. "Hi, Kate. I like your place."

Kate looked up in surprise. "Oh! Zach! It's nice to see you again. How's your vacation so far?"

"Well, a little lonely, to be honest. I was wondering if you could help me with that."

Was it her imagination, or was there something suggestive in his words? He meant books, surely. He wanted her to liven up his vacation by helping him to find some good reading.

"Um … What kind of genre were you looking for?"

"Genre?" He looked confused. Not a good sign.

"Action, suspense? Crime? Historical fiction? I've got some really great new releases." She came out from behind the counter and started to lead him to the New Fiction section. "What do you usually like to read?"

"Well." He rubbed a hand over the ridiculously sexy stubble on his chin. "I'm not much of a reader, actually. I'm more of an active guy. Hiking. Skiing. That sort of thing."

"Oh." Kate felt a kind of punch in the gut whenever someone told her they didn't read. How was it possible that someone didn't enjoy reading? That was like saying *I don't enjoy breathing.* It just didn't make sense.

"Actually, I …" He chuckled. "I'm trying to get up my courage, here. I came to see you."

"Me?"

"I was wondering if I could take you to dinner. They say Neptune's good. But I'm sure you've been there hundreds of times, since you live here and all."

Kate stood there with a book in her hand, looking at Zach, trying to hide her surprise. After their disastrous meeting at Jitters, she'd assumed he'd go back to wherever he lived and she'd never see him again. He was tall and muscular, with dark, thick hair and eyes like she'd seen on the does that grazed in her backyard. He was wearing a pair of faded Levi's that fit like they'd been made for him, and a muscle-hugging black T-shirt that showed just how devoted he must have been to his gym routine. His obvious heartbreak over his divorce notwithstanding, she should have been excited at the prospect of an evening out with a man who was as physically magnificent as Zach. But all she could think was that she needed to apprise her friends of this latest development as quickly as possible. She thought it would probably be poor manners to whip out her cell phone and spread the news right in front of him.

"Well, this is unexpected," she said, stalling for time. "And you've heard right; Neptune is excellent. The head chef is a friend of mine. Well ... *friend* might be too strong a word."

"So, what do you say?" he asked.

She hesitated. "I'd have thought ..."

"Thought what?"

She might as well just say it. "I'd have thought that you wouldn't be looking to date anyone, since you're still in love with your ex."

He nodded his head and avoided her gaze. Then he stuffed his hands into his jeans pockets and looked at his shoes. "Yeah. I just ... I just thought it would be nice. I liked talking to you at the coffee place. It was good having someone to listen. I thought maybe we could talk some more, over dinner."

She didn't know what to do, what to say. More than thirty years of female programming had conditioned her never to refuse a date with someone who looked like this. But instinct—

informed by the memory of him getting misty-eyed over the photo of his ex—told her to flee like a bunny from a cheetah.

"Let me check my schedule over the next few days and give you a call. Would that be all right?"

"Sure." He pulled a business card from his wallet—Zach Lockwood, Realtor—and handed it over. "It's got my cell and my email. Let me know." Then he smiled at her. The smile, all white teeth and sincerity, definitely worked in his favor.

The minute he was out the door, Kate rushed into the back room to get her cell phone out of her purse. On red alert overload, she didn't know who to call first. She decided it should be Lacy, since she'd orchestrated their meeting at Jitters in the first place.

"Red alert! Red alert!" Kate announced into the phone as soon as Lacy picked up.

"Oh my God! Where?"

"Here! In the store!"

"Right now?"

"No! A few minutes ago! Well, since he's gone now, I guess it's not a red alert anymore. More pink."

"Well, what's the point of a red alert if he's not there anymore? The whole red alert system …"

"He asked me out," Kate interrupted.

Lacy's end of the line was silent.

"Lacy?"

"What did you tell him?"

"I said I'd check my schedule and get back to him."

"Hmm."

" 'Hmm' what? What's the 'hmm'?"

"We need a meeting."

"I can't have a meeting right now. Althea's not here. I'm alone in the store."

"Hmm."

"Again with the 'hmm.'"

Lacy ignored that. "I'll call the girls and set up a plan. Call you back."

Lacy called Gen, and Gen called Rose, and both of them called Kate, and when everyone had hashed out their work schedules and evening plans, they all agreed to meet at Kate's house at seven p.m. Lacy would bring the Chinese food. Rose, of course, would bring the wine.

Kate reflected briefly on the sorry state of her love life that it required committee meetings. Did Gwyneth Paltrow need a committee to decide whether she should "consciously uncouple" with Chris Martin? Probably not. But then, she was Gwyneth. Kate was just Kate. And any excuse was a good one to get together with her friends.

Chapter Four

"He's hung up on his ex. He's a tourist, which means he's leaving soon. And he *doesn't read.*" Kate held up three fingers, ticking off the reasons she should say no. The four of them had pulled her small dining table out onto the back deck, and they were eating moo shu chicken, egg rolls, and sweet and sour pork as the sun dipped toward the ocean. Rose had selected a German Riesling, and they were most of the way through the first bottle, with a light breeze on their faces and the sound of crashing waves in the background.

"But, God, there's his looks," Gen said. A stray strand of curly red hair had fallen into her face with the breeze, and she pushed it away as she took another sip of wine.

"Yes. The looks count for at least three items on the plus side," Rose said before crunching into an egg roll.

"Also on the plus side," Lacy said, "is the fact that you need practice."

Kate lifted an eyebrow. "Practice?"

"You really do," Rose said, pointing one black-lacquered fingernail at Kate. "You haven't dated anybody since Marcus. And that was, what? Two years ago?"

Marcus Hoffman, Kate's husband for six years, had been a cheater and a manipulator. When he'd finally left, it had been more a relief to Kate than a trauma. But the way he'd treated her for their entire marriage had left her so wounded that she hadn't even been able to think about men until recently. When she'd told her friends that maybe—not for sure, but *maybe*—

she might be ready to get out there again, they'd thrown themselves into the task of shoving the baby bird out of the nest.

"Yes, I have!" Kate demanded. "I've dated!"

"Okay. Name them. Who have you gone out with since Marcus?" Gen asked.

"I … Well …" Kate put up her hands in surrender. "Okay, maybe I haven't dated much since Marcus. But I know how to date."

"Of course you do, honey," Lacy said soothingly, putting a hand on Kate's arm. "But you might be a little rusty, that's all."

Kate stalled by shoveling some more sweet and sour onto her plate and opening the second bottle of Riesling. After she'd poured some into her glass and offered it to the others, she sighed. "So, what we're saying, then, is that Zach could be, what, a refresher course? Fine. But isn't that kind of unfair to him? If I know it's not going anywhere, isn't it wrong for me to use him for practice?"

"No! That's the beauty of the situation!" Rose insisted. "He's going home in a few days, and he's in love with someone else, so he's not planning on it going anywhere anyway!"

Kate considered this. "Well, I guess that's true."

"Look, you're not out to marry him," Rose said as she arranged a delicate moo shu pancake on her plate. "But if you get a nice dinner at Neptune while enjoying a little eye candy, what's the harm?"

Despite the unassailable logic of their arguments, Kate stared into her wine glass and felt glum. "If this is such a great idea, why don't one of you go out with him?"

"He didn't ask us," Gen said. "He asked you."

"Well."

"You're going," Lacy announced, as though the decision had been hers to make all along. "And then we'll have a post-game debriefing after."

Rose sighed. "I love a good post-game debriefing. Especially if we get to talk about sex."

Kate pointed at her. "We *won't* be talking about sex. There won't be any sex to talk about. It's a first date. And probably the only one with this guy. Jeez."

"Yeah." Rose seemed to deflate slightly. "Well, maybe we can just talk about sex in general."

"Sure, honey." Kate rubbed her arm. "We can do that."

Kate and Zach met at Neptune at seven p.m. on a Wednesday. Gen had insisted on coming up from her downstairs apartment to help Kate dress for the occasion. She was wearing a silky knee-length slip dress in royal blue with a pair of low-heeled silver sandals. Her dark hair was carefully styled, and the color of the dress brought out the intense blue of her eyes. When she'd finished dressing, Gen had sat back, sighed, and said she looked stunning.

When she walked into Neptune and saw Zach sitting at the bar waiting for her, she had to admit that Gen's choices might have been effective. The look on his face when he took in the sight of her—the way his gaze traveled over every inch of her—suggested that she'd achieved the desired effect.

Falling on her face the first time they'd met might have been good strategy, but she didn't think it would play as well a second time, so she was glad she'd chosen shoes that were attractive but more sensible.

"Kate," he said, standing to meet her. "You look gorgeous."

So do you, she thought. He was wearing a black dress shirt, open at the collar, and black slacks. He was sporting a day or two worth of stubble that gave him a rugged look, as though he'd just come from a day of rock climbing. His dark eyes and chiseled jaw could have come straight out of a *GQ* ad. Other women in the restaurant were stealing covert looks at him. Some were less covert than others.

He put a hand on her arm. "Shall we get our table?"

"Of course."

He flagged the hostess, an acquaintance of Kate's from her Thursday yoga class. Janie, a tall blonde who proved to be far more strong and flexible than Kate when performing everything from downward dog to the side plank, took them to a table in the center of the room.

"You look fabulous, Kate," Janie said as she seated them and placed menus in front of them.

"Thanks." Kate accepted a menu and got settled into her chair. "It's no thanks to yoga, though. I've missed class the past couple of weeks."

"You should come back," Janie said. As she talked to Kate, her eyes kept cutting toward Zach and the way he looked in a close-fitting shirt. "We've got a new instructor, and she's really good."

"I will."

"I'll tell Jackson you're here. Enjoy your meal!"

Janie swept off to attend to other customers before Kate could protest. She did *not* want Jackson Graham to know she was here. That's all she needed while on a date—to have him come out and grouse over her choice of wine, or which appetizer she chose to precede which main course. The man thought he was the only one qualified to *eat.*

And maybe that wasn't the only reason she would prefer for him to stay safely tucked away in the kitchen. If he came out here to say hello, her female hormones might implode over having both him and Zach in such close proximity. Zach, with his movie star looks, and Jackson, with his—well, everything.

She was in her own world pondering this when she realized Zach was saying something.

"I'm sorry. I was distracted. What was that?"

"I was asking, who's Jackson?"

"Oh, he's the head chef. Jackson Graham."

"And how do you know him?"

Kate arranged the menu in front of her. "It's a small town. Everybody knows everybody."

"Ah."

The waitress—someone Kate also knew, but not well enough to force the need for small talk—came to take their drink order. Zach chose a bottle of wine without asking Kate's opinion. To her horror, it was a white zinfandel. She personally didn't mind drinking white zin, but she knew without a doubt that if Jackson came out to their table to say a friendly hello, there'd be hell to pay. Jackson placed white zinfandel on the same level of taste and sophistication as Red Bull or cherry Kool-Aid, and she knew from her conversations with Rose that he strenuously protested its presence on the Neptune wine menu at all. Well, at least if he came out here spitting fire, she'd be able to say that Zach chose it. The results might be fun. She smiled privately at the thought.

They studied the menu, placed their orders—porterhouse steak for him and sea bass for her—and settled in to begin the excruciating ritual of first-date small talk.

"So, Zach, how long are you staying in Cambria?" Kate sipped at her wine, reflecting that she would have preferred a nice chardonnay.

"Oh, I've gone home already."

She raised her eyebrows at this, surprised. "Really?"

"Yes. I was only at the B&B for a few days. I came back to see you. I live in San Luis Obispo. Less than an hour on Highway 1, and here I am."

Taken aback, Kate said, "Oh."

"Look," he said. "I know I talked a lot about Sherry when we met before. But I really think it's time for me to move on. And I'm very attracted to you."

Suddenly, everything Kate had assumed about this date was no longer true. This ... whatever it was didn't have a built-in expiration. He lived close enough to Cambria that a relationship was on the table, if they wanted it. Which she did not. He didn't read, he ordered white zinfandel—and there was also the ex-wife thing. Why was she even here? Then she looked up at his face, which appeared to have been chiseled out of marble. *Oh, right. That's why.* Was she really one of those people who went out with someone just because of their looks? Not entirely. She was here partly because her friends had insisted on it. And they were right about one thing. She did need practice with men.

It's just dinner. It's practice.

Still, she felt a bit smarmy. Was she using him as arm candy? Was she just like the popular guys she knew in high school who were interested in girls only because of nice hair and a good pair of breasts?

Okay, I am not *interested in him for his breasts.* She felt a hysterical laugh start to bubble up, so she drowned it in white zinfandel.

"What are you thinking?" he asked. "Seems like you've got a lot going on in there." He pointed to his own temple.

"I'm sorry. I'm thinking about the store," she said, covering. "Sales have been down, and we've got a big event coming up that could give us a much-needed boost if I handle it right. I can't screw it up."

"Oh yeah, the Art Walk," he said.

"Right. The thing is, it's kind of turned into a competition. The shop with the most impressive Art Walk event gets bragging rights for the whole year. It's gotten bigger and bigger every year. It's silly, but ..."

"You want to win."

She laughed. "Yeah. I really do."

"It's like real estate," he said.

"Really? How so?"

He explained. He began explaining before the entrees arrived, he continued explaining after their plates were placed on the table, and he explained some more as they ate. Kate was halfway through her sea bass while he was still explaining. She suddenly remembered why real estate agents had such a reputation for being blowhards. He told her about his biggest sales, his sales average, how that compared to the sales averages of other Realtors in San Luis Obispo, his strategy during an open house, his strategies for staging, and his philosophies on how to select a client to work with. By the time he got to, "... and the way I look doesn't hurt," Kate was ready to climb out the bathroom window.

She didn't enjoy rejecting men—he didn't seem like a bad guy, after all—but it was clear this wasn't the man for her, even for a fling. She decided to steer the conversation in a direction that might give her a clear way out.

"So, tell me more about your ex-wife."

His face changed, going from arrogant know-it-all to vulnerable child, and Kate hurt for him. "You don't want to talk about her, do you?" he said.

"Well, I just … Back at the store, you said you might need someone to talk to."

So he did. He began with how they'd met, then proceeded with their courtship, wedding, and early years together. By the time he got teary-eyed over the tale of their breakup, Kate was no longer thinking of it as a date. She was thinking of it as somebody comforting a broken-hearted friend. And she was a hell of a lot better at that than she was at dating.

Jackson Graham was in the middle of bitching out the salad chef for a wilted piece of red leaf lettuce when Janie breezed by, mentioning that Kate Bennet was in the restaurant with a date.

The information filtered into his brain in stages. The mention of the name—Kate Bennet—made his hands and feet tingle in a not unpleasant way. But then the next word to penetrate—date—made the blood pound in his ears so that he could no longer hear the excuses being made by the salad chef.

He wrapped up his diatribe with "Just goddamned fix it," and the salad chef took the opportunity to get himself out of sight as quickly as possible.

Kate Bennet is here with some guy?

He was torn between his need to see the guy and the impulse to simply throw himself into his work and pretend he'd never heard what Janie had said. When another waitress came into the kitchen and said some local muckety-muck wanted to give Jackson his compliments, he decided it was his opportunity to do a little sleuthing.

Not that he cared what Kate Bennet did, or who she dated.

Oh, hell, who am I kidding?

He took off an apron stained with Bearnaise sauce and stormed out of the kitchen in search of the muckety-muck. On his way to the man's table, he searched the dining room with his peripheral vision, and he saw her almost immediately. It was funny how that worked. His eyes were instantly drawn to her wherever she was in the room. He'd have found her if she'd been hiding in a closet, buried under a half-dozen blankets. Something about her energy drew his attention. It always had. It likely always would. The air around her buzzed with electricity, with light. It was impossible not to see her.

The first thing he noticed was that she looked beautiful. No surprise there. The second thing he noticed was that the asshole with her was insanely, stupidly handsome. He felt a surge of anger inside his cave-man brain, wanting to pound the guy into dust right next to Table Five. Since that would have been bad from a career standpoint, he shut down the part of his mind that was glaring red and proceeded to the muckety-muck's table to hear that his portobello risotto was genius. Which it was, obviously.

Having exchanged pleasantries with the local official, who was a city councilman or a county supervisor or some damned thing, he took a moment to weigh his options. He could skulk back to the kitchen and pretend he hadn't seen her. Or he could go by her table on the pretense of inquiring about her meal. At first he leaned toward skulking, but then he got mad at himself, thinking, *Why should I sneak around? This is my damned restaurant.*

And so, to spare himself the humiliation of sneaking on his own home territory, where if anyone should be sneaking, it should be *her*, he took a deep breath, steeled his resolve, and strolled over to her table—it was a stroll rather than a skulk— and presented himself as though he were just doing his job.

"Kate." He smiled, though it felt strange as it was not his usual facial expression, and looked down at her. The next words he had planned to say fled from his brain like sparrows from a nest as he saw how she looked. "Uh ... I ... wow."

"Hello, Jackson."

She was looking at him expectantly, and he realized he was supposed to say something. "I ... um ... Janie told me you were here, and I wanted to check and make sure everything was satisfactory."

"It is. The sea bass is delicious." She smiled, and he felt the smile like warm honey spreading through his chest.

He turned to the date and extended his hand. "Jackson Graham. Head chef."

"Zach Lockwood. Kate mentioned you. The food is great."

Kate added, "Zach has really been enjoying this bottle of white zinfandel with his porterhouse steak."

White goddamned zinfandel? With a goddamned steak? There were no words. Such an offense against taste and reason called for violence, but again, there were career concerns to consider. Speechless and outraged, he looked toward Kate, and saw that she was smirking at him, a delicate hand shielding her mouth as she tried to suppress a giggle.

She was playing with him, a state of affairs he would have welcomed under different circumstances.

He took a deep breath and called upon his inner calm.

"You know," he said, turning toward Zach and gesturing toward the bottle on the table, "this isn't one of our better wines. Please allow me to send something out to you as my gift."

"Thanks—that's really nice—but we're enjoying this. Right, Kate?" Zach looked to her for affirmation.

Kate's mirth was barely suppressed. "Oh, yes. It pairs so well with everything. Steak, sea bass ... Wouldn't you agree, Jackson?"

He felt much like a cartoon character in the moment before the pig or frog or whatever turns bright red and flies into the air and steam comes pouring out its ears. This was probably why Neptune's owner had urged him repeatedly to stay in the kitchen where he belonged.

"So, have you got a house here in Cambria?" Zach asked.

"Uh ... I live in an apartment above the restaurant, actually. Why do you ask?"

"Zach's a Realtor," Kate added helpfully, the amusement in her eyes telling him that this, right here—this painful exchange—was far and away the best part of her night.

"Here, take my card." Zach thrust a business card toward Jackson. "You know, you really should consider buying. It's been proven time and again that real estate is an excellent investment. Despite the ups and downs, over time, it's the safest place to put your money. Now, Cambria's a pricey area, no question, but there are still some good bargains if you don't mind being a little bit away from the beach. Also, if you don't mind doing a little fixer-upper work—a little DIY, am I right?—then that increases the range of what you can get for your money. You really ought to let me ..."

He was still going on when Jackson mentally flailed around for an escape. "Zach, I hate to interrupt, but I have to get back to work. I don't want to let the kitchen staff get backed up."

Zach looked around at the abundance of empty tables. "Not too busy tonight, a weeknight and all, I'd have thought you …"

"Enjoy your meal!" he said, and hurried back to the relative safety of the kitchen without waiting for a response.

Holy hell.

He went back to work, only partly focused on what he was doing. As he simmered and sautéed and corrected the inevitable errors of his staff, he kept peeking out at the dining room to see what Kate and Gorgeous George were doing. When he caught a glimpse of her heading toward the ladies' room, he handed off what he was doing to an underling, slipped out the door into the dining room, grabbed Kate by the arm, and pulled her into the hallway that led to the restrooms, away from Zach's line of sight.

"Excuse me," Kate said, reclaiming her arm.

"What the hell are you doing with that guy? He's a stiff." Up close and standing beside him, she was even more beautiful tonight than he'd realized. Her eyes were hypnotic. He tried to focus on his line of thought.

"What am I doing? I'm on a date. I'm an adult, single woman. I date."

"Yeah, but *him?*" He noticed her smell, and it threw him off. She smelled of jasmine and warm, clean skin. It almost made his knees weak.

"Is this because of the white zinfandel?" Her lips quirked up into a grin, and he couldn't help it—he had to laugh.

"You did that to me on purpose."

"Well, he did choose the wine on his own, with no prompting. But I maybe did poke at you a little. For fun."

Back to the topic at hand. "Listen, what do you want with that guy? He's a Realtor, for chrissakes."

They gazed at each other, an electricity building between them.

"Jackson?"

"Yeah?" He almost couldn't find his voice.

"I really do need to visit the ladies' room, if you don't mind."

"What? Oh." He backed off and let her go. When she was gone, he peeked into the dining room, and looked at the guy, this Zach.

Christ.

Chapter Five

The post-game analysis took place two days later as the four women walked together at Fiscalini Ranch, a nature preserve with paths that meandered along the bluffs above the rugged, crashing surf. Golden, wild grasses swished in the wind amid wildflowers of yellow and purple. Below them, sea lions reclined on rocks, barking and occasionally scuffling with one another. Some tourists wandered the paths here and there, their cameras on straps around their necks, but mostly this area was for the locals. The early morning sky was clear and dazzling, and a light breeze touched their faces as they walked.

None of their shops opened before ten, except Jitters. But Lacy had the late shift today, so after a flurry of phone calls back and forth, the scheduling for their walk was worked out with relative ease.

"So, really no question that he's hung up on his ex, huh?" Gen asked as they climbed a hilly path, squirrels scurrying out of their way.

"Oh, that's been established." Kate arranged her wide-brimmed hat to shield her face from the sun. "The whole last half of the date was him pining over her. Really, I felt bad for the guy. I mean, breakups are hard. I know that as well as anybody. He's trying to get out there and move on, but ... he's not ready. Even he knows he's not ready."

"Well, that sucks." Lacy, in yoga pants, a tank top, and a baseball cap, looked at Kate in sympathy.

"It's fine. From my end, anyway, it's fine," Kate assured her. "This was just practice, remember? It was never going to work. He wasn't right for me."

"Yeah."

"At least you got a good meal at Neptune, though, right?" Rose tried to inject some optimism into the discussion.

"I did."

"What did you have?"

"Sea bass."

"Mmm." Rose made appreciative noises that one usually heard only during sex. "That's one of my favorites." After a moment, she added, "Jackson says he saw you there."

Rose and Jackson were friends, partly because he ordered wines for the restaurant from De-Vine, so the two consulted regularly. Over time, Rose had grown fond of the prickly chef, finding that his frequent fits of pique came mostly from a desire for excellence. She could admire that.

Kate giggled, remembering the evening. "Oh, he saw us, all right. I'm sure he mentioned the white zinfandel."

"Ugh, white zinfandel?" Gen wrinkled her pale, freckled nose. "Even I know that's a no-go, especially to him."

"Zach ordered it. Jackson saw the wine and I could see that he wanted to throw a fit. It was all he could do to contain himself. I might have poked at him a little bit."

"He said you poked." Rose shook her head with a wry smile. "Brave woman."

"But that wasn't the funny part," Kate said. "Well, yes, it was the funny part, in terms of amusing funny. But it wasn't the strange part."

"What was the strange part?" Lacy asked. Kate assumed Lacy was looking at her with interest, though it was hard to tell with Lacy's enormous sunglasses.

"Here, let's take a break," Kate suggested. They stopped at a bench crafted from driftwood that was positioned above a breathtaking view of the surf. They sat, and she continued. "The strange part was that Jackson pulled me aside when I was on my way to the bathroom, and he seemed really worked up. Even for Jackson."

"About the wine?" Rose asked.

"No. About Zach. He went all alpha male on me. 'What are you doing with that guy?' 'That guy's a stiff.' 'Why are you dating him?' I mean, it's not like it's any of his business. Yes, it's true that Zach did try to sell him real estate. But still."

Rose looked thoughtful. "Hmm."

" 'Hmm' what?" Kate demanded.

"Just hmm."

"I think what Rose is trying to say," Lacy broke in, "is, have you thought about Jackson?"

"What do you mean, have I thought about Jackson? Of course I've thought about him. I'm thinking about him right now. We're talking about him."

Rose raised one eyebrow. "No. I mean, have you *thought* about him?"

"Huh." Gen appeared to be in deep thought. "Now, that could be interesting."

"What are you two talking about?" Kate demanded.

Lacy said, "You have to admit, Kate, it sounds like he's interested in you. Why else would he have cared that you were dating a guy who looks like ... well, like Zach? When guys ask, 'Why are you with him?' what they really mean is, 'Why aren't you with me?' "

"Yeah." Gen nodded. "They do."

Kate felt a little jolt in the center of her chest at the idea that Jackson Graham might possibly be attracted to her. She shrugged in a way that was supposed to be casual. "Oh, come on. He's never been anything but ... irritable when he's around me. That's the word," she decided. "Irritable. Last time I talked to him before Neptune, he called me an idiot."

Rose shook her head. "No, that's not how I remember it at all."

"What do you mean?" Kate said.

"The way I remember it, he *accidentally* called you an idiot, and then when he realized what he'd done, he looked like he'd swallowed his tongue."

"Oh, that's interesting," Lacy interjected.

"No," Kate said. "It's not interesting. I mean, yes, he's somewhat attractive, if you like broad shoulders and thick, wavy hair, and ... and raw male magnetism. But he's slept with pretty much everybody in Cambria. I mean, the man has a reputation. I don't know if I want to deal with that."

"At least he hasn't slept with any of us," Lacy said.

Rose looked uncomfortable. "Well ..."

"Oh, no," Kate said. "You had sex with Jackson?"

"No," Rose said. "No, no. But there was some making out. And there might have been some groping. Okay, a lot of groping."

"Well, then I definitely can't go there," Kate said.

"Sure you can," Rose reassured her. "Look, it was nothing. We fooled around a little, then we decided we were better as friends. I don't have any lingering feelings, or resentment, or anything like that. We're good."

"Really?" Kate realized that she'd felt an ugly surge of jealousy at the thought that Jackson had been with her friend. Rose's explanation made her feel a bit better.

"Really," Rose said.

"You and Jackson," Gen mused. "Wow. I hadn't thought of that, but ... yeah. Wow."

Kate waved her hands around in front of her. "There is no 'me and Jackson.' There is no 'wow.' "

"Well." Rose sounded thoughtful. "There could be a wow."

Jackson and Daniel were playing basketball at Shamel Park, an expanse of lawn, playground equipment, a few sports fields, and a public pool adjacent to the beach. They'd called two friends to make it more interesting than one-on-one: Ryan Delaney, whose cattle ranch provided grass-fed beef for Neptune, was on Jackson's team, and Will Bachman, caretaker for a mansion just up the coast, was on Daniel's.

Jackson and Ryan had lost the coin toss for who'd keep their shirts on, so now their bare torsos glistened with sweat as they played. This displayed Ryan to a certain advantage, since his tanned, fit physique was drawing appreciative glances from women at the park. Jackson, on the other hand, wished he could just put his damned T-shirt back on. With his fair coloring and the fact that he was at the restaurant almost every waking hour, his skin was so pale it practically glowed. He'd had to slather himself with 50 SPF before even thinking about starting the game. To add to the hilarity, the other guys had taken to calling him "Casper." At least he hadn't let himself go like a lot of chefs did, being around food all the time. He usually made it to the gym, and he constantly reminded himself— with some success—that his job was to cook it, not to eat it. So he'd have looked pretty good if he hadn't been so goddamned *white*.

Like he could give a shit what the girls at the park thought of him, anyway. He wished he did. But despite all his best efforts, the only woman whose opinion he cared about was dating a Realtor-slash-supermodel. The thought of that made him want to bash somebody's head in. Preferably, the Realtor supermodel's. But since he couldn't do that, he played with unusual ferocity instead. This didn't escape the notice of Daniel and Will, who'd been shoved, elbowed, and generally abused during the course of the game and were starting to feel a little put out about it.

"Hey, Casper, take it easy. This isn't the NBA," Will said after taking a forearm to the face.

Jackson, breathing heavily, wiped the sweat from his face. "Sorry." And he was. He wasn't roughing people up on purpose. He was just … getting in there a little bit more than usual. And, hell, it was working. At the end of the game, they were up six points, mostly because of Ryan, who'd played varsity basketball in high school.

"What's got you all worked up?" Daniel asked after the game ended and they were toweling off and drinking deeply from bottles of water. The four of them walked toward some nearby benches, still breathing heavily.

"Nothing," Jackson insisted.

"Bullshit," Ryan said. "After that last foul, I thought we were gonna have to call 911 for Daniel."

Jackson threw his towel onto the bench. "Ah, shit."

"So, what is it?"

He peered at the others, hesitated, and then decided he had to talk to someone. "She came into Neptune a couple nights ago with a guy. This …" He gestured vaguely. "This *guy* who sells real estate and orders crap wine and looks like this goddamned Adonis. I guess it's been bothering me."

"We're talking about Kate," Daniel said.

Jackson was annoyed. "Of *course* we're goddamned talking about Kate. I'll tell you what. I've got to get past this … this *thing* I have for her. I oughta find somebody new to go out with. Have some fun. Get my mind off her."

Ryan shook his head. "You asshole."

Jackson blinked at him, surprised. "What? Why am I an asshole?"

"Because it's never once occurred to you that one way to deal with the feelings you have for her is to go out with *her*."

"Ah, that's just … "

"True," Daniel interjected. "That's what it is."

Jackson ran a hand irritably through his hair. "Yeah. I guess it is."

"Look. I get it," Daniel went on. "At least, I think I do. Your last few relationships haven't worked out … "

"That's an understatement."

" … So you've stopped trying. Especially when it's someone who matters to you."

They sat on a bench drinking water and cooling down, watching some moms pushing their toddlers on the swings.

"If it's just somebody to date—some pretty face—then it doesn't matter if she gets tired of your bad moods and your diatribes and moves on sooner rather than later. But when it's Kate … " Daniel left the thought dangling in the air.

"Thank you, Dr. Freud," Jackson said wryly.

"Just ask her out," Will insisted. "Stop being a wuss."

They were silent for a moment while Jackson pulled his shirt back on. He leaned forward, elbows on his knees, avoiding Daniel's gaze.

"Let's say I want to," he said finally.

"Okay, let's say that," Daniel said.

"Why the hell would she ever say yes? Every time she sees me I'm yelling at her or calling her an idiot."

"Yeah, you might want to stop doing that," Ryan said.

Some kids with a big, red rubber ball accidentally kicked it toward the bench. Daniel scooped it up and tossed it back to the kids, who ran off to resume their game.

"You know what you need?" Daniel said after a while.

"Yes," Jackson answered. "But no one's invented personality transplants yet."

"Very funny. Seriously. You need an icebreaker."

Jackson looked at Daniel. "An icebreaker?"

"Yeah. He's right," Ryan said. "You need to be around her in some sort of casual setting, without yelling at her or calling her an idiot. Act like a guy with manners for a change. Let her see the other side of you."

Jackson scoffed. "I don't know if I have another side. And anyway, what makes you guys experts? Last time I checked, Ryan, you hadn't done even one thing to get closer to Lacy. Besides making moony eyes at her, and that doesn't count."

Lacy, who'd lived in Cambria her entire life with her parents and her extended family right there in town, was tall, blond, blue-eyed, and gorgeous. The fact that she was more comfortable in a pair of frayed, faded jeans and a T-shirt than she was in a little black dress made her all the more attractive to Ryan, who was used to life on a cattle ranch, where expensive clothes just seemed frivolous and stupid. He was crazy about her.

The muscles in Ryan's jaw bunched up. "Let's not talk about Lacy."

"Why not?"

"Because we're talking about you."

The conversation was getting entirely too touchy-feely for Jackson, but on the other hand, his friends were right—he had to do something if he was ever going to get anywhere with Kate. It wasn't going to happen on its own.

"So, this 'icebreaker' idea."

"Yeah?" Daniel said.

"How would it work? What would I do? What's the plan, geniuses?"

Daniel grinned and nudged Jackson with his shoulder. "Give me a day or two to think about it."

Chapter Six

Kate got off the phone with Zach and sighed. She was sitting in her pajamas, cross-legged on her sofa with a glass of wine (not white zinfandel) on the table beside her. She and Zach had decided that dating wasn't right for them—they'd never make a good couple—but once he'd started talking to her about his ex-wife, Sherry, he'd found it difficult to stop. He'd been calling her almost nightly to talk about his heartbreak, and to ask for Kate's advice.

She really did feel bad for the guy. It seemed that his problems with Sherry came down to issues with communication, priorities, and timing. She wanted children. He wanted them, but not yet. He wanted to build his career and put together a nest egg for the family they'd eventually have. She wanted him to spend less time working and more time at home. She wanted to go back to school and get the college degree she'd missed out on the first time around. He thought the reason she wanted it was because she didn't trust him to provide for her. He used his looks to advantage in his work, flirting with female clients to get a listing or make a sale. And Sherry was a jealous woman who didn't appreciate that particular strategy.

To Kate, it seemed like the problems were not insurmountable, especially knowing how much Zach wanted to win Sherry back. If they would only take some time to talk about things. To be together without distractions and discuss what they both wanted out of the relationship.

Suddenly, Kate had an idea—a crazy matchmaking idea. In general, she didn't believe in people getting involved in other people's love lives. But on the other hand, she also didn't want to be Zach's over-the-phone therapy buddy for the rest of her life. She felt bad for him and she wanted to help him, but his calls were seriously cutting into time she could have spent eating Ben & Jerry's and watching Netflix.

Inspired, she went out the front door, made a right, hurried down the stairs, and pounded on Gen's door.

"What? I'm coming! Hold on!" Gen called from inside the apartment.

When the door opened, Gen looked at her with squinty eyes.

"What's going on? Is the house on fire?"

Kate pushed her way into the tiny kitchenette, then on into the bedroom-slash-sitting room. Right now, it was set up as a bedroom, with the pull-out sofa made up into a queen-size bed with springs and bars that poked the crap out of your back whenever you slept on it. For some reason, Gen didn't seem to mind the arrangement.

"I just need your opinion on something," Kate said, plopping onto the bed.

"Okay, shoot."

Gen looked bleary-eyed. Maybe she'd been sleeping. *Already?* Kate glanced at the clock on the mantel and was surprised to find that it was past eleven o'clock.

"I have to get Zach back together with his ex."

"Tonight?"

"No, but soon. The sooner the better."

"And you need my opinion on that?" Gen wandered into the kitchen, got a glass of water, and brought it into the bedroom.

"Not exactly. I need your opinion on how I'm going to do it."

"Oh. Okay. Just let me … " She rubbed at her face vigorously, took a deep breath, and opened her eyes wide. A waking-up ritual. "All right. Ready." She plopped down on the bed next to Kate.

"What if I set up a romantic evening for them?" She held up her hands to forestall the objection she thought was coming. "Just wait. Listen. What if I had him invite her to my place for an evening? I won't be there, of course. Obviously. But we could set up dinner on the deck at sunset, with music and some great food. Candlelight. Nice table linens. The whole deal. They can even stay the night. I'll set up the bedroom with rose petals and champagne and … and … okay, I really don't want to think about them having sex in my bed, but I have to get him to stop these hours-long phone conversations where he tells me how miserable he is. So? What do you think?"

Gen scrunched up her nose in thought. "Whose house will she think it is?"

"Oh, good question."

They both thought about that.

"He could say he's selling it."

"Oh! He could say he's renting it!" Kate waved her hands excitedly. "That's plausible, right? There are a ton of vacation rentals around here."

Gen shook her head. "How's he going to explain all of your stuff? Unless you want to move out everything but the furniture for a weekend."

"Oh. Jeez. No, that won't work." Kate's eyebrows shot up. "He could say he's housesitting."

Gen nodded. "Yeah, maybe. That could work. Would she agree to it? I mean, she's his ex for a reason, right?"

"Yeah, but from what he says, the whole 'ex' thing isn't a hundred percent. They talk. They're friendly. He could probably make it happen."

"Huh."

"Yeah."

They sat together on the bed, Gen sipping her water, Kate splayed out across a pile of pillows. "Jeez," Kate said. "This bed is like torture. You're being tortured. Why do you sleep on this thing?"

Gen looked at her wryly. "In case you haven't noticed, this apartment is about the size of a broom closet. There's no room for both a sofa *and* a bed."

"Well, there's that. But at least you have a great landlady."

"I don't know." Zach sounded skeptical over the phone as Kate laid out her plan for him. "We're divorced. She divorced me. Now I'm supposed to ask her for a date?"

"Not just a date!" Kate, standing behind the counter at Swept Away, considered the best way to make her case. "It's … it's a grand gesture! You haven't seen my place, but it's got the best view in Cambria, I swear to you. Breaking waves. Barking sea lions. Gulls soaring overhead. I've even got deer on the lawn. Sometimes. I can't promise the deer, they kind of come and go at will."

"And so this would be dinner, and … "

Clearly, she was going to have to give him the vision from her own imagination, since he had none of his own. "Dinner at sunset, overlooking the ocean. With candlelight, wine, soft music. Rose petals in the bedroom, chilled champagne, more candlelight. And, you know, you're going to have to take it from there, because I'm not describing the rest."

"And where will you be?"

"Somewhere else, obviously." She rolled her eyes.

"I'm supposed to make dinner for her? I don't cook."

"I'll cook!" Kate didn't cook either, but he didn't have to know that. She could work that part out later. "But, listen. If you really want her back, you're going to have to decide up front what you're willing to give her."

"Give her? You mean, like a gift?"

"I mean, like the things she wanted out of the relationship that you said no to. The stuff that broke you up in the first place. What does she really want that you're willing to give her to make this work?"

He was silent.

"What about kids? She wants kids, right? And you said you wanted to wait. Well, what are you waiting for? Tell her you're willing to start trying. Is that something you'd do to get her back?"

"Yeah. We could do that," he said, his voice a little more confident now.

Kate had two customers browsing through the store—middle-aged tourists, the guy in cargo shorts and a Cambria baseball cap, and the woman in a flowing sundress and sandals. Kate knew she needed to help them—needed to get back to work—but she felt like Knute Rockne giving an inspirational speech at halftime. She couldn't stop now, before the deal was sealed.

"That's great, Zach. Tell her you're willing to start a family now, and … and tell her you'll work shorter hours and spend more time with her."

"Well, now, I don't know … "

"Okay, if not that, then tell her she can go to college."

Silence.

"Oh, come on, Zach. She doesn't want to go as some kind of plan B, because she doesn't trust you as a provider. She wants to go because … because she's stagnating at home. She wants to use her mind! She wants to prove something to herself, that she's smart, that she's capable. She wants to grow as a person! For God's sake, let her grow!"

He hesitated for a moment longer.

"Zach. Jeez. You're miserable without her. What's a little college if it will bring her back home?"

"But what about the kids? If we have kids, when is she going to go to college? She'll be busy with all these new kids we'll have."

Kate blew out some air, frustrated. "She'll figure it out. Just tell her you trust her judgment. And then you've got to actually do that. You've got to actually trust her judgment."

"Okay."

"Okay?"

"Yeah."

"You'll do it?"

"Yeah."

She did a silent fist-pump, which caused the tourists to look up in amusement. She put a hand over the phone and mouthed, "I'm so sorry. I'll be right with you."

She returned her attention to Zach. "So, ask her, figure out what night you want to do it, and let me know. I've gotta go. I'm ignoring my customers."

"Okay. Kate? You're the best. Really. Thank you. I don't even know why you're doing this."

She knew. It was because she couldn't take any more of his sad-sack, endless phone calls with him whining like a love-sick puppy. But she didn't tell him that.

"It's no problem, I'm happy to do it. Now ask her. Bye."

She ended the call and turned to her customers. "Thank you for your patience."

"He'll never regret having kids," the woman said. "We have three kids and five grandkids. Here. I have pictures."

Zach got back to her a day later, giving her a date for his romantic evening with Sherry. He seemed surprised that she'd said yes, but Kate wasn't. Things clearly weren't finished between these two, and sometimes a woman needed to be swept off her feet by a guy who'd taken the time to make special plans. Sherry didn't have to know that Kate was the one who'd made the plans.

With that done, she had to deal with the fact that she'd said she would cook. Kate's idea of cooking usually involved two slices of bread and some lunch meat, or maybe putting a Pop-Tart in the toaster. She called Neptune to see if they would cater the dinner, but was disappointed to learn they were booked up weeks in advance.

Crap.

She thought about whether any of her friends could cook. Gen was a good baker, but Kate wasn't at all sure how she'd do with actual dinner food. Rose *knew* food—as in what went well with what—but she rarely made any herself. That left Lacy. She was clearly the best cook of the four of them. She sometimes even marinated things.

During a slow period at the store, Kate called Lacy at Jitters and explained the situation. Lovelorn couple, special evening, nobody to cook the dinner that would prove to be the key to Sherry's heart.

"Oh, wow." Lacy seemed impressed with Kate's plans. "You put all that together? For a guy you went out with and then rejected? I've never been that nice to my bad dates."

"It's not as selfless as it sounds. His 'I can't live without Sherry' phone calls are getting old, especially when I could be rewatching *Breaking Bad*. So, how about it? Can you cook a meal to get these two crazy kids back together? Zach will pay for the food."

"Maybe. What night is it?"

"Friday."

"This Friday?"

"This Friday."

"As in, five nights from now?"

"Yeah. As in, Friday. The day after Thursday. Can you do it?"

The silence on the line didn't bode well.

"I wish I could," she said finally, her voice full of don't-want-to-let-down-a-friend misery. "I've got a family thing that night. My grandparents' golden wedding anniversary. I'm really sorry."

Kate sighed. "Listen, don't worry about it. I'll figure something out. Even if I have to order pizza and serve it by candlelight."

Daniel was at the gallery talking with Gen about some new pieces he was working on when Kate called to update Gen on her plans for the dinner. Daniel's ears pricked up when he heard Gen talking about Kate and Zach.

"What's this about a fancy dinner?" he asked after she hung up the phone. "I like fancy dinner."

"It's for a friend of Kate." She blew a red curl out of her eye in a gesture of frustration. "She's trying to get him back together with his ex. She set up a romantic dinner for them, but … no food. Neptune's booked."

"Hmm. Is this the guy she went out with that one time? The guy she had dinner with at Neptune?"

"Yeah. How do you know about that?"

"Word gets around," he said. "So, what's the plan?"

She looked at him curiously. "Why do you want to know?"

"I just do."

"But why?"

He shrugged. "Just think of it as gossip. Think of me as one of your girlfriends."

"Okay. Can we paint our nails after?"

He flashed her a grin, and she told him the plan.

"Listen. This is perfect. You do her a favor, show her what a good guy you are. She'll owe you one. She pays you back by taking you out to the movies or something. All you have to do is not act like an ass. You think you can manage that?"

"Hmm. Maybe."

Daniel was standing in the dining room at Neptune, an hour before the restaurant opened for lunch. He'd hurried down Main Street to the restaurant after his talk with Gen and banged on the door, saying he needed to talk with Jackson. The chef was rushing around, supervising prep, dealing with whatever chefs dealt with before the doors opened. He'd stopped his work, interested, when he'd heard what Daniel had to say.

"Come on," Daniel urged. "You don't want to miss a chance to be a big hero."

Jackson sighed. "Well, if it's going to get that Zach asshole back with his ex and away from Kate, that's a plus."

"It is," Daniel agreed. "Should I tell Gen to tell Kate you'll do it? I can pass her a note after fifth period."

Jackson scowled at him. "When's the dinner?"

"Friday night."

"Aw, Jeez. You know I can't on a Friday. It's our busiest night."

"Right." Daniel gave it some thought. "Can you make it ahead and have her freeze it and reheat it or something?"

Jackson looked at Daniel as though he'd taken leave of his senses. "Freeze my food? Are you serious?"

Daniel put up his hands in a gesture of surrender. "Sorry, sorry. I should have known better."

"Yeah, you should have. Look, it was a pretty good idea, but … "

"Teach her to make it!" Daniel had the look of someone who'd been struck by inspiration. "Yeah, that's it. Teach her to cook something for them. You'll be working closely together in the kitchen, tasting, stirring. Maybe even sautéing. Your hands brush together over the chicken cutlets."

"What are you, a girl?"

Daniel's brow furrowed. "That's the second time today someone has suggested that."

"Well, if the Prada pump fits … "

"But seriously. You can see the possibilities."

"Maybe," he said again.

"Screw maybe," Daniel said as he headed for the door. "I'll tell her you'll do it. When's your night off?"

"Tuesday."

"Great. Tuesday!" Daniel rushed out the door before Jackson could change his mind.

"Wait. *Jackson* is going to teach *me* to cook something for Zach and Sherry?" Kate was in the shop, and Gen had just walked down from the gallery and popped her head in the door to tell her the news.

"Right. On Tuesday night after you close the shop. It's all set."

"But what … " She closed her eyes and waved her hands around in front of her. "There are so many things wrong with this picture. First, why would Jackson Graham, the top chef in Cambria, want to bother with Zach and Sherry's dinner? And second, if he *does* want to do it, why would he be teaching *me* to do it instead of just doing it himself?"

"Because it's on Friday night."

"Ah. And he has to work on Friday night, obviously. Duh."

"Right."

Kate looked at Gen, her head tilted like a dog who heard something strange. "But why does he want to do it in the first place? Am I paying him a bundle of money I don't have?"

"Nope. He's volunteering."

"But why?"

Poised in the doorway, Gen looked at her with sympathy. "Honey, I love you, but you really can be dense sometimes."

Kate stared at her. "What are you talking about?"

Gen changed her posture and her facial expressions, and started doing her best Jackson Graham impression. " 'Kate, what are you doing with that guy? He's a stiff! White zinfandel? My God!' " Then she became Gen again. "He's too big of a wuss to ask you out on a date, so he's going to teach you to cook instead, because he gets to spend time with you, and, hopefully, he also gets Zach out of the picture by getting him back together with his ex. Jeez. I shouldn't have to draw you a picture."

Kate started to say something, then stopped. She cocked one hand on her hip. "Oh. Really?"

"Yes. I'll tell Daniel to tell Jackson you'll do it. Tuesday night, your house. He'll bring the food." She started to leave, then hesitated. "And wear something pretty. But not something that looks like you're trying too hard. I mean, it's a date, but it's not a date. It's a cooking lesson that's also ... Oh, never mind. I'll pick something out for you. Gotta go." She sped off, leaving Kate and Althea looking after her questioningly.

"What in the world was that all about?" Althea asked, a stack of new releases in her hand.

Kate shrugged. "I guess I'll find out Tuesday."

Chapter Seven

The shop closed at six on Tuesday, and Jackson had sent word—through Daniel and then through Gen—that he'd be at Kate's place at seven. That left little time for Kate to rush home, change into the outfit Gen had picked out for her—a blue cotton sundress and low, strappy sandals—touch up her makeup, and clean up the house so it would look presentable.

Obviously, the kitchen took top priority, cleaning-wise; Jackson would probably turn around and leave, scowling, if it wasn't spotless. Fortunately, that didn't take much, since Kate rarely used the kitchen for anything but toast and frozen pizza.

With the counters wiped down and the sink scoured, she rushed around picking up various pieces of her life from the countertops, the tables, the sofa. Magazines, books, used water glasses. She scooped up a pile of discarded clothes from the bedroom floor, considered putting them away, looked at the clock, and opted instead to stuff them inside the closet and close the door. When she was finished, she gave the place an appraising look. Not bad.

As she worked, she thought about exactly what it was she was hoping to gain from spending time with Jackson. Like Zach, he wasn't relationship material. He didn't use women, exactly—those who had dated him tended to think well of him even after things ended. But end they did, and usually after a very brief time. But who was to say that wasn't just what Kate needed? She was getting back into dating for the first time in years. She wasn't ready to jump into anything serious. A brief and mutually satisfying fling with a man who revved her engine could be exactly the right thing for her at this point in her life. There was no harm in it. They would both have fun, and then they would part on good terms.

At six forty-five, Gen came in to give Kate and the place her assessment. She looked Kate up and down, then gave her a thumbs-up. "Good. You look good. Really pretty, but also casual. Just hanging around, being yourself, living your life, not at all concerned that a really hot guy is about to knock on your door."

Kate gave her a half-grin. "That's just the look I was aiming for."

Gen, looking serious, appraised the house. "Okay, wait." She went to Kate's bookcase, plucked a couple of books from the shelves, and arranged them artfully on a side table. Then, reconsidering, she selected one, opened it to the middle, and placed it pages-down on the arm of the sofa. "There."

"What's that for?"

"*The Unbearable Lightness of Being.* Sexy and intellectual. You're all set."

Gen wished Kate luck and went out the door.

Kate could hear Gen's footsteps going down the stairs to her apartment, and part of Kate wanted to go hide down there, too. What was she doing? Yes, a fun fling might be nice. But Jackson Graham had rarely been anything but foul-tempered and rude to her. Why should she think that he was attracted to her, just because someone told someone else that he was interested?

Just relax, and forget all of that. He's doing me a favor. He's coming because I promised Zach a romantic dinner with Sherry, and I don't know how to cook.

Fine. She'd stick to that. This was a guy just helping someone out. Something he'd have been unlikely to do if he weren't interested in her. But still.

She looked at the clock. Five minutes to seven. She felt a little fluttery feeling in her chest, and took a deep breath to steady herself. Okay, so maybe the very sight of him made her stupid and sweaty-palmed. Maybe it always had. So what? There was no reason to act like this was anything more than a cooking lesson.

After all, it would be foolish to get her hopes up about anything that had to do with a man. She'd learned that the hard way.

Kate hated to be a cliché, but she knew she was one. Burned by a man two years before—having been cheated on, emotionally manipulated, belittled, and used—she'd been left so emotionally fragile that she hadn't ventured out there since then. Gen, Rose, and Lacy had tried to fix her up numerous times, but she just hadn't been ready for that. Was she ready for it now?

Only one way to find out.

She poured herself a glass of chardonnay to steady her nerves. She was only two sips into the glass when Jackson arrived. She opened the door to find him virtually hidden under bags of groceries and kitchen supplies.

"Wow! Let me help you with that," she said, taking a bag from his arms and ushering him in.

"Thanks. I didn't know what you had, so I thought I'd better bring a few things."

They put the bags down in the kitchen and she peered inside: one contained the food they'd be preparing, and another, a thick canvas carry-all, contained a sauté pan, a sauce pot, a set of knives in a leather sheath, and other various implements Kate couldn't name.

"I have a few things, but … mostly I don't cook," she said.

"I was afraid of that."

"That's why I was so desperate for help. Thank you, by the way. I appreciate you coming to my rescue like this." She looked up at him. Instead of replying, he'd stuffed his hands into his pockets, looking uncomfortable. She couldn't help but smile at his awkwardness. Who'd have thought he would be awkward, given his vast and varied experience with women?

There was that fluttery feeling again. Something about the guy. At six-foot-two, with broad shoulders and a powerful build, he towered over her. His wavy, ginger hair was attractively unkempt. He wore close-fitting jeans and a deep emerald button-down shirt that made his green eyes all the more dazzling.

"Should we get started?" she prompted.

"First, let's go over the … Wow." He stopped midsentence as his gaze wandered over the sliding glass doors that led to the deck and the breathtaking view beyond. He walked across the room, opened the door onto the deck, and stepped out. "From the neighborhood, I figured you had a view. But this … "

He took in the breaking waves, the sounds of the sea lions, the grassy expanse on the slope below the house, the hummingbirds flitting to and from a tree just off the railing of the deck.

"It was my mother's." She came out onto the deck to stand beside him.

"The house?"

"Yes. She left it to me when she passed away five years ago. The bookstore, too. When she died, I figured I'd sell both of them and get back to my life. But then … this became my life. I couldn't bring myself to leave." Standing close to him, she could smell a hint of his cologne on the early evening breeze.

"Any regrets?" he asked.

"Actually, yes. I regret that I didn't spend more time here, with her, before she passed. I was too busy. Busy, busy, busy." She shook her head at the thought.

He turned toward her, leaning one hip on the railing of the deck. "What did you do before this? What kept you so busy?"

"Oh," she waved a hand dismissively. "It all seemed so important at the time. I went to grad school. I wrote a book. I had an adjunct teaching job at a university. I was very involved in being an intellectual. Going to cocktail parties to be seen with the right people. That sort of thing."

His eyebrows rose. "You wrote a book?"

"I did."

"Published, or in a drawer somewhere?"

"Come inside. I'll show you."

They went into the house, and she rummaged around in a bookcase. "Now, where did it … " She looked over at the books Gen had stacked on the side table. "Oh. Of course." Naturally, Gen had put the book out where it would be visible. Kate walked to the side table and took the book from the stack. "Here."

She handed the book to Jackson.

He looked at it—a trade paperback with the simple, elegant image of a tree in fall foliage on its cover—and then looked at Kate, surprise on his face. "This is you? You wrote *Beyond the Boundaries of Desire*? You're Katherine Hoffman?"

"It's my married name. Before I changed it back. You've read it?" Kate felt an electric jolt of pleasure at the thought that he knew and had enjoyed her work.

"Years ago, when it came out." He opened the cover and looked at a handwritten inscription on the title page.

To Mom,
I couldn't have done this without your love and support.
All my love, Kate.

"This is your mom's copy."

Kate reached out for the book and held it in both of her hands, tears welling up in her eyes. "Yeah." She swiped at her eyes. "Sorry. She's been gone five years, and it's still hard."

"Of course it is."

They looked at each other with charged intensity before she changed the subject. "So, what did you think of the book?"

"Are you kidding? It was brilliant."

She wondered if maybe he was bluffing—either hadn't read it, or had read it and forgotten about it—when he quoted from the last chapter:

"*And then Wallace understood what she'd meant when she'd said she couldn't live, couldn't breathe. It was a saddening of the soul, a heartache unthinkable in any other place.*"

Kate looked at him, and then at the book. "Well, I … Wow."

"That's what I was going to say about the book. Wow. I couldn't get over the ending, where the kid walks into the river. I almost wrote to you about it."

"You did?"

"Almost. But then I figured a big-time writer like Katherine Hoffman wouldn't want to be bothered by a guy like me." There was that awkwardness, that vulnerability, again. It made her smile.

She turned away from him to hide her mounting emotions. "Are you kidding? I'd have loved it. You were one of about fifty people who read it."

"That's not true. You got reviewed in the *New York Times*."

"You read the *Times* review?"

"Sure. The guy raved about it. Called it a promising debut."

"Well." She shook her head. "That doesn't always translate into sales."

"Is that all it's about, sales?" He sounded disgusted, outraged. "Is that why you stopped writing? Because it didn't sell? That's just ... I mean, if you've got a gift, and it's just about money ... "

She turned back toward him, defensive now. "I didn't stop writing. I stopped getting published. Sales do matter when a publisher is deciding whether to offer you a contract. They matter very much."

She could see him mentally backpedaling, trying to rein in his aggressive attitude. "Yeah, I guess that's true."

"Anyway. I'm glad you liked the book." She changed the subject. "So. What are we going to cook?"

The menu he'd selected for Zach and Sherry's dinner was elegant and sophisticated, but none of it required advanced cooking skills. They'd start with an appetizer of mushroom pizzette—a kind of small pizza topped with button, crimini, and shiitake mushrooms—then move on to a main course of herb roasted pork shoulder with parmesan polenta and a salad of escarole and radicchio with fennel. Dessert would be poached pears with fresh whipped cream.

Kate looked at the menu and her face fell. "This is … I don't know if I can do this. It sounds amazing, but if it doesn't come in a microwaveable tray, I'm pretty much adrift."

"No." He waved off her objections. "The whole point of this menu is that it looks and sounds impressive, but anyone can do it."

She still wasn't sure. "Really?"

"Sure. And it all works well to make ahead the day of the dinner, so you can get it ready and then get out of the way before they get here."

She poured him a glass of chardonnay as they started pulling food and supplies from the bags he'd brought. She'd worried about how he'd react to the wine—would he call her an idiot again? But when he took a sip, his eyebrows raised in appreciation.

"Mmm, not bad. Did Rose get you this?"

She nodded. "Yeah. She's my go-to guy for wine."

He grinned. "Mine too. Okay, let's get the pork roast into the oven first thing, because it takes a while to cook. Then we can work on the side dishes and the appetizer."

She'd expected him to make the food while she watched; she'd heard stories about how controlling he was when it came to cooking. Instead, he showed her how to score the skin on the pork roast, directed her in rubbing it with garlic, rosemary, and sage, gave her tips on the best way to roll the roast and tie it with twine, and then nodded with approval as she slid it into the oven.

"Well, that wasn't so hard," she said. "How long will this take? I haven't eaten since lunch."

"The roast? About three hours."

She gaped at him. "Three *hours*?"

"Yeah, but don't worry. We'll make the mushroom pizzette next. It won't take long, and it'll give us something to munch on while we work."

Together they sliced mushrooms, grated cheese, and stretched out the ball of pizza dough he'd brought. (He suggested premade dough, to make the process easier for her on Friday night. She was grateful.) They placed the pizzette on a baking pan and slid it into the oven and onto the rack beneath the pork roast. While they waited for it to bake, he discussed the importance of organization and cleanliness, showing her how to clean up as she worked so she wouldn't have an enormous mess at the end of the evening.

When the pizzette came out of the oven, Kate inhaled the scent, eyes closed in bliss. "God, that smells fantastic."

"Well, as it happens, we have a break now, because we don't have to make the polenta until the roast is nearly done. Here, let's have some of this." He rummaged around in her kitchen drawers for a pizza cutter. When he found one, he sliced the pizzette into six neat wedges and arranged them on a plate. They refilled their wine glasses and took them and the food out onto the deck, where the sunset was in its full glory. Kate put the plate on a side table between the two Adirondack chairs she kept on the deck, and they ate and sipped wine while the sun washed the sky and the ocean in oranges, pinks, and reds.

"This is amazing," Kate said, munching on a piece of the appetizer they'd made. "But I'd have expected no different, coming from you."

He shook his head. "What's amazing is this view. Jesus. This spot has got to be one of the best lots in town."

Kate nodded and took another sip of wine. "It's one of the original houses in this part of town. It seems like one by one, all of the older houses are being torn down and replaced with architectural showpieces. Of course, the small size of the lots here, combined with restrictions on blocking other people's views, means none of them are very big. But still, this place is starting to look like an eyesore next to the neighbors. I need to get some renovations done, but there never seems to be enough money."

He shrugged. "I don't think it's an eyesore at all. It's a little older, sure, but I think it's great. I like what you've done inside, too. It's homey. Comfortable."

She flushed with warmth at the compliment. "I think so, too. I haven't changed it much since it was my mother's. Most of the furniture, the décor, is hers. Being here, with all of her things, makes me feel closer to her."

"How did she die?" He looked at her cautiously, clearly gauging whether this was an acceptable avenue of conversation.

"Ovarian cancer. She was sick for a long time before I even knew."

His eyebrows furrowed in concern. "She didn't tell you?"

"She didn't know. She'd been having symptoms for over a year, but she kept ignoring them, thinking it was just aging." She shook her head. "By the time she decided to see someone, it was too late. She didn't have a chance." Tears filled her eyes, and her vision blurred. She swiped at them. "I'm getting emotional. Sorry."

"Hey. We don't have to talk about this if you don't want to." He put a hand on her arm.

"No, that's okay. I can talk about it. It's just, I've always wondered if it would have made a difference if I'd been here more. If I'd seen her more. I would have known something was wrong. I'd have made her get help sooner."

He shook his head. "You don't know that."

"What do you mean?" She sniffed a little and looked at him. He was leaning toward her, all concern and intense attention. She caught his scent, cologne and soap and white wine, and something more earthy and manly.

"What I mean is, maybe you wouldn't have seen it. Maybe you'd have thought what she did—that it was normal aging. Or maybe you'd have nagged her to get help, and she still wouldn't have done it. You don't know. Also, and maybe most importantly, her health wasn't just on you. It was her responsibility, too."

She looked down into her wine glass. "I guess."

"Also, shit happens. No matter what you do. It just happens."

From his tone, she could guess that he wasn't just talking about her and her mother. He was talking about himself, and the shit that had happened in his own life. It made her want to know more about him.

She nodded. "Yes. You're right. I know that." And she did. Still, she started to cry. She struggled to keep the emotions inside, but the tears started to flow freely. "I'm sorry," she said. "This is stupid. It's been five years. Excuse me a minute. Let me just … "

She rose from her chair and started to go inside, thinking that she would compose herself in the bathroom, wipe her eyes, blow her nose, make herself presentable before emerging again. Instead, he rose with her and caught her arm in his hand.

"Kate, wait."

She turned to him. He was standing close, his broad chest inches from her, his hand gently resting on her arm. He looked down at her, and she could feel his breath on her, smell his warm male scent.

"I know what it's like to lose people," he said. She could feel his voice in the trembling of her skin. "I know how hard it is. I'm sorry about your mom." He put his arms around her and drew her into a warm embrace. His heartbeat thrummed under the sounds of the breeze and the surf.

"Thank you," she murmured, turning her face toward his. "I ... "

That was all she got out, because then his mouth was lowering toward hers. The kiss started gently, a feather-light touch. A surge of heat ran through her body. She'd known it would if she ever touched him, kissed him, but this ... The force of the jolt was unexpected. He pulled away slightly, his eyes gauging her reaction.

Then she launched herself at him.

It had been so long, so long since Marcus, so long since she'd let herself feel this electric current of desire. She claimed his mouth with hers, pulled his body to her like it had always belonged there, pressed against her.

He let out a groan from deep in his throat and advanced, pushing her backward until her back was pressed against the wall, his mouth devouring hers before he released it and began tasting her jaw and the tender skin of her neck.

"Oh. Oh my ... oh. God." Her body was on fire, mirroring the blazing colors of the horizon.

When they pulled apart, he was the one who was pushing her away, holding her at a distance with his hands against her shoulders.

"That was ... Jesus. I need a minute." He scrubbed at his face with his hands, grabbed his wine glass from the side table, downed the contents in one gulp, and then went into the house.

She leaned back against the side of the house, her pulse pounding, all thoughts of grief and sorrow forgotten.

She could feel the stupid grin on her face but couldn't seem to remove it.

Holy hell.

She went into the house and found him emerging from the bathroom, where a bit of moisture at his collar told her he'd been in there splashing cold water on his face.

"Hey there," she said, perching on the arm of the sofa. "Where'd you go?"

"Look, I didn't mean ... I'm sorry."

"What the hell for?"

He fidgeted with his hands. "Well, you were upset, and I took advantage."

"I've got to invite you over and get upset more often."

From the look on his face, he seemed puzzled that his *I'm a cad, you're an innocent, oppressed damsel* script was not working out.

"I should probably go," he said.

"What? Why?"

"It's just, you know. Before things get out of hand."

"Would that be so bad?" She got up and walked toward him, and he backed up until his butt was against the kitchen counter.

"I'm serious."

She could see that he was. They'd shared a moment of high-voltage electricity. And now he wanted to leave.

"Okay." She tried to keep the disappointment and confusion out of her voice. "But what about the dinner? The cooking lesson. You've only showed me ..."

"Take the pork roast out in"—he checked his watch—"about another hour." He headed toward the door.

"What about the polenta? The salad?"

"I'll email you the instructions."

"But your pans! Your supplies!"

"Just keep them for now. You can get them back to me later."

He hit the door at a near run. He was on the sidewalk and halfway to his car when she called after him. "Jackson!"

He stopped and turned toward her.

"Why the hell are you running away?"

He seemed as though he might answer, but then he simply got into his car and drove away, his tires screeching slightly on the pavement as he accelerated.

Chapter Eight

"**A**nd then he ran out of here like there were wolves chasing him."

"Wow." Kate and Gen were sitting at her dining room table, eating the pork roast and the rest of the mushroom pizzette with a bagged salad Gen had brought up from her apartment. They were well into a bottle of wine, and Kate was waving her glass around for emphasis.

"I mean, this kiss was epic. Freaking *amazing.* And then, poof. He shot out that door like his ass was on fire."

Gen looked thoughtful. "That's not the reaction you usually expect after an epic kiss."

"No, it is not." Kate took another bite of pork roast. "Jeez, this is fabulous. But anyway. It's not like I was expecting a night of out-of-control jungle sex, just because we kissed. Though that would have been nice. But maybe another kiss or two. Some talking. Eat the pork roast."

"There's a story here." Gen pointed her fork at Kate.

"What do you mean?"

"I mean, there's something you don't know about him or his history that caused him to, you know, run like his ass was on fire." Gen raised one eyebrow at Kate pointedly.

Kate threw her hands up in frustration. "I don't know *anything* about him or his history. Which I might, if he'd stayed around long enough for, I don't know, a *conversation* about those things. But he didn't. He pulled out all of these painful emotional revelations from me, and then … Oh, no."

" 'Oh no' what?"

"I talked about my mom, and I cried. Right before the kiss."

"So?" Gen poured them each another half glass of wine.

"So, I don't know why I didn't see this before. I talked about my feelings and cried. And then he ran. You don't suppose he's so unevolved that he just couldn't cope with feelings, do you?"

Gen sighed. "God, I hope not. That would be depressing."

"Men can be that way, though." Kate got up and cleared their plates from the table. She carried them into the kitchen, turned back to Gen, and leaned against the counter.

"Yes, they can," Gen agreed.

Kate blew out a breath and ran her hands through her hair. "Well, that sucks. If that's what it is. Who would even want a guy you can't talk to? What would be the point?"

"I don't know." Gen hefted the platter bearing the rest of the pork roast and brought it into the kitchen, where she started running hot, soapy water in the sink. "I guess there isn't one."

"I guess not."

"At least he weeded himself out early, before you got emotionally invested."

"Yeah."

"But?" Gen looked at Kate expectantly.

"But, there was that kiss."

"Ah, that. Well, you could always keep your girly, emotional trap shut and just use him for sex."

Kate had to admit, the idea held a certain appeal.

"God. What is *wrong* with me?" Jackson was gently banging his head against the wall in the pool room at Ted's. Daniel stood across the pool table from him, cue in hand, an amused look on his face.

"She's probably wondering the same thing right about now."

"No doubt."

"Come on," Daniel urged. "It's your turn."

Jackson picked up his cue, surveyed the table miserably, and lined up his shot. "I was so fucking *rude*. I hauled ass out of there without even explaining about the poached pears." He took his shot, and the cue ball sent the nine careening pointlessly.

"Oh, horrors. You forgot about the poached pears!"

"Shut up."

Jackson drank from a mug of beer as Daniel took his turn. Daniel, who wasn't in turmoil over a woman, was beating Jackson handily. He sank several balls, and when he finally missed, he straightened and faced Jackson.

"So, why? Why did you rush out of there like that, especially after what you describe as a very good kiss?"

Jackson shook his head and rubbed at his eyes. "I don't know."

"Yeah, you do."

"Oh, fuck off. You're worse than a shrink."

They stayed silent while Jackson took his turn. He sank the twelve, then missed an attempt to get the fourteen in the corner pocket.

"Yeah, I guess I do know," he finally admitted.

"Okay. So what was it?"

"I was afraid we were gonna sleep together."

Daniel peered up at him from where he was leaning over the table. "You know that if a girl pressures you, it's okay to say no."

"Ah, you're such an asshole. Shut up."

Daniel chuckled. "Sorry, sorry. Go on."

"It's just ... " Jackson took a moment to gather his thoughts. "That's what I always do. I meet a woman, we go out, we sleep together right away. And it's good. But then pretty soon it isn't good anymore. It's what I always do. And I'm afraid if I do what I always do ... "

"It's going to turn out the way it always does," Daniel finished for him.

"Well ... yeah."

Daniel took a slug from his beer and looked thoughtful. "Okay. You're not wrong that maybe you should take a different approach this time. Except that now you've got her thinking the kiss was just so repellent to you that you couldn't wait to get out of there."

The thought hit Jackson with surprising force. "But that isn't ... She can't think that. Does she?"

Daniel shrugged. "It's possible."

"Ah, jeez."

"So what are you going to do?"

Jackson pointed one finger at Daniel. "That kiss was *not* repellent."

"I repeat," Daniel said. "So, what are you going to do?"

"I don't know. But I'll think of something."

The next morning, a Wednesday, Kate was unlocking the front door at Swept Away, putting out her sandwich board sign advertising ten percent off new releases, when Jackson's truck drove by on Main Street as he headed toward Neptune.

She was involved in her tasks and didn't notice him until the truck came to an abrupt stop two doors down. The street was mostly empty at this hour, so he threw the truck into reverse and pulled to a stop in front of her. Jackson put the truck in park, pulled on the emergency brake, and got out, his face stormy and intense.

He stomped over to where she was arranging the sandwich board.

She looked up in surprise. "Jackson, hi. What ... "

That was all she got out before he grabbed her, pulled her into his arms, and kissed her with an intensity that made her toes tingle. In an instant she was hot and limp, melting against him, feeling the rush of pleasure and fire through her veins.

Just as abruptly, he released her, leaving her barely able to stand upright.

"Last night's kiss was *not* repellent," he said, pointing one finger at her.

"Okay. No. I didn't think it was." She leaned against the door of the shop for support.

He got back into his truck, threw it into drive, and sped away, leaving Kate to wave after him with a dreamy look on her face.

Kate didn't see Jackson over the next couple of days—but she did hear from him. He sent her emails detailing the preparation of the dishes he'd neglected to make the night he'd come to her house. Instructions on the polenta, including tips to keep it from sticking to the pan or clumping. A reminder that she could make the poached pears ahead of time and have them finished and out of the way before Zach and Sherry arrived. A course-by-course wine pairing list, along with a note indicating that he didn't expect her to provide a different wine for each course, he simply wanted her to have that option. A note on where she should buy the produce for the salad, and where she could find the most succulent pork roast. Some hints on presentation, including plating and garnishing.

All in all, it amounted to more than a dozen emails between the kiss on Wednesday morning and the dinner on Friday night. On Friday morning, Lacy dropped by the shop before her shift at Jitters, and Kate showed her the long series of emails, some businesslike, some chatty, some with photos attached as visual aids.

Lacy browsed the emails and laughed. "Oh honey, he's got it bad."

"You think?" Kate was peering at the screen over Lacy's shoulder.

"Oh, yeah. No question. Most of these are just so he can be in touch with you. I mean, nobody cares that much about how to make polenta."

Kate considered that. "He's Jackson Graham. He might care that much about polenta."

"Okay, granted. Fair point. But look at this one, about the polenta." She brought up one of the emails and gestured at the screen. " 'Stir with a counter-clockwise wrist motion'? At this point, he's just making stuff up. He just wants to be writing to you."

Kate leaned one hip against the counter, arms crossed, considering. "Do we think that's creepy or cute?"

"Oh, cute, definitely. I wish I had a guy that hot advising me on my counter-clockwise wrist motion." She sighed. "So, what are you going to do about him?"

"What do you mean?"

Lacy clicked the laptop shut. "I mean, this isn't the Dark Ages when women had to wait for men to ask their fathers for permission to take them courting. He can make moves, you can make moves. He can ravish you in front of the store, you can … I don't know. Call him."

"I'm not sure," Kate said.

"Which part aren't you sure about? The part where it's not the Dark Ages, or the part where you call him?"

"The part where I call him."

Kate pulled some new releases out of a carton and stacked them on a shelf. Lacy followed her around while she worked.

"Why aren't you sure?"

Kate shrugged, her arms full of books. "It's just, the way he rushed out on Tuesday night was kind of … strange. I don't know what it means. I don't know what to think about it."

"You could try asking him what it means."

"He's a guy. He probably doesn't know what it means."

"Well. Right. That could be true. We could ask Gen to ask Daniel Reed. She's doing a lot of work with him at the gallery right now, and he's Jackson's best friend."

"No." Kate stopped what she was doing and faced Lacy, her hands full of books. "We're not doing that. We are not in ninth grade."

"Okay, okay." Lacy grumbled under her breath, "But it always worked for me in ninth grade."

On Friday, Kate left Althea in charge in the afternoon and left work early to plan for the evening. She bought the groceries according to the list Jackson had provided for her. She went home, carefully prepared the pork roast as he had taught her, and put it in the oven. She made the salad—all except for the dressing—covered it in plastic wrap, and set it in the refrigerator for later.

She poached the pears just as he'd told her in a particular step-by-step email that had run several pages when printed out.

They smelled fantastic. When those were done, she put them in a decorative bowl, wrapped them, and put them away. She whipped the cream to go on top, and put that in the refrigerator next to the pears.

For someone who didn't cook often, she felt good about how it all was turning out. She burned the edges of the crust of the pizzette, but that problem was solved with some creative slicing of the appetizer. Some of the polenta did stick to the pan, as she'd feared, but enough didn't that it hardly mattered.

When the food was ready, she turned her attention to the house. She tidied everything up, cleaning the kitchen and putting away the pots and pans, sweeping the floor, shoving her own clutter into cupboards and closets until it was out of sight, placing candles strategically throughout the house, and sprinkling dark red rose petals across her comforter.

By the time she had dragged the dining room table out onto the deck and had set the table with white linens and sparkling dishes, she was beginning to feel a little jealous that this dinner was for someone else and not for her. When was the last time a man had made a fuss over her?

Of course, to be accurate, Zach wasn't making a fuss over Sherry—Kate was. But when was the last time a man had gone to the trouble to enlist someone else to make it look like he'd made a fuss over Kate? Never. Or at least, it had been so long that she barely remembered.

Kate hoped that Sherry would appreciate the gesture—regardless of who had actually done the work—and she also hoped that Zach would follow through on his intentions to compromise in the relationship to make it work. While she wanted these things for Zach, so that he could save his relationship and be happy, she wanted it for her own reasons, as well. She wanted to believe that a marriage could work, that problems could be worked out, that love could prevail in the face of differences and disagreements. She wanted to believe in romance. She wanted to have *hope*. Hope for love in general, but also hope for love for herself.

If she could engineer another chance for Zach, maybe someday she could do the same for herself.

When Zach arrived, she showed him around the house and gave him a last-minute briefing on how to reheat everything, which course to serve when, how to plate it—according to Jackson—and how to complete the last-minute prep.

She instructed him to tell Sherry he'd made the food himself, and even gave him some details on the preparation of each dish so he'd be able to sound convincing, should she start asking questions. Then, finally, she'd wished him luck and hurried out of there before Sherry's scheduled arrival.

"Kate? Thank you," Zach had said at the door as she'd rushed down the walkway and toward the stairs down to Gen's apartment. "I mean it. This is great."

"You're welcome. Just don't screw it up. Don't argue with her! About anything. Don't get into that ex-spouses-bickering-about-old-grudges thing. Remember, you're wooing her!"

"I've got it." He went over to her, kissed her on the cheek, and squeezed her hand. "You're the best, Kate."

"Yeah, yeah." She waved him off. "Now, win that woman!"

She spent the evening down at Gen's place, where Kate ate takeout pizza and Gen munched on a salad, and they watched movies on Netflix. Once or twice, when they'd heard Zach and Sherry moving around on the deck overhead, Kate had eased open the sliding glass door and listened to see how things were going. She knew she shouldn't be eavesdropping, but after all her work, she couldn't help it. She'd heard soft voices, but couldn't quite make out what they were saying. It was just as well, since, of course, it was none of her business.

Kate had planned to sleep down at Gen's place, but that turned out not to be necessary. At around eleven, Zach texted her to say they wouldn't be spending the night. At first, Kate had been alarmed, thinking something with the date must have gone wrong. But he reassured her, saying that Sherry had agreed to go to counseling with him so they could try again— mission accomplished. She just hadn't been ready to take the step of spending the night with him.

So, she'd gone upstairs, said goodnight to Zach, put the place back in order—he'd washed the dishes, but there were still the candles and rose petals to deal with—and crawled into bed. Propped up against the pillows, she'd taken one last look at her laptop before turning in for the night.

Logging in to her email, she found a message from Jackson, sent just fifteen minutes earlier.

How'd it go?

She wrote back:

Pretty well. The food looked good. I burned the edges of the pizzette, though.

She looked at the clock. At almost midnight on a Friday night, he was probably just finishing up at the restaurant, preparing to go home. She thought she likely would not hear from him again until the following morning, so she was surprised when a response promptly appeared in her inbox.

Cut off the burned parts?

She grinned and wrote back:

That's what I did. Zach said it went great.

She got no response for a while, and she thought she should shut the laptop and go to sleep. Just as she was about to follow through on that thought, another message came in.

Since Zach and Sherry had a nice date, maybe we should, too.

A little zing of excitement rushed through her. She typed:

What did you have in mind?

His response came in moments later.

I'll call you tomorrow to ask you in a gentlemanly fashion, without the email.

Jackson was going to ask her out, formally, on a date. She thought of kissing him, first on her deck and later outside the shop. She remembered the rush, the liquid feeling of desire.

Okay. ☺

She looked at her unsent response, considered whether the emoticon made her look like a teenager, and deleted it. She tried several alternative answers:

Okay.

Okay!

I'll talk to you tomorrow.

Tomorrow, then.

Talk to you then, big guy.

She deleted them all and laughed at herself. In the end, she opted for:

Thank you for your help with the dinner. Have a good night, and I'll talk to you tomorrow.

She closed the laptop, set it on the side table, and snuggled down under her covers.

Chapter Nine

The following day she had plenty of work to do at the shop. Saturday was one of her busiest days, especially during summer. She opened an hour earlier and closed an hour later than she did during the rest of the week, and she also liked to provide a little something extra on the weekends: an author appearance, tea and cookies, or maybe story time and a craft in the children's section.

Today, she was keeping it simple, with a two-for-one sale on used books and a refreshment table including lemonade and cookies from the bakery case at Jitters. Simple mattered, because she and Althea still had to plan their Art Walk event, and they were running out of time. The more rumors filtered through to her about what everyone else on Main Street was doing, the more she realized she was going to be caught unprepared if she didn't get moving.

She was planning to meet Althea for a brainstorming session at nine a.m. The store would be open, but business usually was slow that early in the morning. It would give them time to think, to discuss, to hash out a solid plan for their event.

Jackson was supposed to call her today, but she willed herself not to think about it. How stupid would it be for a grown woman to wait by the phone, all nervous and moony-eyed? It would be very stupid, indeed. She was a responsible business owner, and she had things to do. Things other than waiting for a man to call.

She dressed for the day—linen capris, a pair of stylish sandals, and a silky sleeveless blouse—gathered her things, and got out of the house by eight-thirty. The morning was clear and warm, with a light breeze coming off the ocean. Temperatures in the low seventies. A perfect summer day.

She parked her car in a space behind the store and walked over to Jitters to pick up her cookie order. Occasionally, when she wanted something special, she had the bakery down the street make her iced sugar cookies shaped and decorated like popular books, but that was too much time and expense for a regular Saturday. The basic shortbread cookies at Jitters would have to do.

When she popped her head into the coffee place, Lacy was behind the counter, apron on, making espresso for a waiting customer. The strong scent of coffee hit her the moment she walked in the door, along with the sounds of easy conversation and the light jazz playing over the speaker system.

"Hey!" Lacy greeted her. "You here for the cookies?"

"Yeah. And, mmm. Maybe a latte. I had coffee at home, but I can't resist the smell."

"Coming right up." Lacy finished the other customer's order and started making Kate's soy latte, with extra foam and a sprinkling of cinnamon. "So, how'd it go last night?" Lacy asked while she worked. "With Zach and his ex?"

"Good. At least, he says it was good. They didn't stay the night—so there's that—but he says she's agreed to go to counseling with him, see if it's worth trying again."

"Well, that's something," Lacy said over the whoosh of the milk steamer.

"Yeah, it is. I hope it works out for him. He's a good guy. Just … you know. Not for me."

"Not like a certain auburn-haired chef I know." Lacy grinned at Kate as she set her latte on the counter in a large to-go cup.

"Oh, stop it."

"What's up with that, anyway?" Lacy leaned forward con-spiratorially, her forearms braced on the counter.

"He's supposed to call me today." Kate took a sip of the latte and sighed in pleasure.

"Post-dinner recap? A critique of your braising skills? De-construction of your counter-clockwise wrist motion?"

"He says he's going to ask me out."

Lacy stood up straight. "On a date?"

"That was my assumption."

Lacy pumped one arm in the air. "Woo, woo!"

Kate shook her head vigorously. "No. Not, 'woo woo.' It's just ... well, I don't know what it is yet. Let's hold onto our celebrations until we see what it is."

"Fair enough."

Connor, a dark-haired guy in his twenties who was work-ing behind the counter with Lacy, emerged from the back room with a pink bakery box filled with Kate's cookies. "Here ya go, Kate. I'll ring you up."

"Thanks, Connor."

As she was handing over her debit card, he said, "It sounds kind of 'woo woo' to me. I mean, I heard about that kiss he laid on you earlier this week. Hot." He shrugged. "I mean, I didn't see it. But I heard it was hot."

Kate looked at him, stunned. "You heard about the kiss?"

"Well, yeah." He handed back her debit card and receipt. "Around here, everybody knows everything. You know how it is. But don't worry, nobody's judging."

"They're not?"

"Nah. They're saying it's about time."

Kate didn't like the fact that people in town were talking about her kiss, but she shouldn't have been surprised. Small towns were like that. And Main Street was a small town within a small town. If Owen at the cheese shop across the street saw something, he'd call Elinor at the clothing boutique next to him, and she'd let everyone in her bridge club know. That's just how it was. There were no secrets on Main Street.

Kate hurried into the shop, where Althea was already waiting, looking vaguely irritated—as she always did.

"We've been open five minutes already," Althea complained.

"Yes, I know. I was picking up the cookies. Help me set up the table?"

"It's ready," Althea replied. "I had plenty of time to get it prepared while I was *waiting* for you."

Annoyed, Kate set the cookie box and her purse on the counter and turned to Althea, fists on her hips. "Althea. Have we had even one customer by"—she checked her watch—"9:07 a.m.?"

The woman looked uncomfortable. "Well, no."

"Then perhaps you can tell me what, exactly, the burden was that you had to bear during the five- to seven-minute period when you were waiting for me."

"Well. It's not about that," the older woman insisted, her face set in an unattractive pout.

"Then what is it about? Because it seems to me that every day, you evaluate my job performance and find me lacking. I suppose you think you could run this place better than I do?"

"Yes!" she exclaimed. "I could! Anyone could! A … a … a *trained monkey* could! At least it would *be on time!*"

The two women glared at each other for an interminable moment. A pair of tourists walked by on the sidewalk outside. Bright morning light filtered in through the windows. A fly buzzed lazily overhead before landing on a stack of books.

"It seems as though you don't really enjoy working here, Althea," Kate said at last.

"I enjoyed working for your mother," Althea said, a defiant, angry look on her face. "*She* knew the value of promptness and professionalism. *She* put her every spare moment into making this store something special. And *she* knew what I was worth!"

Kate tried not to let the words hurt her, but they did. She had always suspected that she fell short of her mother, in so many ways. Here was Althea, confirming that fear. It stung, and Kate felt wounded.

"Maybe if I had some support instead of constant, nagging criticism, I might be better able to meet your expectations, Althea," Kate said coldly. "Maybe it's your attitude that's bringing down my performance."

Althea blanched. She blinked rapidly a few times. "Well. I think it might be time for us to reevaluate our arrangement here," Althea said, pouting. "I'm sure it was time long ago, in fact. I won't put up with this any longer. And I won't be talked to with such disrespect."

Never mind that Althea wasn't the one who had been compared unfavorably to a trained monkey.

Kate felt sudden remorse for the way she'd spoken to the older woman. Althea was annoying and controlling, no doubt, but that didn't mean Kate had wanted to put her out of her job.

"Althea, wait …"

Althea fussed around behind the counter, grabbing her purse, her sweater, and the lunch she had packed. "I'll just be out of your way. If it's all right with you, I'd like to pick up my final check later today." Kate could see tears forming in the woman's eyes.

"Althea, I didn't mean … "

"Yes, you did. I'll just be going. Good luck to you, Katherine." She walked out the door, the little bell affixed to the top of the door frame jingling in her wake. Kate knew that what she'd really meant was, *Good luck keeping this business afloat without me.*

Kate leaned against the counter. "Well, shit."

She felt the hard press of stress against her breastbone as she arranged the cookies on a plate and placed them on a table Althea had done up with doilies and fresh-cut flowers. Under the guilt and the tension, she was a little bit relieved. Althea did a lot around here, but the woman's disdain toward Kate made every day a trial. Why did she dislike Kate so intensely? Althea had a reputation for being prickly and difficult. Maybe it was just her personality. Maybe it had nothing to do with Kate.

In any case, she was on her own now.

She put out a pitcher of iced lemonade and some cups, arranged napkins beside the cookie plate, surveyed her results, and sighed. She'd have to advertise for a replacement right away. She would need help before the Art Walk event. Then there was the fact that the store was open seven days a week, and Kate had no desire to work every day without a break. Once she found someone, it would take some time to train them well enough that they could be left alone at the store on her days off.

Shit.

She didn't think Althea would suffer financially due to losing this job. From Kate's understanding, Althea was retired from a longtime job as a bookkeeper and worked mainly to keep herself busy. She'd worked here because she loved books. She just didn't seem to love Kate.

The phone rang, and Kate snatched it up. "Swept Away, this is Kate. May I help you?"

"Althea quit?"

Rose. "How could you possibly know that already?"

"She came into the wine shop just a second ago and gave me an earful. 'Your *friend* did this, and your *friend* did that.' Emphasizing the word 'friend,' to indicate the absurdity of anyone befriending you."

Kate groaned. "Of course. I suppose you think I was too hard on her."

"Oh, hell no," Rose said. "I don't know how you've put up with her this long. She's always been a pain in the ass."

Kate laughed. "Yes, she has. But now I don't have any help."

"You'll find someone."

"Before Art Walk?"

"Hmm. Good point."

A customer came into the store, the bell jingling. "I've gotta go," Kate said, and hung up the phone.

All morning, Kate helped customers, got caught up with bookkeeping, accepted used books from a customer in exchange for store credit, placed orders for new books, dusted shelves, washed the windows that faced Main Street, wrote Althea's final check—which she did with some grumbling—answered phone calls, and packaged some orders for shipping. By noon, she was hungry and eager to break for lunch—which she usually would have done while Althea covered the store. But now, since she was on her own, leaving would mean closing the store for an hour. She was hesitant to do that, because the stream of traffic into the shop had been steady all day. She didn't want to lose an hour worth of business.

She decided she would call Sal's, the Italian place three doors down, and have them deliver something, just as soon as she got a break. In the meantime, she grabbed a sugar cookie from the plate she'd set out and munched on it to hold her over.

In the back of her mind, she kept wondering when, and if, Jackson would call. She didn't want to be one of those women hanging on the actions of a man, but she couldn't help thinking about what she would say, and what he would say, and where it all would lead. Of course he wouldn't call now. It was noon, the lunch rush. He'd be busy at Neptune, searing scallops, or doing whatever mysterious magic with food that he did. He'd be more likely to call at midafternoon. Lunch over, the prep for dinner not yet in full swing. She'd worry about it then.

Chapter Ten

The phone did ring at around two p.m., just as she'd expected. As she reached for the phone, the dozens of times she'd rehearsed the conversation in her mind escaped her, her mind went blank, and she had no idea what she was going to say.

"Swept Away, this is Kate speaking. How may I help you?"

"Hey, honeybunny." The voice she was hearing was not the one she'd expected. A feeling of dread replaced her nerves.

"Dad."

"So, how's my girl?"

She tried to gauge from his voice what he would need from her this time. Money? Bail? A ridiculously inconvenient favor? As much experience as she'd had with him, she wasn't good enough to peg the reason for his call this early in the conversation.

"I'm good, Dad. What's up?"

"Why does something have to be up for a father to call his daughter?"

She rolled her eyes. They went through this routine every time. He always spent a certain amount of time pretending he was just calling out of love before getting to his real purpose. Any attempt to hurry him along would be fruitless.

"I'm sorry, of course it doesn't. It's just that the shop is really busy today, and ... "

"So, you don't have time for your dad? Oh. I see. I guess that's why you haven't called me in, what is it, two months?"

Another necessary stop on their usual route: him laying guilt on her so she'd be more receptive to whatever it was he wanted from her.

"Has it been that long?" She rested her forehead against the wall as she talked. "I guess time got away from me."

"I guess it must have. Angela keeps telling me, 'Don't worry about her, she's a grown woman. She'll call when she's ready.' But a father can't help but worry."

About yourself.

"How is Angela?"

Besides cold, calculating, and bitchy, that is.

"Oh, you know. Dealing with some health issues. But she's hanging in there."

Angela was always "dealing with health issues." It was her method of keeping Thomas Bennet's attention on her at all times.

Kate calculated that the pleasantry requirement had been fulfilled. She waited for the inevitable request.

"So, we were wondering if we could come by for a visit. Stay a few days. Angela and I could set up in that cozy apartment you've got downstairs, and we could all spend a little quality family time."

The idea of "quality family time" with him and Angela made Kate's blood pound in her veins. Any chance of "quality family time" had evaporated when her father had left her mother—for Angela.

"I'm afraid that won't work," she said. "I've rented out the apartment."

"Whaaat?" His expression of surprise was exaggerated. "But I thought you were keeping that free for visits from family."

She banged her head softly against the wall. "Nope. It's been rented for over a year now." Which he would know if he'd been here even once during that time. Not that she wished he had.

"Well, that's okay. We can squeeze in at your place. I'm sure somebody can take the sofa."

Okay, that was a good one. If "somebody" took the sofa, that meant two people would be in the bed. And since Kate wasn't about to sleep with either her father or Angela, that meant he intended to turn her out of her own bedroom.

"If you really want to visit, there's a lovely bed and breakfast here in town," she said, feeling sick already at the thought of him coming to Cambria. "There are several, in fact. I can give you some names and phone numbers."

He was silent. Letting the guilt sink in, the fact that his own daughter didn't want him to stay with her.

"Dad?"

"Oh. I see. You'd prefer that we stay elsewhere."

A customer walked through the door of the shop, and Kate uttered a silent prayer of thanks. "I've got to go, Dad. I have a customer."

"But I thought ... "

"We'll talk later. Love you. Bye." She hung up the phone, took a deep breath, and greeted her customer. Less than five minutes later, the phone rang again.

"Swept Away."

"Angela doesn't see why we can't just stay with you."

Kate closed her eyes, tight. "She's seen my place. She knows it's very small."

"Maybe your tenant can stay with friends for a few nights. Maybe ... "

"Dad. I am not turning my tenant out on the street so you can use her apartment. I have to go."

"But ... "

"I'm hanging up now."

When the phone rang again five minutes after that, she was out of patience, and dispensed with her usual professional greeting.

"Look. I told you I can't talk right now. I'm *busy*. I have a *business* to run. If you've called to lay on more guilt ... "

"Actually, I called to see if you wanted to have dinner with me. But if it's a bad time ... "

"Oh, God. Jackson."

"Women usually say that to me under happier circumstances." She could hear the smile in his voice.

She groaned. "I thought you were somebody else."

"They usually don't say that." He paused. "Look. You were obviously in the middle of something. Why don't I ... "

"No, wait." She held the phone away from herself, took a few deep breaths, and brought the receiver back to her ear. "Okay. Let's start over. Swept Away, this is Kate speaking. How may I help you today?"

"Do you have any Stephen King?"

"Oh, come on." She found herself smiling, forgetting about the stress she'd been feeling before he called. "You mentioned something about dinner."

"Yeah. I just ... I was wondering if I could take you out some night. For dinner. That somebody else would cook. You know, like a ... a date."

He was nervous. It was adorable that he was nervous.

"We could do that. What night did you have in mind?"

He cleared his throat. "Ah. Monday? I know Monday is a lousy date night, traditionally not a typical night for that sort of thing, but my schedule … "

"Monday is great."

"It is?"

"Sure. I eat on Mondays."

"Ha. I do, too."

"It works out, then."

He was silent for a moment as she enjoyed the charm of his discomfort. "I'd really like a do-over. The other night, the way I rushed off … I think we should do it over. But without the raw pork roast."

"What about the kissing? Would there be a do-over of the kissing?"

"I can always hope."

He told her he would pick her up at seven—it would give her just enough time to close the shop, go home, and change clothes, but not enough time to obsess over how the evening would go.

Though she suspected she would do that anyway.

As she hung up the phone, Jane Austen, the Swept Away cat, leaped onto the counter, and Kate stroked her smooth back. "Oh, Jane Austen. Do you think I'm ready for Jackson Graham?"

Jane Austen simply purred.

On Sunday, Kate knew she had to put thoughts of Jackson aside and figure out what the hell she was going to do for Art Walk. Since a full-scale carnival with a Ferris wheel, cotton candy, and a Tilt-a-Whirl was out of the question, she thought she had better focus on what would be practical and doable in less than four weeks' time.

An author appearance and book reading was the obvious choice—it was what they'd done every year—but it was boring. A tiny store like hers didn't attract big-name authors, and the kind of author she *could* get didn't bring people in the door.

Still, this was a bookstore. It had to be an author.

So, a fun author. An entertaining author. Or at least someone who would arouse curiosity. It also had to be a local author, since she didn't have the budget to fly someone in from New York—or from anywhere, for that matter.

She went to the shop's Local Authors section and scanned the titles. They leaned heavily toward local history, with a few field guides to Central Coast plants and wildlife thrown in. Kate could feel herself nodding off just thinking about it. Sorting through the books on the shelves, she found a couple of biographies of local bigwigs, and a few things on Hearst Castle. That was interesting, but everything there was to say about William Randolph Hearst and the property up the coast had already been said. And anyone visiting Cambria from elsewhere had probably heard it already on a tour of the wildly popular attraction.

Kate was just about to give up hope when she came across one nearly forgotten volume tucked in at the far end of the bottom shelf. *Wild Woman,* the autobiography of Cassidy McLean, a 1980s film star who had opened a refuge for wild animals in Central California.

Hmm. Cassidy McLean. Kate had forgotten about her.

The refuge, less than an hour inland over the rolling hills of Highway 41, had at one time housed a number of lions, an alligator, several species of monkey, a potbelly pig, and a Bengal tiger. Kate didn't know what kinds of animals were there now, but she knew the refuge was still operating. If Kate could get Cassidy McLean to talk about her film career, and maybe bring a small animal, she could attract the adults who remembered the movies and kids who wanted to see whatever creature the woman could coax into a cage and bring out here.

Inspired, Kate opened her laptop on the shop's counter and called up the website for the refuge. After confirming the place hadn't been shut down by local authorities, she composed an email to Cassidy McLean outlining her plan. She promised to stock a good supply of *Wild Woman* for signing, and offered a small stipend—enough to pay for the gas to drive out here and a good dinner in town. She hit SEND and mentally crossed her fingers.

This could work. But first she's got to say yes.

Chapter Eleven

K ate was bustling around the shop at five thirty on Monday afternoon, preparing to close up early to give her plenty of time to get ready for—and obsess about—her date with Jackson, when Gen called.

"Your dad's here," Gen said. She had once told Kate that with difficult news, it was usually best to just blurt it out.

"He's where? Where is 'here'?"

"The house. He's here at the house. With his wife. And all their luggage. They said they'll be staying with you. For … for a while."

Kate closed her eyes and pressed one palm to the side of her head, as though she were in danger of having her brain fly out her ear. "What? *What?*"

"I'm sorry, Kate." Gen sounded miserable. "I just got home from the gallery, and they were sitting on the front porch with this little dog in a carrier, and with a crap ton of luggage. They were waiting for you. I didn't know what to do. I … I let them in."

"You let them *in?*"

"Oh, Kate. Please don't kill me, sweetie. Remember that you love me."

"I do, but … Oh, jeez. I have a date with Jackson! In an hour and a half! I don't have time to deal with … with my father and Angela, and their damned dog!"

"What can I do? What should I do?" Gen was near tears. "I already let them in, but I could … I could … Well, kicking them out would be really awkward. Maybe find them another place to stay? I could call around … "

Kate let out a deep sigh. "No, don't worry about it. I'll be right home. I'll do ... whatever it is I'm going to do. I don't know yet."

"Kate, I really am sorry."

"It's not your fault. See you soon."

On the drive home, Kate considered her options. She'd told her father that he and Angela couldn't stay with her. She'd suggested a B&B. She'd just go with that. She'd find them accommodations for tonight—good ones, a place that made her house look uncomfortable by comparison—shove them out the door, and then make herself busy over the next few days so she couldn't spend time with them.

Or she could just drive her car into the ocean.

She dismissed that last thought, because the car only had 42,000 miles on it. Seemed like too much of a waste.

She thought centering thoughts as she maneuvered her way along the winding roads that meandered through Lodge Hill, down toward Marine Terrace. *This isn't a life or death crisis. This is a minor inconvenience. I can deal with this. They'll be here for a short time, and then they'll go home. One foot in front of the other. Just get through it.*

When she arrived in front of her house, she saw that an unfamiliar car was parked in the tiny, single-space driveway. The car made her do a double-take. It had to be Angela's. There was no way her father owned a powder pink Cadillac with a Mary Kay logo on the back window. Looking more closely, she saw the car sported a license plate frame that said I <3 MY POMERANIAN.

She parked her car on the street, walked to the front door, took a moment of silent reflection, and then went inside. She hadn't gotten both feet on the tile of the entryway before a small ball of dun-colored fur launched itself at her ankles, yipping and growling in a way that made it sound like it might be choking on a Milk-Bone.

"Jazzy! Oh my goodness. Jazzy, you stop that!" Angela came rushing toward the door, where she scooped up the tiny dog and enveloped it in her arms. "What did you do to upset him?"

"Hello, Angela. No, I didn't get bitten, but thank you so much for asking."

Angela narrowed her eyes at Kate. "Jazzy doesn't bite. Do you, Mr. Jazzykins? Huh? Do you?" She cooed to the dog in baby talk, rubbing its head and making kissing gestures.

At a glance, it appeared that Angela had fully adopted the theme of Mary Kay pink. She was wearing a pair of pink pleated trousers, a pink button-down blouse, pink sandals, and a full complement of makeup in various shades of pink. Kate was surprised the woman hadn't dyed her hair pink. Instead, Angela's hair—a shade of honey that, at her age, likely came from a salon—was done in a shoulder-length bob that flipped up at the ends, putting one in mind of Mary Tyler Moore circa the *Dick Van Dyke Show*.

"Where's my father?" Kate asked.

"Now, what kind of welcome is that?" Angela put on her pouting face. "We drove more than seven hours to be here, and instead of greeting me with … "

"Where is my father?" Kate repeated.

Angela pursed her painted lips. "I sent him out to buy some decent coffee. It seems you only have the *bargain brand*." She shuddered delicately. "Cheap coffee makes my diverticulitis flare up."

"Well, when he gets back, we can get you checked in at the B&B, and … "

"Oh, that's not going to work out."

Kate came into the house, closed the door, set her purse on the kitchen counter, and turned toward Angela. "What's not going to work out?"

"The B&B."

"Why not?" Kate sounded whiny to her own ears, but at least she wasn't throwing glassware.

Angela sighed in a beleaguered and world-weary way. "I suppose they must have lost our reservation. They had no record of us, they said. Well, of course we came right here."

They had no record of you because my father never called.

"Okay. I'm sure we can work something out. I'll get them on the phone."

"They're full."

Kate felt anger rising through her body and up to her chest, making it hard to breathe. She controlled her voice. "Well, this is a tourist town. There must be more than a hundred bed and breakfasts, hotels, motels, and guest houses here. I'm sure we can find something."

"I called around, but no one will take us with our dog," Angela complained.

"Ah. The dog. There's a kennel ... "

"What?! I could never put Jazzy in a kennel. The very thought."

Fine, Kate thought. *Mr. Jazzykins can stay here. We'll put you in the kennel.*

Angela bent down and put Jazzy back on the floor. As she rose, she moaned about her lower-back pain. Jazzy ran around in a circle, lifted his tiny leg, and peed on the corner of Kate's sofa. Angela busied herself looking for something in her purse, which allowed her to pretend she hadn't seen Jazzy defile the furniture.

"Your dog just peed on my sofa."

"Hmm?" Angela didn't look up from where she was rooting around in the Coach bag—also pink.

"Your dog. He peed. On my sofa."

Angela waved an arm toward Kate. "Oh, just try a little vinegar and baking soda."

Since it was clear that Angela wasn't going to address the issue herself, Kate sighed and rooted around in her kitchen for the items. Since she didn't bake, it was unlikely she would have baking soda. And since she didn't make her own salad dressing, it was unlikely she would have vinegar. She didn't find the vinegar, but to her surprise, she did locate a box of baking soda in the back of a cabinet. She brought it out to the sofa with a damp cloth, to find Jazzy chewing on one of her throw pillows.

"Angela."

No response.

"Excuse me. Angela?"

"Hmm?" Angela raised her eyebrows questioningly but didn't look up from her iPhone.

"Could you put Jazzy in his carrier, please?"

Now Angela did look up, with an expression of shock and outrage. "But why?"

"Why? Seriously? He's chewing up my pillow."

Angela waved her arm again. "Oh, ha ha. Dogs will be naughty sometimes!"

"Angela! The carrier."

"But the drive took seven *hours*. The poor thing's been cooped up all *day*!"

Kate looked around helplessly, saw Jazzy's little rhinestoned leash sitting on top of his carrier, grabbed it, and thrust it at Angela. "Then take him for a walk."

At the sound of the word "walk," Jazzy ran to the two women and started yipping and spinning.

"He seems to like the idea," Kate said.

Angela shot Kate a look that said, *We're not done here.* She snatched the leash from Kate's hand and snapped it onto Jazzy's collar.

"Fine." She and the dog headed toward the door.

"And don't forget to clean up after him!" Kate yelled after her.

Her adrenaline surging, tension like a vise around her chest, Kate looked with incredulity at the amount of luggage they had brought. Two full-sized suitcases, two carry-on-sized rolling bags, the dog carrier, and three or four totes. It looked as though they planned to move in permanently.

Over Angela's dead body. Or Jazzy's.

She was on her knees scrubbing at the urine-soaked sofa corner when the door opened behind her.

"Katie!"

She looked up, the smell of dog pee wafting around her. "Dad."

Her father was standing in the doorway holding a grocery bag. In his early sixties, Thomas Bennet was an attractive man who presented himself in far better fashion than he could afford. He had dark hair sprinkled with gray. He wore khaki pants, a powder blue golf shirt, and—Kate could see this clearly from her vantage point—a pair of designer calfskin loafers.

"What are you doing down there?" he asked.

"Cleaning up your dog's pee."

"Ah. That's Jazzy for you. He pees on everything." He laughed jovially, as though this were a point of endless good-hearted amusement.

Kate abandoned her efforts with the sofa, stood up, and put the baking soda and rag aside. "Dad. What are you doing here?"

He looked at her in bemusement. "What do you mean? We talked on the phone about us visiting."

"Yes, but we didn't talk about when. And we talked about you staying at a B&B—not here."

He put the grocery sack down on the kitchen counter. As he removed the items from the sack, Kate could see that it contained not only coffee, but also brie, foie gras, and a $50 bottle of Scotch. Same old Dad.

"The B&B lost our reservation."

"So Angela told me. There are other hotels and B&Bs in town. A lot of them." She handed him her cell phone. "Start calling."

"Well." He looked at the phone, and then back at Kate. "I would have thought you'd be more welcoming. I'm your father. We hardly ever see each other. I thought … "

Oh, God, it was working. The guilt. She fought against it, but hell if it wasn't working.

"Dad, I didn't mean … "

"I know we have some issues between us. But I never thought it would come to me not being welcome in your home." He wiped at his eyes. Was he *crying*?

"I just thought you'd be more comfortable at a hotel, somewhere you can have privacy. You can see how small my place is." The argument sounded false to her own ears. As small as her house was, it was far bigger than a hotel room would be.

"Oh, we'll manage." He put the food into the refrigerator, as though the matter were settled. He started rummaging around in her cupboards for a glass, which he then filled with ice and two fingers of Scotch.

At that moment, Angela came back into the house, with Jazzy on his leash. She bent down and freed the dog, who immediately became a frenzied whirlwind of barking, snarling, and yipping. Then he dashed off into Kate's bedroom, probably intending to pee on something else.

"Well, that was a dreadful walk," Angela complained, sighing to indicate her suffering. "It's so *hilly* here. And there are no *sidewalks*. I thought I was going to break an ankle in these shoes."

"There are sidewalks in town," Kate said helpfully. "Where the B&B is."

"Kate ... " Thomas started in.

At that moment, with Angela complaining, Thomas gearing up for an argument, Kate going back onto her knees to take another crack at cleaning up the pee spot, and Jazzy in paroxysms of excitement over something in the next room, they heard a knock at the door, which was still open from Angela's arrival.

They all looked up as a group, and there, in the doorway, was Jackson, carrying a small pink bakery box and looking confused.

"Hi," he said.

"Oh," Kate said.

And from Angela: "Oh, my."

Kate scrambled up from her knees, noticed the foul-smelling rag in her hand, and rushed to dispose of it and wash her hands. "Jackson, come in," she said from the sink, her hands covered in suds. As she dried off, she made the introductions. "Jackson Graham, this is my father, Thomas Bennet, and his wife, Angela Bennet."

"I didn't know we were expecting company," Thomas said. *We.* As though it were his house, and he had every right to approve or disapprove the people who came to visit here.

"Jackson and I have a date," Kate said. "Which I would have mentioned if you'd called ahead to find out if this was a good time for a visit."

"There's no need to be so *rude,*" Angela scolded.

Jackson, looking bemused, held the pink box out to Kate. "Cupcakes, from the restaurant. I was going to bring flowers, but then I thought, why be a cliché?"

Kate took the box from him and peered inside. The little box contained two perfect cupcakes with pale green frosting and a sprinkling of crushed nuts.

"Pistachio," he said.

She felt that same little melting of her heart that she felt every time she was with him. "You brought me cupcakes."

"Yeah."

She looked up at him. "This is so much better than flowers."

He shifted from one foot to the other, smiling, obviously pleased.

Angela peered over Kate's shoulder and into the box. "Mmm, those look delicious!"

Kate snapped the box closed. Jackson said, "If I'd known Kate was having family over, I'd have brought enough for everyone. Maybe next time."

"Listen, Jackson," Kate said. "I got distracted when I got home, and I haven't showered or changed yet."

He shrugged. "I can wait. But you don't need to change on my account. You look beautiful the way you are."

"Oh, please," Angela scoffed. "Do you see what she's *wearing*? Of course she should change."

"On second thought," Kate said, "it might be better to just go. Let me grab my purse."

She put the cupcake box on the kitchen counter, retrieved her purse, ducked into the bathroom to arrange her hair and apply lipstick, and came back out. "Okay, I'm ready. Dad, Angela, we'll figure things out when I get back. Please don't let Jazzy pee on anything else."

As she spoke, the dog, having heard its name, emerged from the bedroom with a red patent leather peep toe pump in his mouth.

"Oh God," she said.

"I'll get it," Jackson offered. He scooped up the dog, gently pried the shoe from its mouth, put the shoe in the bedroom, and closed the bedroom door. Then he put the dog down on the kitchen tile. Jazzy promptly barked at the bedroom door, as though there were an intruder or a rasher of bacon on the other side.

"Let's go," Kate said.

They went out the front door and headed toward Jackson's truck. They got halfway down the driveway before Kate suddenly stopped.

"Hang on," she said.

She hurried back to the house, went in through the screen door, and found Angela with the bakery box in one hand and a pistachio cupcake in the other. Wordlessly, Kate plucked the cupcake out of Angela's hand, put it back in the box, and took the box away from her. She went back outside with the box to where Jackson was waiting for her.

"Now I'm ready," she said.

Chapter Twelve

The evening was warm and slightly breezy, with the tang of salt water in the air. They drove in Jackson's Chevy Silverado, a full-sized pickup truck he sometimes used to haul supplies for the restaurant.

"Where are we headed?" Kate asked. She tried to make her voice sound light and carefree, but the train wreck going on at her house made that difficult. She wondered how long her father and Angela would be staying, where they would be staying, and how many more of her belongings Jazzy would pee on or chew up before she got home. She also wondered why she wasn't better at standing up to them.

"I thought, The Sandpiper," he said. The Sandpiper was a restaurant across a small, two-lane road from Moonstone Beach. Popular with the tourists, the place was generally considered to be the second-best restaurant in town—after Neptune.

"Mmm," Kate responded, without really hearing him.

"That work for you?"

"Yes, sure. That's fine."

They drove for a while in silence. Finally, Jackson said, "If this is a bad night for you … I mean, I could see you had a lot going on at home … "

"What?" She looked up at him, paying attention now. "Oh, no. I don't want to cancel. Home is pretty much the last place I want to be right now. You did me a favor getting me out of there when you did."

"Yeah, I got that sense." He maneuvered the truck along Ardath Road, pausing once to let a deer and its fawn cross the road into the brush. He turned left onto Highway 1 and then made the turnoff for Moonstone Beach.

"Listen, if you want to talk about it … " he offered.

She did want to talk about it—oh God, she did—but she remembered what had happened the last time she'd talked to Jackson about her feelings. It had ended with him running out the door like he was competing for an Olympic medal. She didn't blame him for that. They barely knew each other—acquaintances for years, but on the wave-and-small-talk level—so she could hardly expect him to become her therapist. Especially if he was interested in her, which he apparently was. Everybody knew you didn't start a new relationship by whining about your problems.

"That's okay," she said, again aiming for that light, carefree, I'm-a-fun-girl tone. "Let's just enjoy our evening."

"Sure."

They arrived at the restaurant, and he parked the truck in the tiny gravel parking lot. She reached for her door handle, but she could see from the purposeful way that he was heading around the truck that he intended to open her door for her. She waited, and let him.

Only now that they were away from the circus going on at her house did she notice how good he looked. He was wearing charcoal slacks, a deep blue button-down shirt open at the neck, and a black blazer. His wavy hair was combed back, still damp from his shower. He was tall and broad, and he smelled like soap and a hint of aftershave. Getting out of the truck, with him standing so near her, she wanted to fold herself into his arms. She could hardly do that, though, within the first few minutes of their first date.

She felt unprepared, uncomfortable, somewhat frumpy and trollish compared to him. She was dressed nicely enough—she'd put on a good outfit for work that morning—but she hadn't had the opportunity to shower, change, and primp for him. She should have accepted his offer to wait for her. But if she'd done that, he'd have had a chance to talk to her father.

No, rushing out the door was definitely the way to go.

He held the door for her as they entered the restaurant. The place was usually packed with tourists during the summer season, but now, on a Monday night, the dining room held just a sprinkling of patrons.

"Jackson Graham," the hostess said warmly. "To what do we owe the honor?"

Jackson looked embarrassed, making Kate wonder whether he had a history with the tall blonde.

"Ah, knock it off, Lindsey." He sounded pleased but uncomfortable with her attention. "You know Kate Bennet?"

"Of course. Hi, Kate."

"Lindsey."

"Can you give us a table by a window?" Jackson asked.

Lindsey looked around and fixed her face in mock consternation. "As packed as we are, that's going to be a challenge. But if you slip me a twenty ... " She put one hand on his bicep.

"Very funny," he said.

"Follow me." She grabbed two menus and led the way toward a table for two with a spectacular view of the ocean, now pink and orange with the glow of sunset.

"Your server will be right with you," Lindsey said after they were seated and had their menus open in front of them. She gave Jackson a look and a wink, and then sashayed away.

Interesting.

"So, how do you know Lindsey?" Kate willed her voice to sound idly curious, as though she were simply making light conversation. In fact, she was reading the terrain. Kate knew Jackson's reputation with women, but it was one thing to know, and it was quite another to come face to face with the evidence during a date. Was Jackson so prolific with women that Kate would be encountering his ex-lovers on every corner? And how would she feel about that? It paid to know such things.

"Oh." He looked at the menu as though he were barely listening. He seemed a little too casual to be convincing. "She worked at Neptune for a while. You know how it is, we're in the same business. People tend to know each other."

"So you didn't date her?"

He looked up from the menu. "If I had, would there be something wrong with that?"

"No, of course not. It's just ... "

"What?" He put the menu down.

She shrugged. "I just like to know the lay of the land."

"The *lay*"—he smirked at the choice of words—"is that yes, we did date. A long time ago. It didn't last long."

"Why not?"

He looked at the menu again. "Ah, Christ."

She leaned back in her chair, offended. "Look, if I can't even ask a simple question ... "

"What?" He looked at her. "No, not that. It's this wine list. I can't believe they serve the Cambria Crest cabernet but not the Sapphire Seas. Who'd the guy at Cambria Crest have to screw to work that?" He shook his head with disgust.

Kate tried to gauge whether he was deflecting the conversation away from Lindsey, or if he really did care that much about the wine list. She decided it was the latter, since it meshed well with everything Rose had told her about him.

In a moment, their server, a tall, slender brunette named Ashley, who, Kate thankfully observed, gave off no particular vibe toward Jackson, came to take their drink order. Jackson seemed flummoxed by the lack of Sapphire Seas, but rallied nicely to order a San Simeon Estate Reserve cabernet sauvignon. She ordered the same thing, partly because she figured he knew good wines better than she did, and partly because she feared being yelled at if she made a choice he didn't approve of.

When they had placed their orders, Ashley turned to Jackson. "Max heard you were here, and if you don't mind, he'd like to put together something special for you."

"Max?" Kate asked.

"Max Singer, our head chef," Ashley added for Kate's benefit.

Jackson put down his menu. "Tell him to wow me."

"I think that's the idea," Ashley said.

When she was gone, Jackson said, "Max also worked at Neptune, before he got the gig here. I taught him everything he knows. First I had to undo the damage they did at that crappy culinary school he attended." He shook his head at the memory.

"Well, you must trust him, or we wouldn't be here."

He looked at her as though that were obvious. "I trained him."

Their drinks came, and they settled in, sipping the rich, dark wine and gazing out at the view, which was becoming more colorful with the passing minutes.

"So, how did you become a chef?" Kate asked.

"My mother is an excellent cook. She wasn't trained or anything, she just had a feel for it. I used to help her in the kitchen, and after a while I was better at it than she was. Something about food, it's just … " He reached for words. "You can paint a picture and hang it on the wall, and it just sits there looking pretty. Or not pretty, depending on the kind of art. But food—making a meal that nourishes people, makes them feel full and happy and well-cared-for—that's an art form that *means* something."

Kate nodded appreciatively. "Do you think you might open your own restaurant someday?"

His head swayed a bit in a gesture of uncertainty. "Maybe. But first I need to land a top job in one of the food capitals."

"Food capitals?"

"You know. New York. San Francisco. Los Angeles. One of the cities where a chef can really make a name for himself." He changed the subject slightly. "How is it that you never learned to cook?"

She smiled. "My mother saw cooking as drudgery that you had to endure for your survival. Most of her recipes involved boxed macaroni or cream of mushroom soup."

Jackson winced. "Ouch."

"Oh, I don't know. I liked it at the time. I still do, on occasion. It used to bug my dad, though. He has loftier tastes."

He sipped his wine and then raised the subject they were both thinking about.

"So, your dad … I take it his visit wasn't exactly planned?"

She wanted to launch into the subject, wanted to rail against her father, wanted to pour out her frustrations, seek advice, seek reassurance. She wanted to explain the troubled relationship she'd always had with her father, and the reasons for it, and her repeated, failed attempts to find common ground.

But last time she talked about her family, he ran.

And then, there was the fact that every piece of dating advice she'd ever read warned against dumping your problems on someone on a first date. Keep it light, keep it positive. No discussion of exes, and certainly no airing of long-held family dysfunction. No whining about how your father never fully accepted you, and then left you and your mother for another woman.

She knew that if she started talking about it, she wouldn't stop, and there probably would be tears. And then she'd never see

Jackson again, except when he needed a book or she wanted a meal at Neptune.

"No, the visit wasn't planned. And houseguests can be stressful."

"No doubt." He nodded. "But I got the sense there was something else going on, as well."

"No, not really."

He looked at her skeptically. "No bad blood between you and Angela?"

Oh, you have no idea.

Instead, she said, "What? No."

"Okay."

Ashley returned bearing two plates. She set them down with a flourish. "For your first course, heirloom tomato and haricot vert salad."

After Ashley was gone, Kate looked at her salad. "This looks wonderful. I don't even know what haricot vert is."

"They're the green beans," Jackson said. "A particular variety. You see how they're thinner than the green beans you're probably used to?"

"Okay, yeah."

To Kate, the salad was delicious. The flavor of the tomatoes, combined with the beans and a zesty, citrusy dressing, was fresh and appealing. Jackson was poking and scowling at his.

"What's wrong?" she asked.

"These tomatoes aren't local."

She put down her fork. "How can you tell?"

He cocked his head at her. "How can you tell if a book is a first edition? You know books, I know tomatoes. Among other things. You see the texture here? That means it was harvested probably weeks ago, and then it was sent on a truck to get here. Why the hell doesn't Max use local tomatoes? A salad like this lives or dies on the freshness of the tomato." He shook his head. "I taught him better than this."

She proceeded to finish her salad while Jackson simply poked at his, eating a few beans but avoiding the nonlocal tomatoes.

Ashley cleared their plates, scowling at Jackson's uneaten salad, and returned with their main course. "Merguez with chickpea puree and eggplant jam," she announced.

"Huh," Jackson said, looking at the plate. A long coil of grilled sausage lay atop a bed of puree, with the eggplant jam on top. A garnish of dandelion greens was artfully arranged in an X over it all, as though one might have used a map to find the food.

"Wow," Kate said. She took a slice of the sausage, dipped it in the puree, and tasted it with a bit of the eggplant jam. The combination of flavors exploded in her mouth, making her moan with pleasure.

Jackson was moaning, too, but for different reasons. "The dandelion greens are starting to wilt," he complained. "And the merguez is overcooked. The ends are dry. Ugh."

Kate was starting to get irritated. "Jackson."

"What?"

"Just eat, please."

"All right." He had a few bites, but when she looked up at him, he was staring at the plate with a furrowed brow and stormy eyes.

"So, did you enjoy culinary school? I'll bet you've got a lot of kitchen horror stories." She tried to change the subject.

He didn't hear her.

"Jackson!"

He looked up, startled.

"Good God. Do you just want to leave?"

"No." He shook his head. "No. But I do want to talk to the chef. I'm gonna kick his ass. I'll be right back." He wadded up his cloth napkin, threw it down beside the plate, and stalked off toward the kitchen.

Kate had been abandoned by dates before. Kenny MacElroy stood her up when she was sixteen and they were supposed to go to the movies. Evan Price took her to a party when she was twenty and left with another girl. But never had she been left at the dinner table while her date went off to berate the chef.

She sat there for a while, eating her dinner. Was it bad manners to go ahead without him? Maybe, but his manners were unquestionably worse, leaving her here alone. Yes, the dandelion greens were slightly wilted. And yes, it was true that in some areas, the sausage—whatever fancy name they'd called it, it was still sausage—was a little charred. But that didn't change the fact that she was hungry. And it also didn't change the fact that the mingled flavors of the puree, the fancy sausage, and the eggplant jam were undeniably appealing.

When she was halfway through her meal, she heard raised voices coming from the kitchen, followed by the sound of breaking glass. A couple of possible scenarios there. Jackson and Max were throwing stemware, or maybe some frightened, beleaguered server had wandered through the kitchen at the wrong moment and had become startled.

When she'd had enough—enough food, and also enough of Jackson's shenanigans—she placed her napkin next to her plate, gathered up her purse and her sweater, and walked out.

The evening was mild and clear. A few tourists walked on the wooden trail that led along the bluffs above the beach. The sun was down but the sky hadn't fully given way to darkness. A pale, silvery blue lay across the water, the day's last display of splendor.

Why hadn't she ordered dessert? She should have, should have ordered them all. When he got the check he'd think twice about abandoning a hungry woman at the dinner table.

She remembered the cupcakes. A crappy day, followed by a crappy evening, could maybe be salvaged with some really excellent cupcakes. It wouldn't hurt to try. She went to Jackson's truck, found it unlocked, and retrieved the pink box from the seat. She pulled her sweater on, walked across the two-lane road that separated The Sandpiper from the beach, and went down a rickety set of ancient wooden steps and onto the sand.

This close to darkness, most of the beachgoers were gone. A few people walked along the water line. A family with a small child, a couple holding hands. She found a seat on a piece of driftwood. The sound of the crashing waves was soothing. In the place where the sun had set, the water was a shimmery grey-blue, the color of forgotten dreams.

She pulled a cupcake out of the box and took a bite.

Oh, God. She closed her eyes and her taste buds hummed. Despite the pleasure going on in her mouth, she couldn't help thinking of the chaos of her day.

Her father. Althea. Jackson.

Shit.

That little yappy dog was probably chewing up her mother's copy of *Beyond the Boundaries of Desire* right now, as she sat here.

She heard footsteps on the sand behind her just as she was digging into the second cupcake.

"Kate?"

She turned her head and looked around, her mouth full of pistachio goodness. Jackson.

He sat down on the log beside her.

"You're eating my cupcake?"

She swallowed and looked at him sideways. "Who says it's yours? You brought them for me. That makes them mine. You want a cupcake, go back into The Sandpiper and make one. I'm sure Max won't mind."

Given his temper, she expected a fight. Was in the mood for one, actually. But instead of yelling, he chuckled.

"You're right. Giving up my cupcake is the least I can do. Listen, I'm sorry. I shouldn't have left you at the table. That was rude."

"You think?" She peeled the paper off the bottom of the last cupcake and popped the rest into her mouth.

"Max was pissed."

"He wasn't the only one." She wadded up the cupcake paper and put it back into the pink box.

Jackson turned to her. "Look, Kate … "

"Jackson. I don't know what you thought you were doing, but … "

"I was nervous."

She wasn't sure what she'd been expecting to hear—some defense of his giant chef ego, maybe—but it wasn't that.

"What?"

He looked down at his hands, which were resting in his lap. The posture was endearingly childlike. "I was nervous. About the date. About you. And when I'm nervous … I control things. I'm never nervous in the kitchen. I think I just wanted to be somewhere I felt like I knew what I was doing."

She found his confession confounding. "Now, why would you be nervous?"

"Seriously?"

"Yes. Seriously."

Now he was the one exasperated. "Because. Jesus. Is it possible you don't know that I've had a thing for you for years? My friends know. Your friends probably know. Lindsey back at the restaurant knows. I didn't want to fuck this up. So then I did. Fuck it up, I mean."

The wings of little birds flapped in her chest. Tiny starlings.

"You've had a thing for me for years?"

Still, he looked down at his hands. "Ever since the first time I came into the bookstore."

"You bought a Michael Chabon."

He looked up at her. "Yeah. You remember that?"

"I have a photographic memory for every book my customers buy."

His eyebrows shot up. "Really?"

"No, you idiot." She smacked his arm. "Not really. I remembered because it's you."

"Because ... Oh." He grinned, and it melted her, just a little.

"Jackson. We've known each other for, what? Years. Why didn't you say something before now if you felt that way?"

He picked up a small piece of driftwood from the sand and worried it in his hands. "Because I don't do well with women."

Kate let out a little scoffing sound. "That's not what I hear."

"That's not what I mean. I don't do well with women *long term*. We get together, we have fun, and then ... " He dropped the wood and made a gesture with his hands that might have indicated a magician's trick—*poof, it's gone*—or might have indicated an explosion. *Boom.*

One side of her mouth quirked up, and she glanced at him out of the corner of her eye. "Did you leave them at restaurants?"

"I might have. Once or twice. But, hell, what does it matter what I did in there? It's not like the date was going anywhere in the first place."

She sat up straight, surprised. "What do you mean?"

"Oh, come on, Kate. You wouldn't *talk* to me. Just small talk. Chitchat. It was clear you had a thousand things going on in your head, and they all had a big KEEP OUT sign posted on them."

She looked at him, started to say something, then stopped.

"See?" He pointed at her. "You won't *tell* me anything. I want to get to know you, but you're not letting me in."

"It's our first date," she said, exasperated.

He made a seesawing gesture with his hand. "Sort of."

"What do you mean 'sort of'?"

"Our first date, yeah. But like you pointed out, we've known each other for years. Waving hello, how was your weekend, all of that superficial bullshit. We've already done the chitchat. I'm sick of chitchat."

She picked up the piece of wood he'd discarded and held it in her palm, turned it in her fingers. "Well. I seem to remember talking to you—really talking to you—that night at my house. And you ran away."

"What?" He looked confused.

"I talked about my mom, and how much I miss her, and *that* was real. I *cried,* for God's sake. And you couldn't get out of there fast enough."

"You … That's … " He got up and stood on the sand in front of her. "You thought that's why I left?"

"Well, since I didn't see any bears chasing you, yeah."

He ran a hand through his hair, mussing it. "Ah, Christ. That's … " He gathered his thoughts. "It was the kiss."

"The kiss."

"Yes."

"Usually kissing someone is seen as a good thing. Usually, people stay."

"Uh huh. People stay, and then they have sex, and it's all hot and great, and it lasts for maybe a couple of weeks, and after that … " He made the *poof* gesture again.

Though it was dark on the beach now, a light dawned in Kate's mind. He was scared. He wanted her for more than fun, for more than he'd had with other women. She *meant* something.

"Come here. Sit down." She patted the log beside her. He sat, and she felt the warmth of him amid the cool evening. She scooted closer so that their bodies touched. She reached out and took his hand. He enveloped her hand in his, their fingers entwining. She rested her head on his shoulder, and she could hear him take in a deep, long breath.

"Okay," she said. "You asked what was going on with my dad. He showed up unannounced, with enough luggage to suggest he plans to stay for a very long time. He and I ... It's complicated. He left my mother for Angela when I was twenty-two. In some ways, it was a new beginning for my mom. She moved here, found her place in the world. But at the time, she was devastated. And so was I."

He squeezed her hand.

"Now, our relationship is mostly him seeing what he can get from me. He came to ask for money. I'm certain of that. And every time he shows up with an agenda instead of just wanting to be with me ... "

Tears rolled down her cheek, and she swiped at them with her free hand. "See?" She laughed bitterly. "When I talk to you about real stuff, I end up crying."

He reached out and touched her chin, turned her face toward him, and spoke softly. "I'm not running away. No bears."

"No bears?" Her voice was a whisper.

"No."

He kissed her gently, and she felt a warmth spread through her that was like a hot bath, or a blanket on a cold day. Like the comfort of coming home.

Chapter Thirteen

They walked on the beach in the moonlight, holding hands. He told her about how he'd come to live in Cambria. A guy he'd known in culinary school had decided to open a restaurant in one of California's most scenic towns and had recruited him to become head chef. She told him about her marriage and divorce—the short version. Marcus had been abusive, not physically but emotionally. He'd slept with other women and then gaslighted her, trying to convince her that her suspicions were the result of her own paranoia and emotional fragility.

When they came to the end of Moonstone Beach, to where the sand ends below the bluffs, he kissed her again. He turned her to him and wrapped her in his arms. The kiss before had been sweet, comforting. This one was urgent, sending a surge of electricity through her veins. She felt his heartbeat against her body, tasted his mouth, felt the rightness of it. The inevitability of him.

They walked back hand in hand, Kate feeling an excitement just under her skin. She hadn't expected this, whatever this was. Especially after the restaurant debacle, she hadn't expected to feel this.

By the time they got back to his truck, it was later than she'd expected. They'd been on the beach, talking, getting to know each other, for much longer than it had seemed.

"I guess I'd better take you home," he said, holding her in his arms beside the Silverado.

"I guess you'd better." She rested her head in the hollow of his shoulder. "I'd invite you back to my house, but my father and stepmother are there."

"Mm hmm," he murmured.

"There's your place," she said.

He looked down at her. "Next time," he said. "Or the time after that. Soon."

She nodded. "All right."

He opened the door for her and tucked her inside. Then he drove her home, to the place where she'd have to deal with the reality of her father and Angela.

They said goodnight at the door. She could see in his face that he didn't want to leave her, didn't want the evening to end with a proper, chaste goodbye. But this was new, this was something different. Jackson wasn't going to treat her like the others, and so she watched him drive off, a goofy grin on her face as she went inside.

She had expected to find her father and Angela watching TV or eating her food. She'd expected to find her belongings chewed and their luggage and clothing all over the living room.

She hadn't expected to find that they'd locked her out of her room.

Kate's part of the tiny house had just one bedroom, and they were in it, with the door locked behind them. The only bathroom was in there, too. At first, she thought she must be misunderstanding the situation. Were they even in there? Had they accidentally locked the door before they'd gone out somewhere? But the pink Cadillac was still in the driveway, and she could hear Jazzy snuffling at other side of the bedroom door.

For a minute, she just stood there in exasperation. They took her room. They were sleeping in her bed. She'd known they would try to manipulate her into giving them the bedroom. But it was one thing to know that, and another to come home and find that they'd taken over without discussion, intentionally locking her out so she couldn't get her things, couldn't even pee, for Christ's sake. And she really did have to pee.

She weighed her options. She knew she should bang on the door, demand that they clear out, and take back her bed. But the evening had been so lovely—the part on the beach with Jackson, not the part earlier, when her father and Angela had arrived unannounced. She didn't want to end the night with a family blowout, with yelling and accusations and the laying on of guilt.

Kate put her ear against the door and could hear her father snoring thunderously.

Jesus.

When she'd come in, she noticed that the light was still on downstairs in Gen's place. She checked the clock on the stove and saw that it wasn't quite midnight. She grabbed her purse, went down the outside stairway, and knocked gently on Gen's door.

Gen opened up wearing a leopard print robe and pink fuzzy slippers. Her face was eager as she greeted Kate. "Hey! How was the date?"

"Good. Really good. I need to use your bathroom."

"Okay. What's wrong with yours?"

"You wouldn't believe it."

She stood back to let Kate in. "Is it a good story?"

"It's a story, anyway. Let me pee first. Then the story."

A few minutes later, when Kate and Gen were sitting cross-legged on Gen's bed like a couple of teenagers, Kate's shoes kicked off and tossed aside, Gen said, "Okay, so what's going on?"

"My father and Angela locked me out of my bedroom."

Gen's eyes grew wide. "They *what*?"

"Not only are they staying with me when I explicitly told them they weren't invited, they waited until I was gone on my date, and then they moved into my room and locked me out, so I can't even get my pajamas or use my own bathroom."

"*No shit.*" Gen seemed to be in awe of their audacity. There might even have been a hint of admiration in her voice.

"I don't know what to do. Do I pound on the door, get them out of there, and send them to a Motel 6, or what?"

Gen nodded. "Yeah, you probably should."

"Seriously?"

"Yes. Look, honey, I know he's your dad, and there are some … *feelings* there. But he takes advantage of you. It's what he does. He doesn't call for months on end, and then when he does, it's because he needs money, or he needs a favor, or … "

"Or he wants to stay in my house and take over my bedroom."

Gen reached out and squeezed Kate's arm. "Yes."

Kate rubbed at her eyes. "I know. You're right. But I can't really deal with this tonight."

"Stressful first date?" Gen asked in sympathy.

"Yes and no. Yes, because first dates are always stressful, and also because Jackson abandoned me at the restaurant. But also no, because then there was the beach, and talking, and kissing. And cupcakes."

Gen adjusted her position and leaned back into a pile of pillows, getting comfortable. "Ooh. Kissing."

"Oh, God, yes, the kissing. Jackson is … he's just … " Nothing she could say to Gen would adequately describe the kissing.

"I see," Gen said.

"He's all blustery and angry and intimidating, and I think he threw some glasses in the kitchen. But he *listens,* and he's so … just so … " Kate held out her arms to indicate the enormity of what Jackson was.

"Oh, sweetie. You're gone."

"I know!" Kate flopped down on the bed and pulled a pillow over her head.

"He threw glasses in the kitchen?"

Kate peeked out from under the pillow. "Maybe. It might have been Max."

"Wait, wait." Gen waved her hands in the air. "Back up. Tell me what happened at the restaurant."

Kate told her, and Gen chuckled, shaking her head. "I've always heard stories about that Jackson Graham temper. Jeez."

"So I ate his cupcake."

"As well you should have, sweetie," Gen cooed. "As well you should have."

"Can I sleep here tonight?" Kate said.

Gen sighed. "Of course you can. But tomorrow, you have to do something about this." She pointed one finger at the ceiling.

"I will. I promise I will."

She fully intended to do something about the father situation the next morning, but she couldn't, because she woke up late, and when she went upstairs at a little after eight a.m., her father and Angela were gone. A note pinned to the refrigerator with a magnet said, *Gone out for breakfast. You need to buy groceries!!! See you when you get home from work. Dad.*

Kate sighed and crumpled up the note. Apparently her hostess skills were lacking. When someone turned up on your doorstep uninvited and took over your bedroom, you were supposed to have fresh croissants and a fruit platter ready for them when they woke up in the morning. Maybe some mimosas.

She peeked into her bedroom. The bed hadn't been made, and the sheets and blankets were in a tangle. An open suitcase lay on the floor, its contents scattered part in, part out of the case. In the bathroom, wet towels lay on the floor in puddles of water from the shower.

At least the dog wasn't here. Kate pictured it in Angela's purse, its fuzzy head peeking out while Angela and Kate's father ate eggs Benedict at The Sandpiper.

Kate checked the clock. She had two hours until Swept Away opened at ten a.m. She knew she should gather up their things, stuff them in the suitcase, put the suitcase on the front doorstep, and lock the door when she left for work. She could leave a note on top with the names of some excellent local hotels.

She seriously considered it for a moment, but the thought of the guilt her father would lay on her for months afterward stopped her. At least they were gone right now, and she could take a shower and get ready for work.

In the shower, she discovered that someone—likely Angela—had used the last of her shampoo.

At the shop that morning, Kate opened for the day. She put out the sandwich board—today's special was biographies, twenty percent off—put out some cat kibble and fresh water for Jane Austen, and cleaned Jane's litter box. Then she checked her emails. Amid the spam, the book order information, and the marketing emails from publishers, she found a message from Cassidy McLean. She clicked it open.

Dear Kate,

I'd love to appear at your Art Walk event. Cambria is so quaint and lovely! I'll bring Samantha with me, she's always a hit at get-togethers. Let's chat on the phone to pin down the details.

Kisses, Cass

Samantha? Who was Samantha? Kate Googled Cassidy Mc-Lean with the name Samantha, wondering if perhaps she was a partner at the wildlife refuge. It turned out that Samantha was a ring-tailed lemur.

Hmm. Okay. That's something the souvenir shop down the street won't have.

Kate returned the email, confirming that Cassidy and Samantha would appear at the Art Walk event and suggesting a time for them to discuss it on the phone. Then she Googled ring-tailed lemurs to have some idea what to expect.

While she was doing that, the bell above the door rang, and Althea came into the shop with a cat carrier.

"Althea." Kate greeted her coolly.

"Kate. I just came by to pick up Jane Austen."

Kate stood there mutely. She couldn't possibly have heard correctly.

"Excuse me?"

"Jane Austen. I came to get her. I'd have taken her with me the day I was *forced out of my job,* but I had to locate a cat carrier. As you can see, I have one. Jane! Jane Austen! Come here, girl." Althea hunched down toward the floor and started hunting around for the cat.

"What makes you think you can take my cat?" Kate demanded.

"*Your* cat? There must be some mistake," Althea said, her heavily lipsticked mouth arranged in a pout. "Jane Austen is, and has always been, *my* cat."

Kate took a moment to think about whether this was true. Two years ago, Jane Austen had walked into the store on a day when Kate had left the front door open to let in the cool ocean breeze. She'd made herself comfortable, climbing onto one of the easy chairs Kate provided for customers who wanted to sit and read. Jane Austen had settled in for a nap, and Kate hadn't had the heart to move her. When she'd returned the next day, and the next, Kate had bought her a bag of kibble, food and water bowls, and a litter box. She'd lived here ever since.

"She's not yours," Kate protested. "She lives in the store. She's the Swept Away cat!"

Althea straightened and crossed her arms defiantly. "Who usually puts out her food and water? Who usually cleans her litter box?"

"We both do that!"

"Hmm. Seems to me that in the last week I worked for you, I did those chores five times out of seven. *Five times* out of *seven*! So if anyone has a claim to this cat, it's me. Now, where is that cat? Jane Austen! Come on, sweetie, Mommy's going to take you home!"

Kate felt helpless. It was true that Althea probably fed the cat more often than Kate did. It was also true that Jane Austen had never lived at either one of their homes—she'd always been the shop's cat. Kate didn't have a bill of sale or papers of adoption to prove Jane Austen was hers. She'd just always thought of it that way.

"I'm the one who took her to get spayed!" Kate offered desperately. "I'm the one who takes her to get her vaccinations!"

"Humph." Althea looked at her with the scowl again. "You did those things because *I* told you they needed to be done. Why, if I hadn't badgered you about it, there's no telling *what* would have become of poor Jane! She'd probably have had two litters by now. Not to mention a nasty case of distemper!"

Althea located Jane Austen under a table and bent down to pick her up. "There you are!" Kate was trying to figure out what to do, how to stop Althea, whether it would be prudent or effective to block the door with her body, when Jackson came in the front door of the shop.

"Hey, Kate." He had a sexy smile on his face as he came in and approached her. "I just thought I'd stop by on my way to work and tell you … "

"There!" Althea said in triumph after forcing the yowling, protesting cat into the carrier and snapping the door shut.

"What's going on here?" Jackson asked.

"I'm taking my cat," Althea announced.

"She's taking *my* cat," Kate said miserably. "She quit, and she's striking out at me by *stealing my cat.*"

"If you don't like it, call the police!" Althea said, picking up Jane Austen's carrier and facing Kate in defiance. "You can explain to them how she's your cat even though she *loves me more!*"

"Oh, come on," Kate protested. "That's just … "

Althea headed toward the door, and Jackson took a couple of steps and stood in front of her, blocking her way. "Put down the cat," he said.

Oh, God. The last thing Kate needed was Jackson blowing a gasket and kicking an old lady's ass in the middle of her store. "Jackson … " she began.

"If you'll just step aside," Althea said.

"I'm asking you to put down the cat," Jackson said again, his voice calm—for the moment.

Kate could see this all heading downhill faster than an Olympic skier. Jackson would yell. Althea would cry. They might engage in a struggle for the cat carrier, each with a hand on the handle, pulling, until poor Jane Austen either got shaken violently inside the carrier or crashed to the floor.

Althea's face was turning red in indignation. "Jackson Graham, don't you bully me. This is my cat, and I'm leaving! Get out of my way!" Her shoulders were squared and her face was set in an expression of grim determination.

Jackson was gearing up for battle—Kate could see it in his face, as well. He'd sort of puffed up, like certain animal species did when they wanted to appear bigger to a potential rival. Which was ridiculous, since Jackson already was a foot taller than Althea.

"Althea. I told you to put down the cat. Don't make me take that carrier away from you." His voice was so intimidating, Kate could practically see his restaurant staff quaking in their kitchen clogs.

"Now, just hold on," Kate said.

They didn't hear her. Althea and Jackson were speaking over each other as the situation escalated.

"I'm leaving with this cat, and there's nothing you can … "

"I'd like to see you get through me, you decrepit old … "

"Stop!" Kate placed herself between Althea and Jackson. She faced Jackson and put her hands on his chest in a gesture meant to calm him. "Jackson, I want you to stop," she said. Without turning around, she said, "Althea, I want you to go out the back door. Please do it. Right now."

"I'm taking Jane Austen," Althea said stubbornly.

"Take her. Just go."

"But my car … "

"Althea, for God's sake."

The older woman must have realized she was pushing things too far, because she hurried out the back door with the cat carrier handle clutched in her fist. As she went, she defiantly looked at Kate, and then grabbed the bag of cat kibble from the counter.

Kate continued to stand with her open hands resting on Jackson's chest. He was breathing fast, his face still reddened by anger. She peered up into his face, worried that he might explode and start throwing books. At least they wouldn't break the way the stemware at the restaurant had.

"Jackson?" she tried tentatively.

"Yeah, what?"

"Take a deep breath."

He did.

"Okay?" she asked.

"Yeah."

"You sure?"

"Yeah."

She lowered her hands and took a step back. "You can't just get into fights with old ladies."

"I can't believe you let her take your cat." His voice was tight, angry.

"I can deal with that later."

"Why did you let her take your cat?"

"Jackson." She took his hand and led him over to the two easy chairs she had set up in her reading nook. "Listen. I appreciate that you were standing up for me, but you can't yell at old ladies in my store. Or anywhere, really."

He took another deep breath and looked at the floor. "Yeah. Okay. I know. But somebody had to do something. You were just going to let her go. You did just let her go."

"What was I supposed to do? Look. I want to see you again. There's ... something ... between us. I want to find out what that is. But you can't make a big, angry scene every time we're together. That just won't work for me." She put a hand on his arm.

He stretched his neck in a calming-down gesture. "Last night," he said. "You stood up to me. You told me I was an asshole at the restaurant. And I was—you were right. People don't usually stand up to me, but you did. Why couldn't you do that with Althea?"

It was a good question. Why *couldn't* she do that with Althea? *And why can't I do that with my father?*

"I guess we both have things to work on," she said.

Chapter Fourteen

Jackson, Daniel, Ryan, and Will played in a recreational baseball league every fall, and in an effort not to embarrass themselves when the season started, they tried to make regular visits to the batting cages in summer, just so they wouldn't look like idiots in September. They had to go all the way down to San Luis Obispo to the nearest facility, but it seemed like a reasonable price to pay to avoid humiliation.

The day after the cat incident was hot and dry, the temperature higher than what they usually expected here on the Central Coast. Ryan was visibly sweating through his T-shirt as he lined up at the plate, waiting for the pitching machine to hurl balls at him.

"So, what's the status with Kate?" Ryan asked Jackson as he swung and missed.

"Morning date next Thursday. Breakfast and a hike. I'd like to see her sooner than that, but it's the only time I can get off from the restaurant when she's not at the shop."

Ryan nodded. "Okay, a beach hike. That can be good. Romantic. Crashing waves and all that."

"Sure."

"Just don't bitch about the pancakes," Will added.

"I know, I know."

Ryan made solid contact with the ball for a decent hit, and Daniel called encouragement to him. "That's the way, Ry! You got it!"

"So." Daniel brought the subject back to Kate. "I guess things are moving along, then?"

Jackson shrugged. "More or less. But she let me know she's not on board with my angry Neanderthal routine."

"Uh-oh," Will said. "Is that still about the first date incident, or did something else happen?"

Jackson grimly watched Ryan hitting some pitches and missing others, and didn't answer.

"Something else happened," Daniel said. "I'm gathering."

Jackson sighed and looked at them. "I came into her shop yesterday morning, and Althea Morgan—the old biddy who used to work there, until she quit—was stealing Kate's cat."

"Jane Austen," Will said.

"Right. She just came in with a goddamned cat carrier, loaded up the cat, and took it." The muscles bunched up in his jaw, tension building just from the memory.

"Jackson, you're up," Ryan said as he vacated his spot in the cage.

Jackson hefted his bat and stepped up to the plate. The pitching machine hurled a ball at him much faster than he remembered from the last time he'd come here. He swung hard and missed.

"So you pulled out your club and your big rock and went after Althea?" Will asked.

Jackson swung and hit a hard ground ball. "Nothing that dramatic. But I did tell her to put down the damned cat and walk away slowly."

"Uh-oh," Ryan said.

Two more strikes, and then a solid fly ball to what would have been left field. "Yeah," Jackson said.

"So you threw down with an old lady to protect Kate's honor?" Ryan said.

Swing, miss.

"Something like that. But Kate didn't see it that way." The bat cracked against the ball. Foul ball to the right. "Told Althea to take the cat and run out the back door, like she thought I was going to go postal on her. Then she gave me a speech about how if we're going to do this thing—which she says she wants to do—then I've got to tone it down. Be civilized. Stop intimidating senior citizens."

Pop fly to the imaginary shortstop. That one would have been an out.

Jackson's turn came to an end and Will took his place.

"It's not an unreasonable request," Daniel said.

"No, I guess not." The hitting practice had taken some of the tension out of his shoulders, but not all of it. He stretched.

"Then what's got you all worked up?" Ryan asked.

Jackson turned to him. "She took the goddamned cat, and Kate didn't do anything about it. She just stood there. Her father and stepmother—who Kate can't stand, by the way—moved into her house after Kate told them no, they couldn't come. I mean, what is that? Why does she let people walk all over her? She's so … But then she just … "

Will, the power hitter among them, smacked a hard fly to left. "And you want to protect her," he said.

"Well … Yeah."

"And she doesn't want to be protected." *Smack.* He hit a ball that would have been over the damned fence.

"No, she doesn't. At least, not by me." Jesus, Will could hit. Jackson felt thankful they were on the same team. "But she's not some milquetoast. I get out of line, she tells me to can it in no uncertain terms."

"Huh," Daniel said. "I'm seeing a certain complement of personalities here."

"Huh," Jackson said.

Kate had to hire somebody. She could handle the shop alone, she supposed, but she didn't relish the idea of working seven days a week, and she also didn't want to have to manage the upcoming

Art Walk without a little help. She couldn't draft any of her friends as temporary employees, because they all had their own jobs or their own businesses to run. A couple of days after Althea's departure, she'd posted a Help Wanted ad online and also on a couple of bulletin boards in town. She'd put a sign in her window, and she'd also been asking people if they knew anyone who needed a part-time job.

Kate was looking wistfully at Jane Austen's bed, vacant but covered in cat hair, when a young man with black dyed hair, two sleeves of tattoos, a pierced eyebrow, and what appeared to be eyeliner came into the store. The guy, who looked to be in his early twenties, was dressed all in black, and had hair that swooped down to cover one eye.

"May I help you?" Kate asked. She'd seen the kid around town here and there. She seemed to recall that he was the son of one of the ladies who came to the monthly book club Kate sponsored.

"Um, yeah." The kid shifted from one foot to another. "I came about the job. My mom said you were looking for somebody, and she sent me over."

"Your mother is Beverly MacPherson."

"Yeah, that's her."

Kate held out her hand. "Kate Bennet."

He shook with her. His grip was surprisingly firm and businesslike. "Fury McPherson."

Kate's eyebrows rose. "Excuse me? Your mother said your name was Brandon."

His head bobbed up and down. "It used to be."

"So, is Fury some kind of nickname, then?"

"No, it's my actual name. I had it changed." He pulled out his wallet, fished his driver's license from the pocket, and showed it to her.

"Huh," Kate said. She handed the license back to him. Beverly hadn't mentioned the name change, probably hoping that if she failed to acknowledge it, then it might not be true.

Kate looked the kid over. He was decidedly out of place in Cambria, where people tended toward conservative clothing—unless they were going the Earth-loving, granola-eating direction of peasant skirts and Birkenstocks. Kate had to imagine that Fury—or Brandon, back then—had been lonely in high school, forming his own little clique of one. Sure, Rose favored tattoos and facial piercings, but she hadn't grown up here.

Kate's hopes were not high when she said, "Okay, tell me a little bit about why you'd be a good fit for Swept Away."

He stuffed his hands into the pockets of his black skinny jeans. "Well, I like books. I read a lot. I'm taking classes at the community college down in SLO, but a couple of them are online, so I'd be available whenever you need me. Just about. Except for Monday and Wednesday mornings."

They discussed his job history—he was a busboy at a local burger joint, and he'd spent time pumping gas at the Shell station on Main Street—and his references. She'd nodded, not paying a great deal of attention, when he'd listed the manager of the burger joint and one of his community college teachers. But she perked up considerably when he gave her the name of his Scoutmaster.

"As in Boy Scouts of America?" she said.

He looked embarrassed. "My mom got me into it when I was this high." He held his hand out at about his waist. "Mostly, it was pretty cool. My Eagle Scout project was kinda awesome."

She blinked at him. "You're an Eagle Scout?"

He shrugged.

"You had an Eagle Scout project." She was getting it all straight in her head.

"You kinda need one to become an Eagle Scout. I organized a group to clean up a hiking trail in Big Sur. We built a bench."

"A bench."

"You know, for hikers. So they can sit."

"Wow."

When they were in the middle of their conversation, an older woman—a tourist, based on the Cambria tote bag she was carrying—came into the store and started browsing one of the bookshelves.

"Let's see how you do," Kate said to the young man.

"You mean now?" He looked nervous.

"Sure. Go ahead. Help that customer." She gestured toward the woman.

He wandered casually over to the woman. "Welcome to Swept Away," he said. "Can I help you with something?"

The woman looked up, blanched at his appearance, and then stammered. "I ... uh ... I was ... I was just looking for a book to read. Something light, for my vacation."

"Right, right." His head bobbed again. "Any particular genre?"

"Hmm." She thought. "Maybe romance."

"Okay. You've probably read all of the Nora Roberts."

"Actually, no," the woman said. "I've never read any of her books."

His eyebrows—the pierced and the unpierced—shot upward. The little sterling silver ring above his right eye bounced. "Dude. You like romance but you've never read *Nora?* How is that even possible?"

The woman looked flustered. "Well, I ... "

"Don't worry, we'll fix you up," he said. He scanned the romance shelf until he found the sizable Nora Roberts section.

He looked at the woman. "Romance plus murder, or just romance?"

"Just romance."

"High conflict or low conflict?"

"Um." She considered this. "Low, I guess."

He nodded. "Humor or no humor?"

"Oh, humor, for sure."

He plucked a book off the shelf. "Here ya go. It's the first in a three-part series, so if you like it, there's more where that came from."

The customer left the store smiling, with a newly purchased book in her tote bag. When she was gone, Kate asked him, "You read romance?"

"Ugh, no." He gave an exaggerated shudder.

"Then how do you know so much about it?"

"My mom reads *everything,*" he said. "And then she talks about it. Endlessly."

Kate chuckled. From her experience at the book club with Beverly McPherson, that description was right on target.

"One thing," she said.

"What's that?"

"It's probably best not to call the elderly female customers 'Dude.'"

Chapter Fifteen

Kate had made progress in some areas of her life, and less progress in others, by the morning of her second date with Jackson. She'd hired Fury and had started to train him. She'd talked on the phone with Cassidy McLean and confirmed her—and her lemur—for the Art Walk. But she'd still failed to get her father and Angela out of her house. It had been one week and three days, and they were still ensconced in her bedroom with their snowdrifts of clothing everywhere and their yappy little dog destroying her things: one shoe, a table leg, two books, and a TV remote, at last count.

As she was getting ready for her morning hiking date—jeans, a cute scoop-necked T-shirt, and sneakers—she tried again to get some kind of read on what her father's plans were. And when he and Angela were likely to leave.

"So," she said, tying on her sneakers and trying to sound casual. "You haven't really mentioned how long you're planning to stay."

"Oh," Thomas said offhandedly, looking up from his newspaper. "We're playing it by ear. It's so nice to finally spend some time with you. Why rush that?"

"Why indeed," she murmured. Then, louder: "It's just, I don't want to impose on Gen any longer than I have to. Have you made any progress finding space at a B&B? I can help with that, if you like."

He shook his head sadly. "They're all so full in the summer. Plus, so few of them take dogs."

She didn't think that was true—it seemed to her that a wide variety of accommodations in town accepted pets—but she didn't say anything.

Angela came bustling in from outside, where she'd been walking Jazzy. She unclipped the dog's leash, planted her hands on her hips, and said, "Is *that* how you're going to do your makeup?"

"It's hiking. We're going hiking. There'll be sweating, and … It didn't seem like a lot of makeup would be required."

"Good lord," Angela said, scowling. "I can see I'm going to have to do something with you." She grabbed Kate's arm and hauled her toward the bathroom.

Twenty minutes later, Kate was sitting across the table from Jackson at a café in town, a croissant and a latte in front of her, her face done up in more makeup than one would expect to wear for a role on Broadway. Since Kate didn't usually wear much makeup—a little concealer, mascara and lip gloss, and she generally called it done—the contrast was striking.

"Wow," Jackson had said when they'd met outside the café. "You know we're just hiking, right?"

"I know, I know." She glared at him. "Angela sells Mary Kay."

Jackson looked bewildered. "And Mary Kay is … "

"Makeup!" Kate had waved both hands in front of her face, drawing attention to Exhibit A. "It's … all this! Ugh. I want that woman out of my house!"

Jackson had chuckled. "It's not that you don't look nice. It's just … a little much for hiking."

"Gee, you think?" Kate had retorted.

Now, Kate was enjoying a warm pastry and a creamy latte while Jackson dug into a thick slice of quiche that he pronounced acceptable. The café was busy with locals at this time of the morning, the tourists mostly still in their plush hotel beds or partaking of the breakfast buffet at the lodge up the hill. It was still early, but the bright morning sunlight poured in through the front window. The café, it's décor rustic with dark wood surfaces and mismatched chairs, smelled of coffee and fresh bread.

By the second date, it was no longer possible to avoid discussing one's ex-husband. So Kate was filling Jackson in on the particulars: She and Marcus had been married six years, separated after five. The divorce had become final two and a half years after he and Kate had moved to Cambria. Cambria had been part of the problem—Marcus had hated it here, feeling that he was stuck in the middle of nowhere. When they had split, he'd gone back to Los Angeles as fast as his car would carry him.

"I don't want to dwell on it, because dwelling on it makes me sound weak and pathetic," Kate said stoically as she popped a piece of croissant into her mouth. "But if we're going to be seeing each other, you deserve to know the basics. Marcus and I got married when I was just out of grad school. That's where I met him— at UCLA. He was engineering, I was English. Anyway. He cheated. A lot. I'd pick up on clues and ask him what was going on, and he'd spin things to make it look like I was so paranoid or emotionally fragile that he was the hero for putting up with me."

"He made you doubt yourself."

"Exactly."

Jackson looked down at his plate, his face showing that Jackson anger that was becoming so familiar to Kate. "I met him a few times right after I started working at Neptune. Seemed like an asshole," Jackson said. "Guys like that give all of us a bad name. I'd like to kick his ass."

"So would I," Kate said.

"But you left him eventually," Jackson said. "So that's good."

She shook her head and sipped at her latte. "I wish I had. I wish I'd shown that kind of sense. He left me. For somebody named Tiffany. Probably one in a long line of Tiffanys. It was only then that I could start to see clearly what he'd done to me. Emotionally, I mean. How he'd manipulated me." She shuddered. "I'm thankful we never had kids. At least I don't have to see him to deal with child support and weekend visits, and … " She gestured with her hand to indicate all the myriad ways parents had to remain involved with each other. "Tiffany would be my kid's step-mother. Or someone like Tiffany. God forbid."

"What if he hadn't been a cheating asshole? Would you have had kids?"

She considered the question carefully before answering. "Not at first. I was very involved in my career for those first years. The novel, my teaching job. I thought I wanted tenure, wanted a life in academia. I was very involved in trying to be somebody. I don't know if kids would have fit into that."

"And now?"

She shrugged. "Now I'm building a different kind of life. A quieter one. And with my mother gone, I'm starting to see how important family really is."

They decided to hike a three-mile trail that started at the beach in San Simeon and curved inward among the grassy hills and the eucalyptus groves. This time of year—the dry season—the hills were golden, with tall grasses that rippled in the breeze. During the rainy season—or, as rainy as it got here, which wasn't very—the grass turned a deep green that covered the rolling hills in a rich emerald. This early in the morning, the temperature was pleasant and cool. Already, a number of people, mostly locals, walked the trails alone or with their dogs.

As they walked, Kate was reminded again why she'd moved here. The beach, the pines, the vast stretches of unspoiled land dotted with grazing cows. This was so different from L.A., which she had once thought to be the center of the universe. Now, after living here for five years, she felt suffocated whenever she returned to the urban sprawl. Concrete, crowds, rivers of cars idling on the freeways, waiting to go nowhere. All signs of the natural world vanquished, even on the beaches, which had been reduced to flat expanses of featureless sand. Her mother had given her a gift by coming here and leading Kate to follow her. It was a simpler life. A better one. A life with a sense of peace, of meaning.

"What are you thinking about?" Jackson asked as they walked among the trees, the ground crunching beneath their feet, the sound of the crashing waves behind them.

"This place," Kate answered, gesturing around her. "I still can't get over how beautiful it is here. You'd think that after five years, I'd have stopped noticing, stopped seeing it. But this ... " She shook her head in wonder.

"You don't miss L.A.?" he asked, glancing back at her from his place ahead of her on the trail.

"Not a bit. Well," she amended, "sometimes I do when I want to shop at Nordstrom. But otherwise, no. I didn't understand it at first when my mother just picked up her whole life and moved here. I thought she was having some kind of late-midlife crisis, reacting to the whole mess with my dad. But I get it now. She knew what she was doing."

"Yeah." He nodded. "The Bay Area's different. Beautiful in its own right. I do miss it sometimes. The night life. The restaurant culture—it's exciting for a chef. When Gavin—my friend from culinary school—opened Neptune, I thought I'd come down here, put in a few years, then take my expertise and parlay into something in San Francisco. But once you're here, it's hard to leave." He looked around at the stunning beauty that surrounded them. "This is a lot to give up."

When the trail widened so that they no longer had to go single file, he walked beside her and reached out to hold her hand. His hand was big and warm around hers. She felt a tingle of joy at his touch.

They'd been walking for about a half-hour, a light sheen of sweat mixing with Kate's Mary Kay makeup, when a tall, blond woman wearing tight spandex workout shorts and a sport bra came toward them on the trail. She was wearing earbuds, and at first she didn't see them. Then she looked up, spotted Jackson, and smiled in surprise.

"Jackson!" She pulled the earbuds from her ears, came forward, went up on her tiptoes, and planted a kiss on Jackson's cheek.

"Melanie." Jackson looked uncomfortable. Kate took in the body language—Melanie and the way she positioned her sculpted hips and tilted her body toward him, Jackson and the way he'd become fidgety, the way he was leaning slightly away from her. "Uh … This is Kate Bennet. Have you two met?"

Melanie's eyes swept over Kate from head to toe and apparently found her lacking. "Not formally, but I've been into the bookstore a few times," she said.

"Lovely to see you again," Kate replied.

Melanie turned the considerable wattage of her attention back to Jackson.

"You never called me," she said to him, her voice a sinewy purr. "My number hasn't changed."

Jackson shot a glance at Kate. "Ah … This isn't really the best … "

Melanie looked at Kate and smirked. She stretched up toward Jackson's ear and whispered to him. Kate could just make out what she said: "When you're done with her … give me a call."

The admirably fit blond bimbo bounced up the trail, and Jackson faced Kate, apology and embarrassment in his expression. "Kate, I'm sorry about that."

Kate stood with her arms crossed over her chest, head cocked to one side, gazing at him. "Is this going to happen often? This running-into-women-you've-slept-with thing? Twice in two dates—that's a pretty impressive start."

He ran a hand through his hair. "I'd like to say no, but … it might."

"You've been busy," she said.

He walked to a nearby bench and sat down, looking uncomfortable. She sat beside him.

"I have kind of a history, I guess," he said. "Is that going to be something you can live with?"

Kate shrugged. "Well, I can't say that I enjoyed that encounter with Melanie. But I know about your 'history.' Word gets around."

He nodded. "I guess it does." He looked at her. "I want this to be different." His face was so open, so earnest, that she believed him.

"And that's why we didn't sleep together that first night? When you were teaching me to cook?"

"Yeah. Kate, I don't know where this is going to go, if it's going to go anywhere. But I do know that all of the sex, all of the casual two-weeks-and-then-move-on shit, it's not what I want anymore. I want to get to know you. I want you to get to know me. And then, I want this thing between us to succeed or fail based on something real."

The way he was looking at her, the honesty and yearning, tugged at her core. A wave of warmth ran through her. And oh, God, the irony. She found herself wanting him more than she'd wanted any man in longer than she could remember—precisely because he'd said he was not going to sleep with her. Or, really, it was more the way he'd said it. Either way, she needed to touch him, to taste him. She felt like her skin was on fire.

"Jackson ... " She drew toward him. He hesitated, and then kissed her. And the world around them vanished as her body ignited. The desire was no longer something she felt; the desire was a living thing inside her. The kiss grew deeper, more urgent. Her arms wrapped around him, the warmth and strength of his back humming beneath her spread fingers.

He crushed her to him, his mouth on hers, and she felt light, small, alive in a way she could barely remember feeling before. He groaned, and she could feel the vibration of it through her body.

Gently, he put his hands on her shoulders and pushed her away.

"Kate. God." He pulled back from her and took a deep breath.

"We could go back to my house," she whispered. Then she remembered her father and Angela. "Or, no. Your apartment?" The hot, seething yearning made her forget how early it was in their relationship, how unwise it might be to jump into something, the things he'd said about wanting this to be different. She forgot everything but this. Everything but him. "Please."

He stood, backed away, put some distance between them. "I want to. God, you have no idea ... But ... "

"So, we're just going to ignore this thing we've got between us?" Her frustration put an edge into her voice. "We're just going to have nice, chaste dates? Maybe you can strum your guitar on the front porch swing while Aunt Bea brings us lemonade."

One side of his mouth quirked up. "You're teasing me."

"I'm not the one who's a tease."

He came back to sit beside her, and put his hands on her shoulders. "You matter, Kate. That's why this has to be different. Because you matter."

She softened, knowing he meant what he was saying, knowing she was more to him than all of the Lindseys and the Melanies and whoever else was lurking out there having been in Jackson's bed.

"How long?" she said.

"How long what?"

"How long do we have to wait in order to make this different than the others? To get to know each other? To ensure that when we do take that step, it's about more than just shallow sex? I mean, even though it would be *fantastic* shallow sex."

The look on his face suggested that he was having trouble focusing because he was thinking about the fantastic shallow sex.

"Jackson?"

She could see him come back to the present. "Well, I hadn't really thought about putting a number on it."

"So, think about it now." Her pulse was coming back down to normal, but her mind was still foggy with the force of wanting him. She urged herself to get back on her game. "It'll work better for me if I know what we're dealing with."

He rubbed at his chin with his hand. "Five dates?"

"Five."

"Yeah, why not?"

"That's still not exactly old-fashioned courting." She grinned.

"It's about four dates better than I usually do."

She got up from the bench and paced a bit, thinking. "Does the first one count?"

"The first one what?"

"The first night we spent time together. The cooking lesson. Does that count as the first date?"

He shook his head. "Nah. That wasn't a date. The Sandpiper was the first date."

"And that makes this the second, not the third."

"Right," he confirmed.

She went over to him and pressed her body against his, her hands resting on his hips. She grinned up at him.

"Think you're going to make it that long, big guy?"

"I'll make it," he said, his voice almost like a grunt.

She pressed a quick, light kiss to his lips. "We'll see."

Chapter Sixteen

"He's a man whore," Kate said. She was sitting with Gen, Rose, and Lacy at The Wild Orchid, a sushi place a block off Main Street, gesturing with a piece of California roll pinched between two chopsticks. "But can I use that to my benefit, have some much-needed fun? Get a little happy stress-relief? No, I cannot. Because he's got some ridiculous—but, yes, sweet—notion that I'm different from all the other women. I'm not! I like sex just as much as the other women!"

"And you haven't had it in a long time," Lacy said soothingly.

"So long!" Kate agreed. "After Marcus, I was so ... so ... " She searched for the word. "So *stunted* emotionally that I didn't even want to. I couldn't even go there with anyone. Couldn't even feel *attracted* most of the time, because ... "

"We know, honey," Rose said, rubbing Kate's upper arm.

"But Jackson!" Kate said. "Oh my God. It's like I'm sixteen again with the raging hormones, and the *urgency,* and the feeling that the world's just going to freaking *end* right now, today, if I can't get him into bed. You know?" She popped the California roll into her mouth.

"I wish," Gen murmured.

"God, sixteen," Lacy said dreamily. "I remember that. Steven Ford. Prom night." She shuddered happily at the memory.

"Steven Ford?" Rose piped in. "Steve from the bank?"

"Oh, yeah," Lacy said. "He wasn't always so ... paunchy."

"Let's get back to me and my pent-up sexual tension," Kate said.

"Okay, let's," Gen agreed. "So, he's withholding sex for five dates."

"Well, it sounds bad when you say it like that," Kate said.

The restaurant, in the bottom floor of what was once a Victorian house, was half-filled with a mix of locals and tourists. Kitschy décor, including paper lanterns and a giant Buddha, contrasted with the cozy feel of the low ceilings, the chair railings, the fireplace on one wall, the squeaky wood floors and the small doorways.

Lacy picked up a piece of raw salmon and considered Kate. "Okay, let's rephrase it then. He's taking a traditional, respectful approach to the first five dates."

"Better," Kate said. "But, yes. That's the deal. I may have kind of, I don't know"—she waved her chopsticks around, considering how to say it—"issued a sort of challenge."

"A challenge?" Gen looked at her curiously.

"What kind of challenge?" Rose asked.

Kate shrugged. "I might have suggested, in a kind of playful way, that he might not make it to Date Five."

"Oh, boy," Lacy said. She chewed thoughtfully on the salmon. "That makes things interesting."

"It does," Gen agreed.

"Sort of sounds like you're planning to ring his bell before the end of the round," Rose said. "So to speak."

"Oh, I don't know." Kate toyed with her pile of white rice, thinking. "I mean, it's really sweet and kind of flattering that he wants to treat me differently from all his other women. And, jeez, there are a lot of other women."

"Well, we knew that," Lacy said.

"Sure," Kate said. "But knowing that is one thing. Running into them out in the world when I'm with Jackson is another. Did I tell you about Melanie?" She said the name in a high, mocking voice, the way she might have if the name had been Bitsy or Muffy.

"Melanie Taylor?" Rose inquired. "I heard they used to have a thing."

"Right." Kate pointed a chopstick at Rose. "She *propositioned* him while I was standing right there!"

Rose gaped at her. "Really? Could you have misinterpreted something?"

Kate batted her eyelashes and did her Melanie voice. " 'Oh, Jackson. When you're finished with *her*, give me a call.' " She batted the lashes again.

Lacy let out a guffaw. "Well, that took some lady balls."

"No kidding," Kate agreed.

"So, what's your plan to seduce him before Date Five?" Gen asked, leaning forward eagerly. "Do tell. I'm having a dry spell. I have to live vicariously."

Kate slumped a bit, feeling grumpy. "I don't know. I might have an idea if my father and Angela would get out of my house. It's kind of hard to lure a guy into my bed when my father's already in it."

"Ooh." Rose waved her hands in front of her face. "Now I need brain bleach."

"That is a problem," Gen agreed. "So, what *are* you going to do about your dad? Has he said when he's leaving?"

"Nope."

"Oh, honey," Lacy said sympathetically. "With *your* dad, that could only mean one thing."

"He lost his condo and he has nowhere to go? I've already thought of that," Kate said.

"All that and you can't even get laid," Gen said.

"We'll see about that," Kate said, picking up her glass of wine.

❖

The whole cold shower thing was overrated, in Jackson's opinion. It didn't work. It didn't stop him from thinking about sex, all the time. Specifically, sex with Kate.

This was different than what he'd experienced with other women. You met people, you liked the way they looked. You had an itch, you scratched it. Everybody was happy. Well, the women didn't usually stay happy once the fun was over and they had to live with him on a day-to-day basis. But still.

Sex, and thinking about sex, was great, but it usually didn't interfere with his daily life. Usually, he could compartmentalize. Sex was one thing, work was another. Even when he'd slept with someone he was working with—not an infrequent occasion—he was able to put all that aside and focus on his job.

But this was different. Not since his adolescent obsession with Debra Ferguson when he was in twelfth grade had he been this preoccupied with a female.

The kitchen staff at Neptune probably knew something was up, though they couldn't know what. Jackson was off his game, forgetting things, burning things and then having to redo them. But the most conspicuous red flag was the fact that he wasn't yelling. Jose at the fish station sent out some undercooked salmon, and a server brought it back, and Jackson barely quirked an eyebrow.

He was distracted, unfocused. And he had sharp knives in his hands.

"Jackson? You okay, man?" Esteban, the salad guy, put a hand on Jackson's back.

"What?" Jackson looked up at him like he'd barely heard.

Yeah, he was fucked.

The five-date thing had been his idea, and right now it seemed like a stupid one. She'd wanted to go back to his apartment. She'd said *please,* for Christ's sake. And he'd responded with his wussy *let's do this the right way* bullshit.

He'd wanted to show his respect for her.

Well, respect was going to get him burned or cut if he couldn't get his head in the game.

"I'm good," he told Esteban. "Yeah, I'm good."

He was going to have to fire somebody or throw something pretty soon, just to prove it.

Kate decided it was time for a come-to-Jesus talk with her father. He and Angela had been in Kate's house for almost two weeks, with no indication of when they might leave. Kate was tired of sleeping with Gen, tired of not having access to her bedroom, her things. Tired of leaving the house every day with a face full of Mary Kay makeup that was definitely not her style.

And she really wanted them out before her fifth date with Jackson. His apartment was probably great and would likely serve their needs just fine. But she wanted options.

She wanted her damned house back, and she wanted her father and stepmother safely back in Los Angeles where she couldn't suddenly snap and kill them.

Which was always a possibility.

"Hey, Dad?" She approached him as he was sitting at the dining table drinking coffee and reading the morning newspaper. He was the only person she knew who still read a newspaper instead of getting news on the Internet. It was early, and he was still wearing his bathrobe—a navy blue velour number with his monogram on the pocket. Angela was out walking Jazzy—walking apparently was good for Angela's sciatica—which gave Kate a window of opportunity.

"Hmm?" He raised his eyebrows to show he was listening, but didn't look up from the paper.

"Can we talk for a minute?" Her pulse sped up, and she realized she was nervous about talking to her own father in her own house. Ridiculous.

"Sure, honey."

She sat down in the chair across from him and began carefully. "I just thought we should discuss your plans."

"Ah. Well, today I thought Angela and I would visit Hearst Castle. Looks like it's going to be a beautiful day for it. Would you like to join us?"

She cleared her throat. "Thanks, but I have to work. See, I didn't mean your plans for today. I meant your plans for when you thought you might go ... you know. Back to Los Angeles."

He looked at her blankly.

"It's just, this house is really small," she said.

His expression perked up, and he folded the newspaper and set it down. "It's small, but the location is prime. Did you know your property values have soared over the last couple of years? What with the water issues in Cambria—the de facto moratorium on new construction because of the drought—existing homes near the beach might as well be made of gold. Have you ever thought of selling?"

The conversation had taken a turn she hadn't expected.

"What?"

"You just said the house is too small. Why, you could sell, make a huge profit, and buy a much bigger place inland for less than what you make on the sale. You could have a bigger house and a nice savings account."

He looked at her expectantly, as though she might bubble over with excitement at his idea.

"I don't want to sell my house," she said.

"It's worth more than six hundred thousand on Zillow. For a two-bedroom!" he said excitedly.

"Wait a minute. You looked up the value of my house on Zillow?"

He avoided her gaze, fussing with the paper and the coffee cup. "Well, I ... "

"Why were you looking up the value of my house?"

He took a deep breath, entwined his fingers in front of him, and said, "Kate, since you asked, I think it's time we talked about this house."

"What about it?"

"As you know, Angela and I have had some financial problems. A couple of investments that didn't go the way we wanted, the foreclosure."

"Foreclosure?" This was the first she was hearing of it. "You never ... "

"And the thing is," he went on as though she'd never spoken, "I never would have been in such a bind in the first place if it hadn't been for the divorce settlement I had to pay to your mother." He spread his hands plaintively. "It was excessive, the settlement, especially considering we had no minor children."

"So you're blaming Mom for your money troubles?" Her face was starting to feel hot, and she could hear her pulse pounding in her ears. "She's not the one who wanted the divorce. You were."

"Of course. Of course. But ... "

"She'd have stayed forever. She'd have ... "

"Kate." He looked at her with the calm, piercing gaze he used when he wanted to dominate an argument. "You can't know what went on in our marriage. No child can ever know what happens in private between her parents."

"Okay." She took a deep breath and tried to calm herself.

"What I'm saying is," he went on, "ultimately, most of the settlement she received from me went into this." He spread his hands to indicate the house surrounding them.

"My house."

"Yes."

"And since the settlement was unfair to begin with … "

"Wait. Oh, wait." She was starting to get it. It was all starting to come clear. And the picture that was forming was enough to make her blood rush to her head, make her see red. "You want me to sell the house and give you the money?"

"No, no." He shook his head. "Not all of it."

"But some of it."

The little smile on his face was that one that said, *You're being irrational but I'm humoring you.* "Just enough to get me back on my feet, Kate. It's only fair."

Fair.

"What about all of the money I've given you over the years? All of the loans you've never paid back?" Her voice was rising. "What about that, Dad? What about the fact that this is *my god-damned house,* and I'm not going to sell it and give the *goddamned profits* to *you!*" She was standing now, the force of her outrage having propelled her to her feet.

Her father, still calm, shook his head sadly. "I knew you'd react this way."

"Why?" Kate demanded. "Because I'm *sane?*"

"I was afraid you wouldn't be able to see reason," he said.

"*Reason?!*"

"You're so emotional about anything that has to do with your mother," he said, as though that were a great and terrible character flaw.

With sudden clarity, Kate could see that this, right here—this man sitting at her table and his way of manipulating her—was the root of her problems with men. When he wanted something un-reasonable and she didn't want to give in, he spun the situation to make it look like she was irrational, overly emotional, inherently damaged and stunted. Was it any wonder she'd married a man who had treated her the same way? She knew what was happening—knew exactly what he was doing—but just as she hadn't been able to leave Marcus, she couldn't seem to detach completely from her father, either. She was angry with him, but she was angry with herself, too, for letting herself be treated this way.

"You know what?" Kate said, rising from her seat at the table. "I think your vacation's over. I need you and Angela to pack up and go."

He sighed and did the sad head shake again. "As I was just explaining to you, we had to give up our condo. We're between addresses."

"If *between addresses* means you're homeless, that's not my problem. I need you to go. I want my bedroom back. I want my house back." Her anger was like a heavy, hot weight on her chest.

He picked up the newspaper and began reading again. "As soon as we find another place to stay. Perhaps something here in Cambria, hmm?" He turned to the sports page and sipped his coffee.

All that day at work, Kate obsessed over her father and what to do about him. When she'd told him to leave, it was as though he hadn't heard her. That patronizing smirk he'd given her was the same one he'd used on Kate's mother while Kate was growing up. Kate wondered how her mother hadn't suffocated him in his sleep.

While her outburst at him had been cathartic, she was no closer to getting him out of her house. How could she get him to leave if he refused to go? If Jackson were in this position, he'd probably have picked him up and physically put him on the street by now. Too bad Kate didn't have that kind of upper body strength.

She tried to put thoughts of her father aside, and focused on training Fury at the store. The kid was good. He paid attention and learned fast, and he had some creative ideas. Early that morning, she'd sent him to write a two-for-one promotion on the blackboard that stood on the sidewalk outside the store. He'd taken longer than she expected, then beckoned her to come and look. He'd drawn a charming picture of a pigtailed girl in a chair absorbed in a book, and in careful script, he'd written, *Tell us the first line of your favorite book and get two for the price of one!*

"First line of your favorite book," Kate said thoughtfully.

"Yeah. I thought it would be fun. Get people in the door."

She nodded. "Okay. Let's see how it works."

Now, by lunchtime, they'd heard "Call me Ishmael," "It was the best of times, it was the worst of times," "In a hole in the ground there lived a hobbit," and, from a tiny girl, "The sun did not shine, it was too wet to play."

When a middle-aged man came in and offered, "Once upon a time and a very good time it was there was a moocow coming down along the road," Fury scowled and said, *"Portrait of the Artist?* Dude, that is *not* your favorite book. That's not anybody's favorite book!" And the two had gotten into a lively discussion about literature for entertainment versus intellectual enlightenment.

He had some good ideas for Art Walk, too. He'd suggested a contest: He or Kate would read a paragraph from an unnamed book, and the first audience member to name the book would win it. There could be age divisions: adult, young adult, and children.

"Hmm," Kate considered. "If they know the book well enough to name it, they probably already have it."

"Doesn't matter," Fury said. "Everybody loves to win things."

"That's true," she said.

Within a couple of days she felt comfortable leaving him alone in the store during her lunch breaks. That allowed her to slip out to have a salad with Rose, or to do some quick shopping in the boutiques on Main Street—things she'd been missing since Althea's departure.

Something else she missed was Jane Austen. Every time Kate looked at Jane Austen's empty bed, she felt a sad little tug in her chest. It wasn't just the fact that she didn't have the cat to keep her company in the store, though that was a factor. She was also bothered—more so than she would have expected—by how the cat's absence reminded her of her own lack of assertiveness. Why had she let Althea take the Swept Away cat? Who did Althea think she was? Was Jane Austen happy at Althea's house? Did she miss the attention she got at the bookstore, the customers stroking her and cooing soft words into her ears?

Kate considered getting another cat, but she knew it wouldn't be the same. You couldn't just replace a pet the way you'd replace a broken lamp or a lost set of keys. She was used to Jane Austen, was comforted by her presence and her quirks.

"You could get a snake," Fury suggested when he saw Kate gazing sadly at Jane Austen's empty food and water bowls, now stacked on a shelf in the back room.

"A snake?" Kate asked.

"Sure. I had a boa constrictor when I was in high school. I thought it would impress girls."

She looked at him, amused. "Did it?"

"Not really. Girls are too sympathetic."

She looked at him questioningly.

"Live feedings," he said. "Mice, usually. Marcy Ellison cried and called me a murderer."

"Ah."

"Might not be the best thing for the store, after all," he said.

Chapter Seventeen

Sunday nights at Neptune tended to be moderately busy during the summer tourist season. The crowds of out-of-towners in cargo shorts, souvenir T-shirts and flip-flops, staying until Monday to make a long weekend, congregated in groups of four to six outside the restaurant's front doors, making him long for the days—far in the past—when elegant dining meant you put on a coat and tie. Where was the respect for the food, for the ambiance, for the artistry that went into each plate that left the kitchen? But this was a beach town, you had to remember that. And tourists paid the bills.

Jackson had been going hard since early in the morning, meeting with his produce supplier, talking to the fish guy about why there was no goddamned fresh crab, tweaking the menu for the coming week, working with the prep crew. Now he was in the middle of it, in the heat and the steam and the bustle of the kitchen during the height of dinner service.

This was when he came alive, when he truly felt like himself. Something about the creative act of cooking, combined with the rush of doing it for hundreds of people in a night, made him forget everything else. The laser-like focus the job required pushed out the static and the noise of all of his petty problems, and that was therapeutic. Meditative.

Even when he lost his shit over some dumbass mistake made by someone in his crew—a daily occurrence—it was all a part of the whole, a part of the high-tension team effort to feed people not just well, but with excellence. It was part of the rhythm, like ballet. Like performing a piano concerto.

Around seven-thirty, when he was right in the middle of his stride, in the middle of the zone, he noticed something odd about a ticket Janie had brought in.

"Janie, is this right?" He held the ticket in front of him, peering at her scratchy handwriting.

"Which part?"

"At Table Twelve, one guy, two appetizers?"

She nodded. "Yep."

Could be nothing, but it raised an alarm bell. When the same single diner at Table Twelve also ordered two entrees, Jackson knew the guy wasn't just especially hungry. The guy was a food critic. He had to be. People rarely dined alone, and when they did, they didn't order enough to feed an army—unless they wanted to sample an array of menu items.

Gavin Hughes, the restaurant's owner, noticed about the same time Jackson did. He popped into the kitchen and made a quick stop to talk to Jackson.

"Table Twelve?" he said.

"Yeah, I got it," Jackson told him. "Guy's gotta be a critic."

"I don't recognize him," Gavin said.

"Yeah, well, we better assume he is. Jose!" Jackson yelled to his sous chef, who was busy searing some bacon-wrapped filets.

"Yes, chef!"

Jackson went over and told Jose—a short, compact, middle-aged man of boundless energy whom Jackson had come to think of as his right hand—about his suspicions regarding Table Twelve.

" ... And nothing goes out until I see it. Got that? Do *not* fuck this up." He gave Jose a friendly, encouraging smack on the back and went to work on the seafood portion of Table Twelve's meal.

❖

Two nights after the Table Twelve triumph—and Jackson knew it was a triumph when Janie reported to him that the guy had eaten with obvious pleasure and gusto—Jackson and Kate had their third date, which was dinner at Jackson's apartment.

Kate was surprised he'd invited her there, since it presented a threat to his plan to stay abstinent for five dates. With the chemistry between them, what were the odds that they'd be able to keep their hands off each other in a private, relatively comfortable environment?

Kate wore her good underwear and shaved her legs, just in case.

Jackson's apartment was on the second floor of a big brick building about a mile down Main Street from the bookstore. The first floor housed Neptune—an arrangement that probably made Jackson even more of a workaholic than he otherwise would have been. The building was a boxy, imposing structure that had once been a bank, with an outside staircase leading to Jackson's door.

She knocked on his door at six p.m. on a Tuesday—the restaurant's slowest day—wearing a silky red top, a strappy pair of sandals, and jeans that made her ass look great. At least, Gen said they made her ass look great. But who knew? Friends had to compliment your ass before a date—it's what they were there for.

He opened the door dressed in Levi's and a button-down shirt left untucked, his feet bare, hair combed back from his face. He leaned in for a hello kiss, and he smelled like soap, mouthwash, and essence of Jackson Graham.

"Come on in." He took her hand and brought her inside.

The bones of the apartment were appealing. Hardwood floors, white walls with crown moldings, plenty of windows letting in natural light, even a fireplace with an elaborately carved surround. But the décor was in the style of workaholic man, with little in the place to indicate that someone considered it home. He had a sofa that had probably come from a thrift store or from a friend's garage, a big-screen TV, some side tables, some lamps, a small dining table and chairs, and not much else. The expanse of floor was unbroken by any sign of a rug, and the walls were bare except for the mounted TV.

The kitchen, though, was different, as Kate might have expected. It was too small for professional-quality appliances, but she could see at a glance that it was stocked with gleaming stainless steel pots and pans and knives that probably cost more than her car.

"This is an interesting place," she said, looking around. She gestured toward the sparse living area. "Did you just move in?"

He looked confused. "What? No. I've been here three years. Why?"

She raised her eyebrows at him. "Most people would have bought a rug by now, that's all."

He shrugged. "I don't spend much time at home."

"I gathered."

He went to the kitchen, poured a glass of chilled white wine, and handed it to her. The taste was crisp, with a hint of apple.

"Even when I try to spend time at home," he went on, "it doesn't usually work out. Some kind of crisis downstairs, and I'll have a sous chef banging on my door. Which is *not* going to happen tonight. I told them not to bother me unless the building's on fire. And even then, it better be a fire they can't put out on their own." He picked up a chef's knife. "You want to sit down and make yourself comfortable while I get things ready?"

"I can keep you company in the kitchen," she said.

He started slicing vegetables—some zucchini and mushrooms—and she was fascinated by his fluid, practiced motions, his speed, as though the knife were an extension of his hand.

"Wow," she said.

"Nothing fancy," he told her. "Just a simple stir-fry."

"Still," she said.

They chatted about his day—he'd worked a little at the restaurant in the morning and then went jogging with Daniel—her day, her plans for Art Walk, the catering jobs he had coming up. As he continued to cook, she took her glass of wine and wandered around the apartment. Though he had no homey touches, he did have books—a dark, hefty bookcase full of books. She perused the titles and found her own, *Beyond the Boundaries of Desire*. She wondered at first if he'd gotten it just to impress her, but noticed that the pages looked well-worn and dog-eared.

"Do you usually bring women here?" she asked impulsively. She didn't know why she'd said it. She didn't want to put him on the defensive about his history with women. She just wanted to know.

"Never," he said.

Her eyebrows shot up. "Really? Never?"

"Never." He carried two steaming plates of stir-fry to the table, which had been set before her arrival. "You're the first."

"I'm the *first*?" It didn't seem credible, considering how prolific he was with women, but on the other hand, a glance around said it was true. This wasn't a place he'd created to impress his dates. This was just where he slept, where he kept his things.

The stir-fry was delicious—she would have expected no less—and she made happy noises as she savored the first bite. "Oh, God," she said. "This is fabulous. What's that flavor?"

"It's probably the fresh ginger."

"Oh, wow. Yeah. And I like how it's got a little kick, but not too much."

"It's not hard. I can teach you to make it."

She grinned. "That would be good, since our last cooking lesson was cut short."

"Well ... " He fidgeted.

She changed the subject to let him off the hook. "So, you said you're from the Bay Area. San Francisco?"

He took a sip of his wine and shook his head. "No. Oakland."

"How was that?"

He shrugged. "My dad was a dock worker at the port, my mom was a nurse at the children's hospital. They worked hard, but never got much to show for it. Public schools in Oakland aren't the best, so I learned to keep my head down, try not to be noticed."

"Do they still live there?"

He nodded. "Yeah, same house. My dad's retired—you can't do that kind of work forever—but my mom's still nursing. A city like that, she sees a lot of rough things at the hospital. Shootings, drug overdoses, domestic violence. And this is all kids." He shook his head, his mouth set in a grim line. "She used to say, 'Jackson, you get your education and get out of here as soon as you can.' And that's what I did. I offered to bring them down here, but they said no. Home is home, I guess."

"I guess it is." She thought about mothers and fathers, and what it would be like to still have both of hers in a place she could think of as home. "This is my home now," she said. "Though it took a while for anywhere to seem like home after I lost my mom. She was it. She was home. Now I have to be that for myself."

"I hear people talk about her sometimes," he said thoughtfully. "Your mom, I mean. Here in Cambria. All good things. People miss her."

The thought of that collective memory, that joining together of people who knew her, made Kate feel warm inside. She smiled. "That's good to know."

"Speaking of parents … " He asked her what was going on with her father, and she told him the short version.

"He needs money. Again. Apparently, his condo has been foreclosed, and he and Angela have nowhere to live. So … " She took a deep breath. "He wants me to sell my house and give him the money—not all of it, he says, oh so generously—but enough to get him 'back on his feet.' Says I owe it to him because the divorce settlement was unfair."

He stared at her. "Jesus."

"Even *he* would be pissed with my father right now," Kate said.

Jackson set down his fork. "Please, for the love of all that is holy, tell me that you're not thinking of doing it."

"Oh, God no. That house … it's more than a house. It means a lot to me. It's … "

"It's a connection to your mother," he supplied.

"Yes. It is. There's no way I'm selling it, not for him, not for anyone. I told him that. But when I talk, he doesn't seem to hear me. I told him he needed to leave, and he said, 'As soon as we find somewhere else to stay.' Which, considering how hard he's looking, could be never."

"You need to make him leave."

"But how … "

"Kate."

She looked at him.

"You need to make him leave," he said.

"He's my dad," she said. She sighed, and looked down into her wine glass. "I wish I knew how to be more assertive with people. I don't like being a doormat. I guess somewhere down deep I think that if I act the right way with him, he'll really see me—he'll appreciate me for who I am. But it never happens." She looked at Jackson. "How do you do it?"

"Do what?"

"Well …" She shifted in her chair, thinking of how to say it. "You never take any crap off of anyone. You don't seem to care what anybody thinks. If someone needs to have their ass handed to them, you just …" She gestured with her hand. "You just do it."

He got up, went to the kitchen, and retrieved the bottle of wine they'd started. He poured more for both of them, sat down, and folded his arms on top of the table. "Kate. I never told you how I ended up going to culinary school."

"No, you didn't," she said, puzzled by the abrupt change of topic.

"Well. As I mentioned, my parents were struggling financially, and as you might be aware, culinary school—especially one in San Francisco—costs an absurd amount of money."

"Right."

He took a deep breath before going on. "I paid for it with the settlement from a very bad car accident I was in."

"Jackson … " She could see that the story was hard for him to tell, that this was going to be a story that mattered. She reached out a hand toward him, and he took it in his.

"I was in the car with a guy I knew from high school. Not a close friend, just a guy I hung out with. You know how it is. Anyway, we'd both been drinking. Not a huge amount, we weren't shitfaced. But we probably shouldn't have been in the car."

He kept his eyes on the table, avoiding her gaze, as he continued.

"He was driving. We were on a two-lane road, late. Some fog on the ground, so it was hard to see. The guy in the other lane swerved into ours, hit us head-on, with the main impact on the driver's side of the car." He rubbed the back of her hand gently with his thumb as he continued. "I had my seatbelt on, he didn't."

"Oh, Jackson." She knew what was going to come next, and she braced herself for it.

"My friend—a guy named Logan Walsh—was killed on impact. I was in the hospital for a while, a concussion, some broken bones and whatnot."

He paused, collecting his thoughts, before he finished.

"Even though the accident wasn't Logan's fault, I could never help wondering what would have happened if he'd been completely sober. Would he have seen the guy coming? Would he have been able to swerve out of the way in time?" He shook his head. "I will never—and I mean ever—forget the way his mother screamed when she got to the hospital and they told her he was gone. And I *knew* he shouldn't have been driving. I *knew* it. But I was too big of a pussy to say anything. Didn't want him to be mad at me." He looked disgusted with himself.

"How awful," Kate said. But she knew there really wasn't anything to say.

"Yeah. Anyway. My point is, that was about the time I decided that I was never going to hold back what I thought about things again. People think I'm an asshole … "

She started to protest, and he gave her a wry grin.

"Don't argue," he said. "They do. But that's okay. That's fine. If that's how it's got to be, that's how it's got to be. Because I'm never holding my tongue again about anything that matters." He laughed lightly. "Though, maybe I've got to learn to hold it more often about stuff that doesn't matter."

She considered that. "You said you never hold back what you think. But you also said you've had a thing for me for a while now. You kept that secret pretty well." She smiled at him playfully.

"Yeah, well … "

"Why didn't you tell me sooner how you felt?" She was curious, but she also was grasping for some clue that would tell her what this all meant, where they were going, whether she would be just another in his long line of not conquests, precisely—she could see he wasn't like that—but perhaps serial efforts to find connection and meaning.

"I didn't think I had a chance with you," he said.

She raised her eyebrows, surprised. "Why not?"

He shrugged. "You're very together. You're beautiful. You're a serious person. I'm … Well. I'm still trying to figure out what the hell I'm doing."

She stood up from the table and reached out a hand to him. He took it, stood up, and enfolded her in his arms.

"Seems to me like you're doing okay," she said.

"I'm working on it."

Chapter Eighteen

Gen was starting to lose patience with sharing her bed. She was a doll about it, of course—Kate would have expected no less from her best friend—but there was a certain crankiness in the mornings, a certain resigned acceptance when Kate came home at night, that told Kate she'd better figure something else out soon.

It didn't help that Kate had become a restless sleeper. Since Jackson. Since she'd regularly begun going to bed at night having been with him, or having spoken to him on the phone, without the benefit of sweet, sleep-inducing sex. He was sticking to his five-date plan, despite Kate's efforts to persuade him otherwise on his couch on Date Three. His self-control was maddening. And hers was at its breaking point.

The sexual frustration was becoming harder and harder to live with, and it usually resulted in Kate thrashing around at night, trying to sleep, but failing.

The night after the third date, Gen flipped the light on at two a.m., bleary-eyed and irritated. "Oh, for God's sake," she said. "Just screw the man already!"

"I want to," Kate said, groaning and pulling a pillow over her face. "He won't do it! Shit, I'm like a seventeen-year-old boy trying to persuade his virgin girlfriend to put out. 'You'd do it for me if you loved me.' Ugh!"

"I thought it was cute at first," Gen said. "But the whole not-sleeping thing? Less cute."

"I know. I'm sorry. This whole thing with my dad … You're putting up with a lot. Have I told you what a great friend you are?"

"You have. But tell me again."

Kate sat up and looked seriously at Gen. "You are. You really are. You're a great friend. And I'll figure something out soon. I'll fix all of this. I promise."

Gen flopped back onto her pillows. "Soon, okay? I'm getting unsightly circles under my eyes."

"You are not."

"But you are."

Kate sat up straight, alarmed. "Am I?" She got up and went to the bathroom, turned on the light, and peered into the mirror. "Oh, God. I am."

"I know what'll cure that."

"What?" Kate poked her head out of the bathroom to listen.

"Sex. And then sleep."

In the final run-up to Art Walk, both Kate and Jackson were busy with preparations—her for the event at the store, him with catering jobs for the big night—and so they were not able to dispense with Date Four and get down to business as quickly as they might have liked. She was swamped with work during the day, he couldn't get away from the restaurant in the evenings.

They talked on the phone, texted, and emailed a lot, but it wasn't getting the job done for either of them.

"We have to do Date Four, so we can do Date Five! The all-important Date Five!" Kate told Jackson on her cell phone during a lull at the store. "Do not make me wait any longer than I have to for Date Five, Jackson. I might have to kill you."

He let out a low, seductive laugh that made the blood rush straight to the body parts she was trying to forget. "Who said Date Five was the all-important one? I thought we'd agreed to hold out until *after* Date Five. Which means the all-important stuff will happen on Date Six."

"Six?" Kate sputtered. "But that's ... I ... You ..."

He laughed at her again, his voice a deep purr. "I'm joking," he said. "It's Date Five. It's definitely Date Five."

"If I haven't already evaporated into a puff of frustration and broken dreams," she said.

His voice was serious now. "Jesus. It's so sexy that you want this as much as I do. There's something to be said for waiting like this."

"Not much," she said. "Gen hasn't slept in a week."

"Gen?"

"I'll explain another time," she said. "The point is, we've got to get this show rolling. When are we having goddamned Date Four?"

" 'Goddamned Date Four,' " he echoed. "That has a nice ring to it."

"When?" she demanded.

"Hmm. I'm working every night until Art Walk. But I've got a window of time Tuesday afternoon. Can you get away?"

"I work Tuesday afternoon."

"How about the new guy at the store? Can he handle it for a couple of hours? We could ... I don't know. Drive down to Morro Bay and see an early movie."

"That works."

"Anything you want to see?" he asked.

"Whatever will get us to Date Five."

"Amen."

In the last days before Art Walk, Kate worked with Fury to prepare for the store's event. They ordered folding chairs for their guests. They couldn't get catering from Neptune, which was all booked up, so they arranged for a place down in Morro Bay to bring a selection of canapes and beverages. They double-checked with Cassidy McLean to make sure she was still free and that she hadn't forgotten. Kate discussed with Cassidy what she would talk about during her presentation—and did some research on ring-tailed lemurs to make sure she wasn't inviting some crazed wild beast into her store that would terrorize the guests. Once she was satisfied that the lemur would do little more than climb around on Cassidy and look cute, she checked on whether she would need to provide anything for the animal. Cassidy assured her she'd bring everything Samantha needed.

That left advertising and cleaning the store. She and Fury put out flyers about Cassidy's appearance, put notices about the event on the store's website, and hung a sign in the front window. The success of the event would not rely on advertising, though. The nature of Art Walk was that everyone—locals and tourists—would be out on Main Street, walking from venue to venue and discovering things as they went. People who didn't know about the Swept Away event would stumble upon it. Cassidy had agreed to give her presentation twice that evening to accommodate those who trickled in at different times.

By Tuesday, Kate felt that she had enough of a handle on things to turn the store over to Fury to free her up for Date Four.

That didn't stop her from fussing around with him, though.

"Are you sure it's okay for me to go?" she asked, already gathering up her purse and her other belongings.

"Sure. It's no problem. Go." He bobbed his head in the affirmative.

"I know you've taken over during my lunch breaks, but this will be longer."

"Right. Movies usually last longer than lunch."

"Is that sarcasm?" She raised an eyebrow at him.

"Dude. Go. Have your date. I'm fine."

"When I go on lunch breaks, I'm right here in town. If you need anything, you can call and I can come back. This time … "

"You'll be farther away."

"Right!"

"I'm not gonna burn down the store or anything. I'm not gonna invite my friends in here to party." He rolled his eyes at her.

"I hadn't thought about that last scenario. It concerns me that you did."

He placed his hands on her back and gently pushed her toward the door. "You're gonna be late if you don't get going."

"But … "

"You're gonna miss the previews. It sucks when you miss the previews."

He finally got her out the door, and she met Jackson at Neptune for the drive down to Morro Bay. She let the hostess know she was there, and in a few minutes, Jackson came out of the kitchen, removing his chef's coat and smiling when he saw her.

The sight of him, the smile, the way the look in his eyes warmed for her, made something small and gentle hum inside her belly. He took her hand, and she felt a sense of rightness, of belonging.

"Should we go?" he said.

"Absolutely." She turned her face toward him, and he kissed her. He tasted like comfort and promise. She'd been wrong about Date Four: It wasn't something to be dispensed with. A few hours of Jackson in the middle of her day was a gift worth savoring.

Traffic was light, and the drive down to Morro Bay took about half an hour. Everyone in Cambria was so familiar with the drive they could have done it blindfolded. While part of Cambria's charm was that it lacked chain restaurants, drive-throughs, and many of the other establishments that stole a town's character and made it look just like everywhere else, there were times when you just wanted to shop at a well-equipped grocery store or get a Starbucks Frappuccino. Or see a movie.

The day was bright and clear, and Jackson seemed to be in a good mood. He hummed whatever tune was playing in his head, tapping out the beat on the steering wheel as he drove.

"You seem happy," Kate told him.

"I'm with you," he said simply. His response made her grin like an idiot.

The only movie theater in town was a one-screen place that had been open since 1942. It had been updated in the interim, no doubt, but it retained a feeling of nostalgia, of grandeur, and it evoked the spirit of the thousands of helpings of sticky fake butter and spilled sodas that had gone before. Because there was only one screen, Kate and Jackson had no options regarding what they would watch. The sole offering was an action-adventure flick that, they learned with dismay, had garnered only a ten percent rating on Rotten Tomatoes; the name of the movie was adorned on the website with an ugly green splat.

"Well, that doesn't look promising," Jackson said. "We could do something else."

"I think we should see it," Kate said.

He looked at her doubtfully. "Really?"

"Sure. It'll be fun. We can heckle. Have you ever seen *Mystery Science Theater 3000*?"

"Sure," he said. "But I'm surprised you have."

She punched him playfully on the shoulder. "Come on. Let's get our tickets."

Even the woman manning the box office seemed surprised that anyone wanted to see the film. They got their tickets and went inside, inhaling the smell of stale popcorn and oily hair.

"This place is great. I love this place," Kate said.

"Snacks?" Jackson said.

"Absolutely," Kate replied with enthusiasm.

"Popcorn?" he said.

They both peered uncertainly into the bin containing artificially yellow popcorn that might have been there since the night before, or might have been there through the eons, pre-dating the opening of the theater and even the dawn of motion pictures themselves.

"Better stick with the candy," Kate said.

They bought boxes of candy and giant bathtub-sized vessels of soda from a pimpled kid who looked like he'd just smoked a joint in the men's room. Then they hauled their purchases into the theater and looked around for a seat.

"Where's everybody else?" Kate said.

"Huh. I guess we're it," Jackson said.

The theater was vast, the kind that had filled up completely only for the blockbuster movies of their youth, like *Titanic* and *Jurassic Park*. They maneuvered halfway down the aisle and found two center seats.

"Do you suppose anybody else is going to come?" Jackson asked.

"I hope not," Kate said, snuggling down into her seat. "This is kind of great." She opened her box of candy and popped some into her mouth. "God, Jujubes. I haven't had these since I was twelve. These are the flavor of youth and joy, right here." She washed the candy down with a giant slurp of Coke.

When she looked up at him, he was gazing at her with a lopsided smile on his face.

"What?" she said.

He shrugged. "I just like the uncomplicated happiness you're getting from this. Most women would be pissed if I brought them here."

She nudged him with an elbow. "I'm not most women."

"Yeah, I'm getting that," he said.

When it was time for the movie to start, the theater went dark and the sound erupted with a thunderous boom. Had they made movies louder since Kate was young, or did she just remember it that way? She was certain her ears would be ringing when she left here in two hours.

Because they were alone in the theater, they had the luxury of heckling the movie, just as Kate had suggested, without annoying anyone. Jackson turned out to be funnier than she'd expected, and some of his observations about the acting and the cheesy plot developments had her laughing until her stomach ached. When he made a bad pun, she pelted him with a Jujube. This led to him lobbing a Milk Dud back at her. And that led to her looking at him in the dim light from the screen with amusement and pleasure in her eyes.

He leaned over and kissed her. He tasted like chocolate and caramel.

After the movie, they emerged, squinting, into the sunlight. They walked across the street to a place that sold hamburgers, hot dogs, and french fries through an ancient-looking window surrounded by peeling paint. They bought chili dogs and fries and carried them to a picnic table sheltered by a big umbrella.

Kate dug into her food with gusto. Jackson did, too, to her surprise. She'd have thought he was too much of a food snob to enjoy a good chili dog.

"I hadn't pegged you for a chili dog kind of guy," Kate observed.

"Why? Just because I'm a chef?" He shook his head. "There's a certain perfection to a chili dog, especially one that oozes chili all over your fingers when you eat it. I like a Big Mac on occasion, too."

"Huh," she said. "Who'd have thought?"

They ate in happy silence, and they wiped the chili off of their hands and faces with flimsy paper napkins. Then they sat under the umbrella, enjoying the light breeze and the smell of the ocean.

"So," he said.

"So?"

"So, I want to ask you about this guy Marcus ... "

"My husband. Ex-husband."

" ... But I don't know if that's a sensitive topic. I want to know, but I don't want to ruin a really good date."

Kate shrugged. "It's okay. I don't mind talking about him. I would have minded as recently as six months ago. It was hard for a long time. But now ... " She searched for words. "Now, none of it seems to matter that much anymore. I've moved on."

He nodded. He wadded up their used napkins and wrappers and tossed them into a nearby trash can.

"You said you met him in grad school," he prompted.

"Right. I met him at a party the English department was hosting. He was there with a girl from a seminar I was taking. He was drunk. That should have been my first clue that he wasn't right for me." She shook her head at the memory.

He leaned toward her, resting his forearms on the picnic table. "What was the attraction?"

"He was really charming at first. Attractive. Brilliant. He had this thing, this way of turning his attention on someone and making them feel like the most important person in the world. It's only later that you see that *he's* the most important person in his world."

"Were you ever happy together?" he asked. "Before things started to go wrong?"

She sighed and considered the question. A gentle breeze blew through her hair. Nearby, seagulls picked at a few discarded french fries.

"I thought we were happy," she said. "At first. But what I thought was happiness was just me having not caught on to him. He was cheating from the beginning. Before the wedding, even. I had no idea. And then later, when I did have an idea, he always made it about me. About how I was too insecure to trust anyone. How I was inventing scenarios in my mind to conform with the twisted view I had of men. How he could never win with me, because I was damaged and wasn't capable of a healthy relationship."

She saw the muscles in his jaw flex with what might have been anger. "And you believed him?"

"I didn't know what to believe. When your two choices are to believe that you're emotionally stunted, or to believe that your husband is cheating on you with every woman he can get his hands on and that he never loved you, the first option looks pretty attractive."

He nodded. "I can see that."

"What about you?" she said.

"Me?"

"Have you had any serious relationships?"

He laughed lightly. "Not since Debra Ferguson in twelfth grade."

"Ooh. Tell me about Debra Ferguson."

"She was a cheerleader. With a ponytail. God, I loved her ponytail."

She grinned. "The tiny skirts and the pompoms probably didn't hurt."

"No." He smiled wistfully. "I lost my virginity to her in the back of my dad's 1986 Buick LeSabre."

"Let me guess," Kate said. "You went your separate ways after graduation."

"No." He raised his eyebrows thoughtfully. "No, no. We stayed together for a couple years after graduation. We were engaged for a while."

This was taking a turn Kate hadn't anticipated. "Engaged?"

"Yeah." He nodded. "I had a job busing tables and she worked as a checker at a grocery store. We were gonna get an apartment, have a cheap wedding because it was all we could afford. Then we'd have some kids, the whole bit."

She leaned toward him. "So, what happened?"

He shrugged. "The accident happened."

"The car accident."

"Yeah. I went through ... some things after that. I was in the hospital for a while, and then I had some problems with depression. It was too much for her. She broke it off."

Kate reached out and put a hand on his arm. "That's awful."

"Ah, I don't know. It was for the best. Getting married right out of high school ... it was never gonna work out. Better to know that up front."

"She doesn't sound like a very good person," Kate said.

He shook his head. "It wasn't her fault. She was a kid. We both were."

Before heading back to his truck, they walked toward the water and sat on the beach, wiggling their bare toes in the wet sand.

"I probably should get back to the shop and relieve Fury," Kate said. Overhead, seagulls soared and dipped and soared again. Down the beach, some kids were making a sandcastle with a red plastic shovel and a pail.

"You want to go?" he said.

"No. I want to stay here with you." She leaned over and rested her head against his shoulder. He put an arm around her, and they sat that way for a long time.

Finally, when they knew they couldn't delay it any longer, they put their shoes back on their sandy feet and made the walk to where he had parked. They drove back to Cambria with her hand in his.

Chapter Nineteen

The fact that Date Four was over—and the ever-critical Date Five was looming—ratcheted up Kate's tension even further. She asked Jackson if there was any way they could find some time for a date before Art Walk—any time at all—and he gave her that seductive laugh and urged her to be patient. He didn't want to rush Date Five. It couldn't be a lunch in the middle of their work day, it couldn't be a drink after Jackson got out of the restaurant in the late hours. No, Date Five had to be done right. He had plans, he said. Important Date Five plans, for Monday.

Knowing that Jackson was the one saying no to sex, and Kate was the one urging him to recklessly surrender to passion, was strange and somehow empowering. A lifetime of being female had taught Kate that the traditional roles were for the male to pressure and the female to resist. It was how things had worked all of her teenage and then adult life. Forces ranging from her upbringing to the media said the man was supposed to want it; the woman was supposed to use sex only for procreation and to tip the scales of power in the relationship. She wasn't supposed to have normal, adult desires, and she certainly wasn't supposed to assert those desires.

The way those desires were raging inside her, and having made no secret of that to Jackson, felt freeing. She didn't need candles and rose petals and soft music, but apparently *he* did, and that thought made her smile.

She thought about that, and about the various carnal delights Date Five would have to offer, on Friday night after work as she,

Gen, Rose, and Lacy discussed their plans for Art Walk the next day.

They were sitting around the dining table in the cottage Rose rented in a woodsy neighborhood east of Highway 1. The tiny house, which had been standing for more than a hundred years, was charmingly rustic—though Rose would have used the word "dilapidated." The knotty pine paneling and freestanding cast iron fireplace made it feel like they were at camp.

"A lemur?" Lacy asked. They were sharing a bottle of white wine and a big bowl of popcorn, all of them dressed in their "girls' night in" ensembles of T-shirts and sweatpants.

"A ring-tailed lemur," Kate confirmed. "Did you know they spread this lemur stink all over everything to mark territory and establish dominance? But humans can't detect the smell. Thankfully. Otherwise, that might have been a deal-breaker."

"Huh," Gen said. "It's going to be just like when Johnny Carson had that zoo lady on his show."

"Joan Embery," Rose supplied.

"Right." Gen pointed a finger at her. "That's her."

"The little bugger's going to poop on my floor," Kate said. "I just know it." She asked Gen, "What about you?"

"I'm not going to poop on your floor," Gen said. "Though, you should probably keep an eye on the tourists."

"Very funny."

Gen had an art demonstration at the gallery, with a wine and cheese reception. Rose's wine tasting shop would be presenting a lecture on how to do proper wine and food pairings, with a wine and hors d'oeuvre tasting. Jitters—which expected to do a brisk business with all of the foot traffic—would have live music. An acoustic guitarist, as you'd expect from any self-respecting coffee house.

"I hate Art Walk," Kate declared. "It's always so much work, and this year it's delaying my gratification with Jackson. I don't want my gratification delayed. I want my gratification now."

"You poor thing," Gen said soothingly.

Rose raised her eyebrows, one pierced with a stainless steel barbell. "It's been a while, hasn't it? Since you've been ... you know ... gratified."

"So long," Kate confirmed. "So, so long."

"Hey. You know what would be gratifying?" Gen asked.

"What?" Kate said.

"Kicking your father and Angela out of your house."

Kate groaned. "I know. I need to. I just have to figure out how."

"I'll do it," Rose offered. "Just say the word, and I'll have their asses out on the curb before you can say Daddy Dearest."

"I'll do it," Kate said again. "I will. I just ... I need time."

Gen groaned.

"Oh, honey," Kate said. "I'm so sorry about invading your personal space. But at least after Monday I should be sleeping a lot better."

Gen raised her wineglass in a mock toast. "Here's hoping."

As Kate was leaving her house on Saturday to go to work—it would be a long day, beginning midmorning and ending well after midnight—a grey Toyota Corolla slowed down on its way past her street and paused in front of her house. The window rolled down, and a man in his midfifties poked a smartphone out the driver's side window and started taking pictures.

Tourists. God only knows why they do what they do.

The man with the phone spotted Kate emerging from Gen's downstairs apartment and called out to her.

"Do you live here?" he said.

"I do. How can I help you?" She was slightly annoyed and in a hurry, but the courtesy that came with running a business took over.

"Quite a location," he said.

"Yes, I love it here."

"What are the property taxes like?"

She approached the car, which had Oregon plates. "Oh, are you thinking of relocating?"

"Maybe, if I can get the right deal." He winked at her.

"Well, it's a lovely town," Kate offered.

"It sure is." He pointed at the house. "You got central heating in there?"

"Um … no."

"Ah. Hmm."

"Okay, well," Kate said, trying to end the conversation. "I have to get to work. Have a good day!" As she walked to her car, she saw the man park the car, get out, and stand with his hands on his hips, looking at her house.

A little creeped out, Kate waited in her car until the guy drove away. If he'd intended to burglarize her place, surely he'd have been more stealthy about it. And it certainly wasn't unusual for visitors to Cambria to scope out the local real estate, asking questions and taking pictures.

Still, she had a bad feeling, and somehow, she connected it with her father.

Saturday evening brought perfect weather for the event. Cool but not cold, clear skies, light breeze off the ocean with the enticing scent of salt water.

Kate arranged the canapes, the napkins, and the plastic drink cups; Fury straightened the rows of folding chairs; and Cassidy McLean, who had arrived right on time toting Samantha in a plastic cat carrier, was arranging a stack of her books on a table for signing.

Kate checked her watch: six-thirty p.m.

"Okay," she told Fury. "Open the doors!"

He propped open the front door of the shop and put out the sandwich board announcing that Cassidy McLean would be speaking at seven-thirty and again at nine, with book signings after each presentation. In smaller print, the sign advertised refreshments, a special sales promotion, and Fury's "name the book and win it" contest.

Kate took a deep breath and girded her loins for the evening to come.

It looked like they were going to get pretty good crowds. As soon as the doors opened, people starting coming in and milling around, browsing the books, nibbling on the little cheese puffs and pigs in blankets. Kate and Fury greeted everyone, made small talk, made sure everyone knew Cassidy would be speaking soon. Cassidy did her part as well, chatting with the locals and tourists about her experience in the movies and her life at the wild animal refuge. Kate noted with approval that Cassidy was subtle about pushing her book, letting her own personality sell it rather than shoving it in people's faces. The woman was a pro.

Things were going smoothly enough that, with plenty of time left before Cassidy's talk, Kate left Fury in charge for a bit and went out onto Main Street to see what everyone else was doing for their events.

The Porter Gallery was holding a live drawing demonstration, with an artist sketching a model who was draped gracefully in billowy white cloth, her bare shoulders and legs emerging from beneath the folds of fabric. Gen had briefly considered using a nude model—because, after all, the idea was to create a stir and draw a crowd—but rejected the idea when Kate had pointed out how many children people brought with them for Art Walk.

De-Vine seemed to have a good crowd for the talk on wine and food pairings. Kate ducked in just long enough for a couple of exquisitely presented bite-sized morsels and a few sips of a fragrant, rich cabernet sauvignon.

She made small talk with people she encountered along the way: her regular customers, her neighbors, people she knew from the gas station and the library and the clothing boutiques. Main Street had a festive, carnival atmosphere that almost made her wish she were a tourist instead of a business owner with a job to do.

On her way back toward the shop, she passed a street performer playing the saxophone, a food cart offering fresh-made tacos, and a guy selling helium balloons that lit up from the inside.

She checked the time on her cell phone and decided she just had time to drop in on Lacy before heading back to Swept Away.

The coffee house was about three-quarters full, with a line at the counter and most of the tables occupied. The guitarist was already performing—he was a scraggly looking guy singing a mournful version of James Taylor's "You've Got a Friend."

Kate snagged Lacy as the other woman was taking a couple of lattes to a couple sitting at a round table by the door. After Lacy delivered the drinks, Kate asked, "How's it going?"

"Good." Lacy nodded. "People seem to like Bob."

"Bob?"

"The singer." She gestured. "Though he's a little heavy on the James Taylor. We've already heard 'Fire and Rain' and 'Sweet Baby James,' and it's not even seven-thirty."

People did seem to be enjoying the music; they were looking attentively at the makeshift stage, interested, enjoying their coffees.

"How about you?" Lacy asked. "How's it coming over there?"

"Okay, I guess. Cassidy McLean seems great. But I'm nervous."

Lacy rubbed Kate's upper arm. "Hang in there. It's just one night!"

"Right." She nodded. "Right."

Kate looked around and saw people she knew, and people she didn't know. Peering into the dim light of the coffee house, she spotted a familiar face she hadn't expected to see.

"Is that Zach?" she whispered to Lacy, just loud enough to be heard over the guitarist.

"Uh huh," Lacy confirmed. "Caramel macchiato, no whip."

"Is that his wife?" Kate was curious. The woman sitting with Zach was lovely, all silky black hair and smooth, creamy skin. It was hard to tell in the dim lighting, but she didn't look happy.

"I guess so," Lacy said. "I didn't ask."

"Hmm." Kate caught a glance at her watch. "Shit! Gotta go. Good luck!"

She dashed out the door and back to Swept Away, where the crowd was starting to find seats for Cassidy's talk. Her father and Angela were sitting third row center. Jazzy was poking his fuzzy little head out of Angela's purse. At least that meant he wasn't home eating Kate's favorite jeans.

"Dad," she said. "Angela. You came."

"Of course we came," her father said, puffing up a bit. "I wouldn't miss my daughter's big night!"

"We do this every year," she said. "This is the first time you've come."

"Ah. Well … "

"You know, they've got a terrific guitarist next door. Maybe you should … "

Her less-than-subtle effort to get him out the door was interrupted as Cassidy nodded to Kate that she was ready to begin.

Kate went to the front of the room, where she'd set up a lectern. "If everyone could please take their seats!" She waited while people shuffled around each other and settled into the folding chairs, holding little napkins full of food in their laps.

Once everyone had settled, she launched into her welcome speech: "I'd like to thank you all for coming out tonight. Welcome to Swept Away." There was a smattering of applause. She gave a brief bio of Cassidy McLean, which included the highlights of her film career and the history of the animal refuge she'd opened with her husband. Kate finished up with a hearty endorsement of *Wild Woman,* Cassidy's book. "Let's all give a friendly Swept Away welcome to Cassidy McLean," she said, leading a round of applause and stepping to the side.

Cassidy took the lectern, opened a copy of *Wild Woman,* and started to read a passage she and Kate had picked out beforehand. The plan was that after the reading, she would bring out Samantha and talk about ring-tailed lemurs, as well as the many other species she housed on her property.

While Cassidy talked, Kate surveyed the refreshment table, which was starting to look a little bare. "Could you go into the back and get some more canapes?" she asked Fury. "The iced tea looks a little low, too."

"I'm on it," he told her, disappearing into the back room.

She took a look at the crowd. About thirty people had gathered for the event, which was, frankly, a better turnout than she'd expected based on previous years. She noticed that the audience was mostly older; probably people who remembered Cassidy McLean's glory years in movies.

A steady stream of foot traffic was going by on the sidewalk, and a few more people came in to listen to the talk.

When Samantha came out, the crowd gasped in delight. The black and white creature was about a foot and a half long, with eyes ringed in black and a long, striped tail that she swished about to great effect. As Cassidy talked about how Samantha had come to the refuge, and about ring-tailed lemurs in general, Kate noticed Zach and his ex-wife, Sherry, standing in the open door to the bookstore. Sherry, she of the Miss World bone structure, was scowling, her arms crossed over her chest.

"Is that her?" Sherry said, pointing at Kate.

Zach put a hand on Sherry's shoulder and said something to her that Kate couldn't hear.

"I just want to talk to her," Sherry said.

Again, Zach leaned toward Sherry's ear and murmured something to her.

"I don't give a shit!" Sherry said, causing numerous people in the audience to turn around to look at her. "I just want to talk to this bitch!"

Kate didn't know what was happening, but it didn't seem like anything good. She asked Fury to hold down the fort and charged toward the front door to head off any trouble before it came into her store.

"Is there something I can help you with?" she asked the couple.

"Kate," Zach said. "I'm really sorry. I … "

"*You* shut your mouth," Sherry said, throwing him a look that would have immolated him, had she been gifted with pyrokinesis.

"Maybe we should step outside," Kate said. She led Zach and Sherry out onto the sidewalk. Then, considering, she closed the front door of the bookstore behind them so the customers inside wouldn't hear whatever was about to happen.

"Now. What's this about?"

"It's about you screwing my husband," Sherry said.

"What? I never ... "

"Sherry," Zach said.

"That was your house where we had dinner, wasn't it?" she demanded. "Don't lie, you skank."

"Hey!" Kate protested. "Let's just back up a bit."

Sherry grabbed Zach's cell phone out of his hand and pulled up the lengthy call history between him and Kate. Then, triumph on her face, she pulled up their texts and shoved the phone into Kate's face.

"Did you *read* the texts, Sherry?" Zach demanded. "Because if you did, you'd see there was nothing in there! Just friendly, innocent, how-was-your-day kind of stuff!"

"Why were you asking her how *her* day was?" Sherry said, on the verge of tears. "Why weren't you calling me, asking *me* how *my* day was? And then you took me to her *house* ... "

"Sherry. Honey."

He put a hand on her arm, and she shook it off. "Don't touch me!"

"We planned that dinner for *you*," Kate tried.

"*You* planned it?! *You?!*" Sherry was spinning into near hysteria. She grabbed Kate by the shoulders and started shaking her. "I'm going to beat your scrawny ass!" she screamed.

A crowd was starting to gather as Zach grabbed Sherry and tried to pull her away. Kate was just starting to think about the self-defense classes she'd taken in college—aim for the eyes, she recalled—when Sherry suddenly let go of her and moved backward three feet as though displaced by an alien ray gun. Kate stood there stunned, wondering what had happened, and then she saw Jackson, who'd appeared out of nowhere, setting the other woman down on the sidewalk and standing in front of Kate, blocking Sherry's access to her.

"Where did you come from?" Kate said, stunned.

"What the hell is going on here?" Jackson demanded of Zach.

"I'm sorry, man," Zach said. "My wife, she gets a little jealous."

"Wife?" Sherry demanded. "I'm not your wife anymore, you cheating asshole!"

Jackson looked over his shoulder at Kate. "You slept with this guy?"

"No!" Kate said.

"No, no!" Zach said. He likely would have said that whether it were true or not, considering that Jackson was taller than him and outweighed him by a good fifty pounds.

"Somebody had better make things clear to me," Jackson said, a threat in his voice.

"Sherry saw the phone calls and texts between me and Zach," Kate said. "When we were planning the dinner."

"Then there were the calls to your landline when I was doing comps for the house," Zach added.

"Comps?" Kate said.

"Yeah, for the house," Zach repeated. "I told you before, I was talking to her *dad,* for Christ's sake," he said to Sherry.

"You're selling your house?" Jackson asked Kate, turning to look at her.

"No!"

"You're not?" Zach said. "But your dad … "

"Wait!" Kate waved her hands wildly in front of her face in an effort to clear away her confusion. "My dad? What exactly did he say to you?"

"*Hello!*" Sherry said. "Can we get back to how he's a cheating asshole and you're a skanky whore?"

"I am *not* a skanky whore!" Kate yelled.

As the altercation got louder, people started to come out of the store to watch the much more entertaining scene playing out on the sidewalk. Kate saw that her father and Sherry were among the gawkers.

"Dad. Did you tell Zach I was selling my house?" Kate demanded.

"Well, I ... "

"He said he wanted to know what it would go for, get the ball rolling," Sherry said, now having apparently forgotten about her initial mission.

"Get the ... What the ... " Kate sputtered in her anger and disbelief. Suddenly, the guy taking pictures of her house made sense.

"I just thought ... " Thomas began.

"That is *it*," Kate yelled. "That is goddamned *it*!"

"Don't you talk to your father that way!" Angela demanded. "Oh! My blood pressure!"

At that moment, Jazzy, apparently upset by the yelling, leaped out of Angela's purse and darted into the bookstore, tearing after the lemur, who was cradled in Cassidy McLean's arms. Jazzy barked, yipped and yelped. Samantha let out a loud, wailing howl and sprinted out of Cassidy's arms and into the back of the store.

"Jazzy!" Angela cried.

"Oh, shit," Kate said.

Kate heard crashing sounds from inside the store as guests who were uncertain whether lemurs could be dangerous decided that caution was preferable to hospitalization and high-tailed it out onto the street.

"Samantha!" Cassidy cried, rushing into the back room after the lemur and the frenzied little dog.

Kate pushed her way through the crowd and rushed into the store with Jackson behind her. Bringing up the rear was Angela, exclaiming, "If that little ferret hurts my Jazzy … "

"It's not a goddamned ferret," Cassidy McLean yelled at her. "It's a ring-tailed goddamned lemur!"

Kate grabbed Fury. "Clear out the store," she told him. "Get everybody out of here. The last thing we need is for somebody to get bitten." He nodded and rushed around apologizing and herding people toward the door.

Kate, Jackson, Cassidy, Angela, Thomas, Samantha, and Jazzy all were crowded into the tiny back room. Samantha was on top of a cabinet, letting out her horrific, ear-splitting wail, while Jazzy was on his hind legs, front legs planted on the front of the cabinet, growling and yipping.

Kate scooped up Jazzy and turned toward Angela. "Get him out of here!" she said, thrusting the tiny dog into Angela's hands.

"How dare you talk to me like that!" Angela said, her Mary Kay–coated lips in an angry pout.

"You're right. I'll correct my language. Get him *the hell* out of here." She glared at her father. "And take Jazzy, too."

Behind her, Jackson let out a guffaw.

When Kate's father and stepmother had left with the dog, Cassidy made soothing coos and kissing noises at Samantha. When that didn't work, she offered Samantha some kind of lemur treat she produced from her bag. The lemur scurried down onto Cassidy's shoulder. Cassidy scooped her up and put her back in her carrier.

"Cassidy, I'm so sorry," Kate said.

Cassidy's face was red, her hair askew. "Do you know what could have happened to Samantha? Do you realize how easily she could have gotten hurt?"

"I didn't … I … "

"Come on, baby," Cassidy said to the lemur, carrying the cage back into the main part of the store.

With some semblance of order restored, Kate turned to face Jackson.

"You just appeared out of nowhere and pulled that lunatic off of me. Where did you come from?"

"We got all the food delivered, and I thought I'd stop by."

He looked at her. She looked at him. She was still breathing heavily, her chest heaving. Her emotions were high, her every nerve on high alert.

"Screw Date Five," she said, and launched herself at him.

One second they were feet apart, talking, and the next, she had her body wrapped around him, her mouth on his in an explosion of desire. His arms were around her, his hands in her hair, holding her head to him, his mouth devouring hers. He backed her up against a bookshelf, and books fell to the floor around them.

"Oh. God." Her blood was a river of fire within her. She reached up and grabbed his shirt and ripped it open. Buttons flew.

"Let me just ... the door ... " With one leg, he reached back and kicked closed the door to the main part of the store.

She ran her hands over his chest, feeling the warm, smooth skin, the hard muscles. He tore off the ripped shirt and pressed his body against hers, putting his mouth on hers, then moving down to her jaw, her neck, the V of skin exposed by her blouse.

"Oh, I ... oh ..." She couldn't remember ever feeling this, not with Marcus, not with anyone. This urgency, this need. This desire to climb inside of him and be a part of his beating heart.

He started to unbutton her blouse, but then, impatient, he yanked it off over her head. His mouth traveled lower and pressed its warmth to the top of her breast, his tongue exploring.

Kate moaned, a low and throaty sound.

The door to the store started to open as Fury called, "Kate?"

Jackson separated from her just long enough to close the door and search for a lock. "How do I ... ?"

"It doesn't lock. Here." She grabbed a crate of books and pushed it in front of the door, and they attacked each other again. This time she was the one who shoved him up against the wall. A manila folder of paperwork that had been stacked on a shelf above them fluttered its contents around them like fall leaves.

His hands were on her, all over her, and he roughly pulled her skirt up until it was bunched around her waist. He grabbed her ass and pulled her to him, and she felt his arousal against her body.

"Maybe we should stop. This isn't how I wanted to do this," he began, his voice a husky rasp.

"This is Date Five," she said, desperate to have his naked body pressed against hers.

"What? This is ... "

"You're my date for the Art Walk."

"Kate, that's ... "

"Just go with it, Jackson! For Christ's sake!" She unbuckled his belt, and he groaned with pleasure.

He proved to be surprisingly nimble at removing her bra, and she was reminded that he'd had plenty of practice with that sort of thing. But how could she be anything but grateful for his skill? For the masterful way he handled her as his hot mouth closed over her breast.

She felt crazy, driven mindless by the force of her need. She grappled with his zipper, and then when he was freed of his pants she wrapped her hand around him and heard him breathe her name.

A knock came at the back door leading to the alleyway. This door did lock, and Kate reached out and turned the dead bolt.

"Kate?" Angela rapped on the door. "Kate, open up right this minute. I want to speak to you about the way you treated me and your father. Kate?"

"Ignore her," Jackson murmured into her ear, his body holding her up against the wall. "Just pretend she's not there." His hand went into the waistband of her panties and traveled downward until he found her, all warm and wet for him. He put a finger inside her and she pressed her mouth against the salty skin of his neck to keep from crying out.

"Jackson," she said, her voice a plea. "I can't wait anymore. I can't ... "

"Ah, shit," he moaned.

"What? What?"

"Condoms. I don't have any goddamned condoms."

"Wait!" she said. "I do!"

He pulled back from her slightly. "You do?"

"In my purse! In case we couldn't hold out until Date Five!"

He smiled seductively. "I love a woman who's prepared."

"There's no time for banter! Just get them!"

"Where?"

She pointed a few feet away, to where her purse sat on a shelf. Without releasing her, he lunged for it, hunted around inside, then finally dumped it out, scattering her wallet, pens, lipsticks, tampons.

"There!" She pointed.

He grabbed a little square packet and ripped it open with his teeth. With the business of safety attended to, he hooked his fingers into the waist of her panties and pulled them down, then lifted her up onto him, her back pressed against the plaster wall.

She felt so many sensations. His body in hers, thrusting urgently. The taste of his skin, salty and hot. The feel of his breath on her, the sound of his voice moaning her name. The raw, aching need in the center of her body, building, building, rushing to a devastating crescendo.

When her orgasm hit, she felt like she was flying apart. She cried out, mindless to the fact that someone might hear, aware only of him and the way he made her feel.

He moved into her urgently until his own body shuddered with release.

They clung to each other, sticky with sweat, their hearts beating fast, breathing hard. He brought a hand up to smooth a sweaty strand of hair from her forehead. They slowly lowered to the floor, where they sat propped against the wall, wrapped in each other's arms.

"Kate," he said. "Jesus."

"That was … " she said. "I've never … "

"I know. Me neither." He rested his chin on top of her head in a way that made her feel safe, protected.

"I'm not new at this," she said. "But that was … There are no words."

"I know." He paused. "I wanted to do this right. Not in the back room of your store." He looked around them at the mess they had made.

She laughed. "If that was doing it wrong, then doing it right might kill me."

The pounding at the back door came again. "Kate! I can *hear* you in there!"

Jackson laughed his sexy, husky laugh. "Maybe you should just let her in."

She considered that. "Not a bad idea. It might make her think twice about invading people's privacy."

"Then again, I don't want to share you with anybody right now. Especially her." He kissed the top of her head tenderly.

They sat entwined, naked, floating on the cloud of their afterglow.

"Best Art Walk ever," Kate said.

Chapter Twenty

Kate and Jackson got dressed the best they could. For Kate, only the flush of her skin and the smudge of her makeup gave her away. But Jackson was left without a shirt, having had his ripped from his body in a hail of buttons and torn fabric.

"What am I supposed to do about this?" he said, holding the ruined garment in his hand.

"Oh. Wow. I'm sorry about that," Kate said.

"Don't get me wrong, I liked it. I might have this framed," he said, gesturing to the shirt. "But what am I going to wear?"

She rummaged around in the back room until she found a carton with some promotional T-shirts left over from an event she'd held a few months before. She sorted through the shirts until she found one that would fit him, and tossed it to him.

"Emily Brontë?" He looked at Kate uncertainly. "How am I gonna explain this to my guy friends?"

"If you tell them this story, you'll be their hero," she said, smirking at him. "Or you could always go bare-chested. That would be my preference, actually."

He snapped her with the T-shirt like a guy in a locker room. "Vixen."

"You bet."

When they were at least reasonably put together and Kate had scooped the contents of her purse back into the bag, Angela banged on the back door again.

"What do you say, Jackson?" Kate asked, her hands planted on her hips, empowered by sexual satisfaction, adrenaline, and not a small amount of pure Jackson Graham. "You want to help me kick my worthless father out on his ass?"

"I wouldn't miss it," he said. "Lead the way."

Kate flung open the back door to find Angela with her fist poised in mid-knock.

"Well, it's about time you opened the door. I have some things to say to you." Angela's face was a mask of indignant fury and Mary Kay lilac eyeshadow. "You owe us an apology. You should be ashamed of yourself. The way you treat us … "

Kate grabbed her purse and pushed past Angela, and she and Jackson headed toward her car.

"Do you need to lock up?" he asked.

"Fury's here. And anyway, I'll be back. This won't take long."

"Kate! You come back here and listen to what I have to say," Angela bleated. "Kate!"

Without looking back, Kate went to her Honda, got in, and fired up the engine. Jackson's butt had barely landed in the passenger seat before she pulled out of the tiny parking lot and headed toward home.

"Are you okay to drive?" Jackson asked, buckling his seat belt. "Not too upset?"

"I feel fine," she said, meaning it. It was the first time she'd felt this fine in a very long time.

When they arrived at her house, she pulled into the driveway with a screech of brakes. She got out of the car and power-walked to the front door. She unlocked it, went inside, and headed across the living room toward the big sliding glass door that opened out onto the balcony. She opened the door wide.

With the way cleared, she went into her bedroom, opened the closet and the dresser drawers, and started gathering armloads of her father's and Angela's belongings. Her arms full of shirts, pants, shoes, belts, and the various pieces of their wardrobes, she went out onto the balcony and heaved everything over the side. Garments fluttered to the damp grass below.

"Kate, are you sure about this?" Jackson said.

"Grab a handful and help me." She went back into the bedroom for another load. Shoes, socks, underwear, belts, T-shirts, all took flight over the balcony railing and landed in a heap on the lawn, startling a doe that had been grazing beneath a tree.

"Here, grab this." She handed Jackson the big, wheeled suitcase. "It's heavy."

Jackson took the suitcase and hefted it into the great beyond.

Toiletries, Angela's makeup case, Jazzy's dog bed. Her father's orthopedic pillow. Their special coffee, her sleep mask, his robe and slippers, all of it sailed into the night and down onto the grass, where a pile of alarming size was forming.

When Kate headed toward the balcony with Thomas's laptop computer, Jackson put a hand on her arm to stop her. "Are you sure you want to throw that?"

She looked at the computer, and then at him. "Shit. You're right." Instead of throwing it, she took it outside, walked down the stairs past Gen's apartment, and placed the laptop on top of the pile of her father's things.

Kate was just coming back up the stairs when Thomas and Angela arrived, piloting the mammoth pink Cadillac.

Angela spotted the mountain of miscellany on the lawn and screamed. Neighbors peeked their heads out of their front doors, inquiring whether everything was okay.

"What in the world is going on here?" Thomas demanded. "Is that how you run your store? Is this how you run your home? It's lucky I'm here. There's no telling what you'd ... "

"You're leaving," Kate said.

"How dare you talk to me this way? I'm your father," he said.

"Right. You're my father. Let's just take a look at your performance so far, shall we?" Kate was squared off against him, her hands on her hips, magnificent in her anger. "You were controlling and manipulative the entire time I was growing up. You made my mother miserable. And then you left her for another woman." She glared at Angela. "*This* woman. You left my mother alone, so that when she was facing the worst time of her life, when she was dying of *cancer*,"—her voice broke—"she didn't have the man who had promised to be there until death do you part."

Jackson put a steadying hand on her shoulder, and she took strength from it. "And now, when she's gone, you come here and tell me that you *deserve* to have this house, *her* house, as though you already haven't taken enough from her. From me. You force your way in here, take over my home, my bedroom, my life, showing no respect for me, no respect for anything I've built here. And finally," she said, taking a deep breath, "you try to sell my house from under me so you can take and take and take, because you won't be satisfied until I'm left with nothing. No home, no money, no father, and no self-respect. Does that about cover it?"

For once, he was silent. Angela, however, was not. "How can you ... "

Jackson pointed a finger at Angela, his look deadly calm. "Don't."

Her mouth snapped shut.

"Where do you expect me to go?" Thomas said.

"I don't care. A Motel 6. A box on the side of the road. Hell. Your choice."

"Never in a million years did I think my daughter would treat me this way," he said.

"Well, it'll be the last time," Kate said. "It'll be the last time I'll have to. Because I'm done with you. I'm finished. It's over. Give me my spare key."

She held her hand out for the key and stared at him. After a moment of hesitation, he picked it out of his pocket and placed it in her palm. She walked into the house, with Jackson behind her. She closed the door, and locked it.

Once she was inside, once the adrenaline of the situation started to drain out of her, she started to shake. "Aw, come here," Jackson said, taking her into his arms. "You did what you had to do. It was the right thing. I'm proud of you."

"I know," she murmured into his T-shirt. "I'm proud of me, too."

"But it's still hard."

"It is."

He was still holding her tightly in his arms when they heard the Cadillac start up and drive away.

Sunday was all clear skies and brilliant sunlight. Kate sipped her first cup of coffee in an Adirondack chair on the deck, watching the breaking waves in the cool of the morning. She'd invited Jackson to stay the night with her, but when he'd come to Swept Away the night before, he'd only expected to drop in to say hello; he'd had things to wrap up at the restaurant and didn't expect to be finished until late. She'd had to return to town, too, to send Fury home and reassure him that she didn't expect the chaos of the evening to be righted all in one night.

Today she'd have to go to work and fix everything—the mess, the damage, the broken things, and especially the rampant small-town talk about everything that had taken place. But now, sitting here in the morning light with a truly excellent cup of coffee, she couldn't get the goofy grin off her face.

"Kate?" The voice was coming from the patio right beneath her deck. Gen.

"Hey," she answered.

"Are you alone?"

Kate smiled. "I am."

"Want company?"

"Sure. Come on up."

She heard Gen's feet padding on the stairs and then heard her come in the front door with the key Kate had given her when Gen had moved in. "Good morning, honey," Gen called to her.

"It really is," Kate answered.

Gen made a stop in the kitchen to pour herself a cup of coffee from the pot and came out onto the deck. She was still dressed in flannel pajamas and fuzzy slippers, her wild mass of red curls piled atop her head. She plopped down into the other Adirondack chair and sipped silently for a few moments.

"Aren't you going to ask?" Kate said.

"About which part? I don't even know where to start."

Kate looked at her with one eyebrow raised.

"Okay, maybe I do know where to start. I heard that you and Jackson ... that the two of you went into the back room of the store, and ... there were *sounds*." She left the rest dangling there in the space between them.

Kate nodded. "There were, indeed, sounds."

"So you ... ?"

"We certainly did."

Gen stomped her feet excitedly against the wood of the deck. "Oh, wow! In the back room of the store? During Art Walk? Oh my gosh. Was it awesome? Kate. Was he awesome? Because it always seemed like he'd be awesome."

Kate smiled at her friend's enthusiasm. Then she sighed. "It was ... I don't even know how to say it. I don't have the vocabulary for what it was. It was like he broke me into a thousand pieces and then put me back together again. I'm just ... " A tear rolled down her cheek and she swiped it away.

"Oh, honey." Gen was alarmed. "You're crying."

Kate laughed.

"But they're happy tears?" Gen ventured.

"I don't even know what they are. I don't even know. My Art Walk event was ruined, I got called a skanky whore, I got physically attacked by Zach's crazy ex-wife, I had revelatory sex—the best sex of my life, or of anyone's life, probably—I threw my father out of my house and told him I'm finished with him. There's just so much *processing* to do."

Gen sighed and leaned back in her chair. "Wow. The best sex of anybody's life."

"God. You can't know. It really, really was."

"And you're okay?"

"I am," Kate said. "I honestly think I am. I'm better than okay. I'm better than I've been in a long time, maybe ever."

"Where does that leave you and your father?" Gen asked.

Kate shrugged. "I told him we're done. And that makes me sad, because even when someone treats you like crap, you still have hope that someday they'll change, that someday they'll stop treating you like crap and act like a father is supposed to act. And giving up that hope is hard. It hurts. But there's relief, too. And, I'm worried about him. He said he had nowhere to go. That might not have been bullshit."

Gen rubbed Kate's forearm with her hand. "But you can't solve his problems."

"No, I can't. He made them. He has to solve them."

"And where does all of this leave you and Jackson?"

Kate set down her mug on the deck and rubbed at her face with her hands. "Ah, God. I don't know. I thought I'd be able to just have fun with him, you know? Go on some dates, maybe have some good times in bed. Before he moves on. Because he always moves on. But now ... "

"Uh oh," Gen said.

"Yeah." Kate laughed at herself. "Uh oh." She looked at Gen. "Do you think he's capable of having a real relationship? I mean, we know his history. Do you think he can handle something real? Does he even want that?"

Gen looked thoughtful. She shrugged. "Ask him."

"He says he wants to give this a shot. Says he wants this to be different from his usual hit-and-run. But even if that's what he wants, will he be able to do it?"

Gen shook her head slowly, considering. "Maybe he's ready. And maybe that's just wishful thinking. But I'll tell you what." She looked intently at Kate. "You never could have done what you did with your father before Jackson."

Kate gave a shaky sigh. "You think?"

"He's ... I don't know. He's making you stronger. More confident. He's a good influence."

They sat together in companionable silence, drinking their coffee and watching the hummingbirds hover and flit around the tree right off the deck.

"I'm so jealous right now," Gen said finally.

Kate looked at her. "Jealous?"

"I want this. This aching over a man. This afterglow. This ... Just this. Where's *my* man? I'm thirty-four years old, and I've been looking since I was eighteen. *Where is my man?*"

"You date," Kate reminded her.

"Yeah, but not like this. I haven't felt"—she gestured toward Kate—"this."

Kate gave Gen a wry smile. "If he crushes me like a tin can, you're not going to be so jealous anymore."

"He won't."

"He might."

Since there was nothing to say to that, no comforting words that would actually be true, Gen reached out and took Kate's hand, and they sat together while the sea lions barked out their early morning greetings.

"What the hell happened at Kate's shop last night?" Daniel demanded. Jackson got the call over his cell phone when he was on his way from his meat supplier back to the restaurant. "I was stuck over at the gallery giving a talk, but the stories ... I've heard everything from a wild animal attack to Kate getting beaten up in the street."

Jackson grinned. "Nothing as dire as that."

"Which part?"

"Either." He explained that the wild animal attack was actually a yappy dog and a frightened lemur hiding on top of a cabinet, and that rather than being beaten up, Kate had been accused of shenanigans with someone else's man.

"Hmm. Did she do it?" Daniel inquired.

"No. Well, she went out with him once, and they're friendly."

"I'm thinking the dispute centers on people's varying definitions of the word 'friendly,'" Daniel said.

"Pretty much."

After a pause, Daniel said, "I heard other things, too."

"I don't talk about such things," Jackson said. "I'm a gentleman."

Daniel scoffed. "Since when?"

"Since now. Since today."

"Uh huh. Does this protectiveness mean you're developing real feelings for her?"

Jackson felt uncomfortable with where the conversation was going. He shifted in the driver's seat as he turned on Highway 1 toward town. "I've had real feelings for her for a while now. You know that."

"But now they're *more* real."

Jackson was silent.

"Look, Jackson," Daniel said. The teasing tone that had been in his voice all through the call was gone. "I've known you for a few years now. This thing you do, with the women, the whole two-weeks-and-goodbye thing, it isn't making you happy, and you know it."

"I'm not the one who says goodbye. It's usually the women who say goodbye."

"Because you choose women you know won't stick around. Don't bullshit me and say you don't."

Jackson, irritated, said nothing.

"My point is," Daniel went on, "you might actually have a shot at some happiness here. Don't screw it up."

"I'm not sure I know how. To not screw it up, I mean."

"You know what to do," Daniel assured him. "You've just never done it."

When Kate got to the store that morning, the residual calamity was worse than she'd remembered. The folding chairs were still out and were in complete disarray, their once tidy rows now gone, with some on their sides and others shoved this way and that while people fled the dog-and-lemur melee. It looked as though the chairs had gotten drunk, and many had passed out.

The refreshment table still bore the cold and dried-up remnants of last night's canapes, and someone had spilled the remains of the iced tea. In the back room, books still littered the floor from where Kate and Jackson had upended them during their passionate abandon. The papers from the file folder that had fallen lay like confetti around her feet.

When she'd returned to the store last night after showing her father the door—or, actually, the pile of crap on the lawn—Fury had already started to clean up, and he'd offered to stay and help her. But he'd had a long day, so she sent him home. She had intended to set things right last night, but so many thoughts and feelings were swirling through her that she gave up and left it.

Now, with morning light streaming through the front windows, she started folding chairs and stacking them against the wall for the rental company to pick up later in the day. When that was done, she threw out the leftover food from the refreshment table. She found a rag in the back room and wiped up the spilled tea.

As she sopped up the tea, the cell phone in her back pocket vibrated, and she pulled it out and looked at it. A text, from Jackson. It said:

I'm thinking about you.

Kate smiled, and a warmth spread over her skin. She texted back:

I'm thinking about you, too.

A moment later, another vibration.

There's been some gossip about us, apparently.

She thought about her response, typed something in, then erased it. Finally, she settled on:

The best parts are true.

He sent her a smiley face. ☺ Then, this:

I need to see you again. Soon.

The thought sent a trill of excitement through her body.

Yes, she wrote. Just this. Just, yes. There could be no other answer for him, not now, not when she felt like this.

Kate spent the rest of the day fielding questions about the events of the night before. Rose and Lacy each called, of course, and it seemed that Cambrians from all over town just happened to stop in her store, wanting to chat. Some of the questions she could answer directly—like what happened with the lemur—and others she had to deflect—like what the hell was going on in the back room.

She called Cassidy McLean and apologized, sincerely, for the disaster her appearance had become. Zach called her and apologized, also sincerely, for the way Sherry had accosted her.

By the time Fury came to work, most of the mess had been cleaned up, and the store looked more or less the way it usually did.

"Crazy night," he said, glancing at her quickly and then averting his eyes, a clear giveaway that he'd heard the animal noises coming from the storage area—and not the ones made by the dog and the lemur.

"It certainly was."

"Is Cassidy McLean pissed?"

Kate shrugged. "Oh, I'm sure that wasn't one of the highlights of her career as an author. But she was gracious when I called her on the phone. Samantha's none the worse for wear, apparently. I told her I'd make a donation to the animal refuge."

Fury bobbed his head. "That's nice of you." He was still avoiding her gaze.

"Fury. Look at me." She waited until he did. "We both know what you're thinking about but not mentioning. Could we maybe just pretend that didn't happen, or that you weren't out here listening when it did? Could we just … maintain that fiction for the sake of our work environment, please?"

He grinned and scuffed at the floor with his foot. It was such a childlike gesture coming from him, with his tattoo sleeves and his Goth makeup, that it made her feel an unaccountable affection for him.

"Sure," he said. "We can do that."

"Excellent. Now, Mrs. Singer over on Burton called and said she has some books to trade for store credit, but she can't make it over here because of her mobility issues. Could you run over there and check out what she's got? You know what we need. Don't let her give you her old cookbooks and sewing machine manuals. Because she'll try."

"Got it, boss."

When he was gone, she had time to think about what had happened, and what was to come. She had feelings for Jackson. Back when he'd first come to her house for the cooking lesson, she'd intended this as something casual. A few dates, maybe some easy, fun sex. It would be friendly. Relaxed. A way for her to ease back into dating. She knew Jackson's pattern with women, and she knew that he didn't do long-term. But she liked him, and she was open to some good-natured fun with him.

But all that had changed. It had changed quickly and permanently. It had changed as she'd learned that he loved books; as he'd listened to her—really listened—about her mother, and her father, and her complicated feelings about them; as he'd tried with an endearing earnestness to treat her differently than the other women he'd known; and as he'd touched her and brought her to heights of desire and pleasure she'd never experienced.

Now, she was lost.

There'd be no going back, no reversing course, no way to turn off these feelings, which were real and strong.

That left one problem: Jackson was Jackson. And Jackson didn't do relationships.

He wanted to, she was sure of that. He wasn't setting out to use her or to treat her as disposable. He wanted to try, wanted something more substantial than what he'd had in the past. She believed that. The question was, could he do it? Could he change for her? Wanting something was one thing. Wanting it enough to do what it took to get it was entirely another.

Kate was leaving herself wide open for getting hurt. She knew that. And if she did get hurt this time, if he did decide that he was only cut out for short-term flings, it wasn't something she was going to get over quickly. But she couldn't walk away just to save herself from the risk. Walking away was no longer an option.

She'd just have to let this play itself out. She'd stay open, she'd give herself to him, because it was what her heart was telling her to do. If he didn't prove to be up to the challenge, then she'd just have to deal with those consequences when they came.

Chapter Twenty-One

J ackson had already planned Date Five, and it would have been a waste to discard a perfectly good plan just because the climactic finale had already happened. On the Monday following the Art Walk fiasco, Kate would leave Fury in charge of the store, and Jackson planned to pick her up at her house at midmorning for a drive to Big Sur. He'd made lunch reservations at a fine dining restaurant with a breathtaking view of the coast, and then, on the way back to Cambria, they would stop at McWay Falls to take in some scenery. For natural beauty, it was hard to beat Cambria, but if there was any place that could accomplish that, it was Big Sur.

He was just getting ready to leave his apartment on Monday morning to head for Kate's house when his cell phone rang. He snatched it up, hoping it wasn't Kate calling to cancel. It wasn't. The number was one he didn't recognize.

"Jackson Graham," he said, the phone propped between his shoulder and his ear.

"Jackson!" a hearty, enthusiastic voice said. "This is Tucker Elway. We met once, back when you were attending the California Culinary Academy. You probably don't remember."

"Yeah, I remember," Jackson said, interested now. "Don't you own Joie in San Francisco now?" Joie was a highly regarded French restaurant that Jackson had seen on numerous Top Ten lists for the Bay Area.

"That's right, that's right. Have you been in to join us?"

"Not since you took over. I'm down in Cambria."

"Yes. I'm aware. I actually was down there the week before last and had a meal at Neptune."

Jackson's eyes widened. "You did?"

"Yeah, a week ago Sunday." He cited the items he'd ordered—two appetizers, two entrees, and three desserts—and it clicked. Tucker Elway was the guy Jackson had pegged as a food writer.

"That was you? I thought it was a critic. Pulled out all the stops expecting to see something in *Sunset* magazine."

Elway chuckled good-naturedly. "Yes, well. I wanted to see what you've got without making too much of a fuss about it. I'm looking for a new executive chef for Joie. I've been making the rounds, checking out candidates who interest me. And you interest me."

Jackson clutched the phone and dropped onto his couch. "Executive chef? Who's there now? Isn't it Kerry de Barra?"

"That's right. He's moving to the East Coast to be closer to his family. Plus, I've been wanting to take the food at Joie in a new direction for a while now."

"Huh," Jackson said. "What new direction do you have in mind?"

"I'd like to get you up here to the city to talk about it. Show you the restaurant, talk over some ideas. What do you think?"

What did he think? A year ago, Jackson would have given his left arm and one of his big toes to be executive chef at Joie. It was exactly the kind of opportunity he'd imagined when he'd been toiling away at culinary school, and later, when he'd been gaining experience making salads and plating desserts. But that was before Cambria had worked its charm on him, before it became something that felt suspiciously like home. It was also before Kate. Though he couldn't make life decisions based on a relationship that was only four dates old. Could he?

"Things are pretty busy at Neptune right now," he said, stalling. "It's the summer tourist season."

"Ah, but surely you could get up here for a day. Sometime next week?"

"Let me check my schedule and I'll call you back."

"I'll look forward to it."

Jackson was quiet as he drove up to Big Sur with Kate by his side. He couldn't help it; he had too much going on in his mind. Executive chef at Joie was the big leagues. It was the kind of job he'd dreamed of when he was still in training. Joie was a restaurant that got you written about in glossy magazines, a job that would ensure that everyone in the culinary world would know his name.

That was a double-edged sword, no doubt. They'd know your name if you made amazing food that had customers making reservations a month in advance, but they'd also know your name if you served trite, clichéd entrees that put one in mind of the early bird specials in Boca Raton.

If he hit a rough patch in Cambria, he could regroup and right his course in relative obscurity. At Joie, he'd succeed or fail in the spotlight. That was a lot of pressure.

But more than that, he was thinking about Kate. This was the first time he'd felt excited about a relationship—truly excited—in as long as he could remember. She was smart and beautiful; she was open and kind; she was *real* in a way the Melanies of the world were not. And the physical chemistry they shared was something he hadn't been prepared for. He'd always loved sex. Hell, who didn't? But what had happened between them on Saturday night had taken the sex he was used to and cranked it up to ten, turned it to full volume, full color, full power. Two days later, he felt like he was still recovering.

He couldn't wait to find out if the lightning strike that had hit them on Saturday was a one-time thing, or if they could replicate it.

If he and Kate had been together for a year, or two years, he could take the job in San Francisco and ask her to go with him. They'd be making the decision together, as a couple. But they were only on Date Five, far too early to consult each other on life decisions. In his experience, relationships didn't last. Women didn't stay. Love was something he heard about from other people.

What if they moved to the city together and it didn't work out between them? She'd be stranded in a place that wasn't her home, her business gone, resenting the hell out of him for up-ending the life she'd built for herself.

He was about halfway through this train of thought when it hit him like a punch to the gut that he was actually *thinking of taking her with him.* He was thinking long-term, which hadn't happened with any other woman in more than a decade. Not once.

The reality of it left him breathless.

Jesus.

And that made him scared. Terrified. Women always left, and that was fine, because by the time they went he was usually ready for it anyway. But this time? This time, if she left, she was going to burn his world to the ground and leave him a charred, smoking wreck.

And then. And then there was Cambria.

He'd come to love it. He'd come to think of it as home. He felt a peace there that he'd never felt in the Bay Area—or anywhere else, for that matter. He loved the pines and the deer and the crashing surf. He loved the tide pools and the sea lions and the squirrels that scampered over the bluff trails. He loved the wild-flowers that carpeted the ground in the spring. He loved the fact that there were no chain restaurants, no drive-ins, no Starbucks. Hell, he even loved the tourists. Most of the time.

But opportunities like this did not come often.

"Jackson?"

It was only a few hours to the Bay Area by car. Could a long-distance relationship work?

"Jackson."

His schedule at Joie would be even more crazy than what he was doing now. But he'd be closer to his parents ...

"Jackson!"

He snapped back into focus. "Hmm? What?"

"Where were you? In your head, I mean. What distant planet were you visiting?"

"Ah," he said, embarrassed. "I'm sorry. I just have a lot going on right now."

"Like what?" She was looking at him, her face earnest and interested.

"Just ... something going on at work."

"Nothing bad, I hope."

"No, no. I just have to think about some things, make some decisions. For the restaurant." It wasn't a lie, exactly. If he did go to work at Joie, it would affect Neptune profoundly.

"Okay." There was an edge to her voice that told him she was annoyed that he wasn't talking to her about whatever was on his mind.

But he couldn't yet. Couldn't figure out how.

They headed up the coast past Hearst Castle, past the stretch of beach where elephant seals congregated to nap on the sand and spar with one another, past Ragged Point, with its show-stopping views—and its crowds of tourists.

The day was stunning, with clear skies, cool temperatures, and light breezes. As the road climbed higher and grew more treacherous with its numerous twists and turns, the view improved exponentially. Pines towered to their right, sheer cliffs peered down onto rocky coastline to their left.

He didn't want to be an ass, didn't want to shut down on their date, which was, after all, Date Five, with its promise of earth-shattering sex at the end. So he brought himself back into the present and refocused his attention.

"Have you heard from your father or Angela?" he asked. This could be a poor gambit, given the emotional nature of the subject matter. But it had to be asked.

"Not yet. But I will."

He spared her the briefest glance before putting his eyes back on the road. "You seem pretty sure about that."

"Oh, I am," she said. "We've been through this before. Right now, he's lying low in the hope that I'll cool down and forget what he did. The hope is that I'll feel guilty for treating him that way, then I'll eventually send him some money."

"Does that usually work?"

"It does." She sounded grim. "I'm ashamed to say it, but yeah, it usually does."

"But those other times, you—what?—you had words? Maybe spoke harshly? I doubt you threw his crap out on your lawn."

"That's true."

"So maybe this time, it'll stick."

"We'll see."

They were quiet for a few minutes, and then she said, "Do you know that I'm getting two or three people a day driving by my house, checking it out to see if they want to make an offer? Before I knew what was happening, it was kind of freaking me out. Now I'm just annoyed."

"Zach didn't list it for sale, did he? Wouldn't he need your signature for that?"

She shook her head. "No, he couldn't list it, but he did mention it to his real estate friends. People think they're going to jump on it the minute it goes on the MLS." She let out a harsh breath.

"Zach's really sorry, by the way. He had no idea my father was playing him. He's not used to getting the Thomas Bennet treatment the way I am."

"What's up with Zach and Sherry?" Jackson asked. "Did he get that worked out?"

"No, I guess not. She believes him that we weren't involved. But she's still pissed that he was calling me as much as he was."

"Huh," Jackson said.

"Do you think she has a point?" Kate asked.

"About what?"

"I just mean, how would you feel if a woman you were involved with had a close male friend? I'm wondering if Sherry has a legitimate beef, if I crossed a line."

Jackson shrugged and shook his head. "You've got to trust somebody, or there's no point in being with them. You want a guy friend, have guy friends. If you want to turn away from me and toward somebody else, that means I wasn't doing my job in the first place."

"Your job?" There was amusement in her voice.

"Damn right."

"And what exactly do you see as the job description?"

He shot a quick glance at her, saw the smile that played on her lips.

"Keeping you so utterly sexually satisfied that you'll scoff at any other man who's ballsy enough to look at you."

She cleared her throat. "Oh."

It was a job he intended to take seriously.

Lunch in Big Sur was exquisite; at least, Kate thought so. If Jackson disagreed, he kept his opinions to himself. Then again, he probably shared Kate's assessment, considering that he ate everything on his plate.

They split a bottle of wine over their meal, which they ate at a window table with a staggering view of the ocean. Kate felt slightly drunk—a giddy and happy condition—when the waiter brought her dessert, a light-as-air hazelnut cake topped with chocolate ganache.

They talked and ate and held hands and drank—Jackson drank just a little, because he was driving, Kate a bit more—with the blue, churning artistry of nature as their backdrop. By the time their coffee arrived, Kate thought that she'd never had a more enjoyable meal.

"Jackson, thank you so much," she said, her hand resting in his on the table. "This was wonderful."

"It's not over yet," he said. He appraised her with his gaze. "You look happy."

"I am."

"The last couple of times we were together, you cried." His voice held a slight tease. "I like making you happy."

"Hmm." She smiled in a way that made her eyes shine. "Maybe you can make a habit of it."

He picked up her hand and kissed it. "I'd love to try."

He'd promised her the date wasn't over, and so on their way back toward Cambria they stopped at McWay Falls, took the short trail from the parking lot, and watched from the overlook as the eighty-foot waterfall plunged from the cliffs onto the beach below. Kate watched from the railing, and Jackson stood behind her, his arms around her. As she marveled at the beauty of the falls, he tenderly kissed her hair.

From there, they walked back across the parking lot and onto a hiking trail that led them to another, smaller waterfall amid the lush greenery of ferns and towering pines. They made their way down to where the water tumbled over rocks and into a stream that flowed gently toward the ocean.

Kate sat on a piece of a fallen tree and started to take off her shoes and socks. "Come on," she told Jackson. "Let's wade in."

"Nah." He shook his head. "It's probably cold as hell."

She tsked at him. "I thought you were tougher than that."

"Bait me all you want. It's not gonna work." He sat on the log beside her, his shoes and socks still firmly on his feet.

She stepped into the water, onto the slippery rocks at the bottom of the stream, and gasped with the cold. "Oh my God! It's like ice!"

"Told you," he said smugly.

"It's refreshing," she taunted. "You'll like it."

"I don't think so."

"Here. I'll show you." Impulsively, she bent down, filled her hands with the bracingly cold water, and flung it at him.

He looked at her in shock, water dripping from his hair, from his face. "I can't believe you did that."

She covered her mouth with her hands and giggled. The giggle turned to a shriek when he came at her, dashing into the water with his shoes still on, scooping up big handfuls of icy water and tossing them at her.

They splashed each other, running through the water and playing like a couple of kids, until he reached out and grabbed her, her foot slipped on the slick stream bed, and they both tumbled headlong into the water.

The cold left Kate shocked and trembling as she lay in the shallow stream, water up to her shoulders, Jackson lying on top of her, holding her in his arms.

"You're shivering," he said, his mouth inches from hers.

"Cold," she said. Then all thoughts of discomfort vanished as his mouth covered hers, sending torrents of heat through her veins.

She clutched at him, wrapped herself around him as he kissed her, not the frantic kiss of desperation they'd shared in the back room of the store on Saturday night, but a kiss that was more deliberate, more intentional; she felt the depth of meaning in this kiss, and her body responded to it.

"Oh," she said.

He dripped onto her from above, holding her, looking into her face. Her breath was heightened from the play, the cold, the passion of the kiss.

"We should probably get out of the water," he said at last, his voice rough.

"Okay."

Her legs felt weak as he got up from on top of her and helped her up. They climbed out of the stream and onto dry land, and he grinned at her. "You look half drowned." He wiped some water from her face with his hand.

She pushed at him playfully. "You should have just gone in when I asked you to."

"That'll teach me."

"I would hope so."

She held his gaze, and felt magic. Pure, giddy happiness, and tenderness, and something else that might have been love.

Chapter Twenty-Two

The drive back to Cambria was long, and by the time they got there, they could barely keep their hands off each other. There was a quick discussion of where they should go—his place or hers. Kate suggested his, because it was marginally closer. But Jackson pointed out that being one floor above his place of work meant a high likelihood of interruption. That settled it. He drove—maybe a little too fast due to a sense of urgency—down Ardath Road to her house at Marine Terrace.

He parked on the street, and they hurried to the front door, his wet shoes making a squishing noise with every step.

"Let me just ... " In her hurry, she had a hard time getting her key into the lock, so he took it from her and opened the door.

"Is Gen downstairs?" he asked. She understood the question. There might be noise.

"Working."

"Good."

They started stripping off their clothes as soon as they got the door closed, and by the time they reached her bedroom, they'd left a trail of wet garments leading from the front door, through the living room, and into her room. Fully nude, she fell onto the bed, and he lowered himself on top of her. She'd been cold in her wet things, but his body was hot, and she devoured him with her mouth, with her hands.

He smelled like stream water and sunshine.

Poised above her, he looked down into her face. "This. This thing with us," he whispered. "This is ... "

She nodded. The way he looked at her told her what he was trying to say.

Now, with the afternoon and evening stretching before them, they took the time to explore each other with their hands, their mouths, feeling, tasting, memorizing the landscape of each other's bodies.

He told her to lie still, and she stretched out like a cat in a sunbeam while he ran his tongue and his fingertips over her throat, her breasts, her belly, her legs. Her skin quivered with need in the wake of each feathery touch. He rose up her thighs and came to rest between them, tasting and touching. The tension rose and grew until she arched her back and cried out.

Sated for now, she turned her attention to him, learning his body the way he'd learned hers. She surprised herself with her own boldness after all this time, this interminable time of loneliness. She used her mouth on him, and he held his hands in her hair.

When he could no longer endure the wait, he rolled her onto her back. He finally, finally penetrated her, and she gasped with pleasure, with satisfaction. She was overwhelmed, overjoyed, and a tear slid down her cheek.

"Crying again," he murmured.

He kissed the salty path of her tears.

Afterward, they lay together beneath the covers in the late afternoon light that streamed through the windows.

"Date Five was awesome," Kate said. "I love Date Five. We should just do Date Five over and over again."

Jackson gave a low laugh and pressed a kiss to her temple. "Works for me."

"Hey," she said after a while.

"Hmm?"

"What was it that you didn't want to talk about earlier? When we were driving up to Big Sur? You were preoccupied, but you didn't tell me what it was about." She snuggled into his arms.

"Just a work thing."

She looked up into his face. "But it's not *just* a work thing, is it?"

He was quiet for a while. Then: "What makes you say that?"

"Because you seem worried about it—whatever it is."

"I'm not," he said.

"But if you ... "

He silenced her words with his kisses.

They took a shower together, and after that, they ordered a pizza and sat out on her deck drinking beer from bottles and waiting for the food to arrive. Jackson's wet clothes were in the washing machine, and he'd tried without success to find something in Kate's house that he could wear until they were ready. Her bathrobe was too small for him, as were her sweatpants. So he lounged on the deck with a tablecloth wrapped around his waist. He'd considered using just a towel, but the relative lack of coverage made him worry about the view from the street below.

By now, it was early evening and the sky was beginning to show its first tinges of pink and orange.

The pizza came. Kate tried to pay for it, but Jackson insisted that he was the Date Five host, and that meant he would pay the pizza guy, even if they were in Kate's house. He scurried around the house in his tablecloth, looking for the wet wallet he'd pulled out of his pants before putting them in the washer.

He paid the pizza guy with a twenty that was still soggy, and they went back onto the deck and ate the pepperoni, sausage, and black olive pizza straight from the box.

"God, you look good in a tablecloth," she said as she munched on a slice of pizza. "You should wear that all the time."

"Maybe I will. Though there could be safety issues at the restaurant."

They heard rapid footsteps coming down the stairs on the side of the house. A moment later, Gen's voice said, "Hey, Kate, are you ... ?" Gen stepped out onto the lawn under the deck and peered up. When she saw Jackson in his tablecloth, her eyes widened.

"Gen." Jackson saluted her with the piece of pizza in his hand.

"Hi, Jackson. I'll just ... I'll see you guys later." She popped back under the deck with a big grin on her face.

"She'll want to talk about this later," Kate said.

Jackson nodded. "I'm sure she will. When you speak of me, speak well."

❖

The next few days passed in a blur of bliss for Kate. Jackson's schedule at the restaurant was brutal, but they talked on the phone often, supplemented with texts and emails. He left the restaurant late every night, but that didn't stop him from dropping by Kate's house a few times after work to make love to her and sleep in her bed.

Kate was looking forward to his next night off so they could have a proper date, even if it was just a lazy night in eating takeout and watching Netflix. So she was surprised—but neither upset nor concerned—when he told her he had to go to the Bay Area the following Monday to visit his parents. He'd be there overnight, returning Tuesday.

"Is everything okay with them?" Kate asked when he told her of his plans over the phone.

"Yeah, yeah. I just haven't been there for a while. My mom is laying the guilt on me whenever I talk to her. 'Jackson? Do I know a Jackson? I seem to vaguely remember that name.' That kind of bullshit."

Kate laughed. "Right. I get it. Well, have a safe drive. I'll see you when you get back."

"I'm counting on it," he said.

There was something in his voice, though. She knew he wasn't telling her everything, but she tried not to worry about it.

Jackson did visit his parents on his trip to the Bay Area. In fact, he spent that night in his old room, sleeping on a futon now that his mother had removed his twin bed and his hockey posters and had brought in her sewing machine and scrapbooking supplies. But he also visited Tucker Elway at Joie.

Elway ushered Jackson through the restaurant, which was sleek with copper-plated ceilings, pale blue walls, and white tuxedo-style banquettes providing seating for blond wood tables. Here and there, small circular café tables were surrounded by high-backed chairs upholstered in purple velvet.

"Wow," Jackson said as they walked through the dining room, which was twice the size of the one at Neptune. The effect of the purple velvet might have been tacky or ostentatious, but instead the pop of color made the place look current and hip. It was midafternoon, so the dining room wasn't full, but neither was it empty. Three couples and two groups of women appeared to be enjoying drinks and appetizers.

"I'm pleased that you like it," Elway said. He was an older, white-haired man dressed entirely in black: black jeans, black T-shirt, black belt, black loafers. His haircut had probably cost more than Jackson's TV, and Jackson suspected that Elway got his eyebrows waxed. San Francisco was a different world than what he'd grown used to in Cambria. "Let's just take a look at the kitchen."

They went through the swinging door into the kitchen, and Jackson stopped, stunned. This kitchen was everything Gavin Hughes, the owner at Neptune, would have provided if he could afford it. The gleaming stainless steel surfaces; the top-quality appliances; the large space that allowed for a level of organization unheard of at Neptune. Only a few kitchen staff were on duty at this time of day, because of the light demand, but the ones who were there worked with efficiency and expertise.

Elway showed Jackson around, introduced him to the kitchen staff, and then ushered him back into an office resplendent with hardwood floors, natural light, and a highly polished mahogany desk.

"Have a seat." Elway indicated his visitor chair—one of the high-backed purple numbers Jackson had seen in the dining room. "Can I get you anything? Coffee?"

Jackson accepted the coffee, and when he was comfortably sipping its enviable richness—this was, undeniably, better than the coffee at Neptune—Elway launched into his pitch.

"I'd like you to rework our menu. What we've got is good— it's gotten us this far—but it's not as fresh or interesting as I'd like. Joie is still a place you come to enjoy a fantastic meal, but it used to be a place you talked about. There was a prestige. Who's been there, who hasn't, what did you have to do to get a table, who was there when you went. That sort of thing. We haven't had that in a while. I want to get it back."

Jackson found himself nodding. "Right. But you don't want to go so avant-garde that the food is a curiosity rather than a meal. People still have to want to eat it."

"Exactly. I'd love to hear your ideas."

They talked about concepts, themes, the practicalities of sourcing ingredients. Jackson forgot he was interviewing for a job. When he talked about food, he became absorbed and animated, and nothing else mattered. Elway pulled out a copy of the current menu, and they went over it item by item, discussing the good, the very good, and the outdated.

"So, when can you start?" Elway said at last, leaning back in his chair.

"I ... What?" Jackson was caught off guard.

"Here's the salary I can offer you." Elway wrote a figure on a piece of note paper and slid it across the table. Jackson took a peek, and his heart did a little stutter. He was sure there had to be one too many zeroes here.

"That's not as high as it seems," Elway said. "The rents here are astronomical."

"I know. I grew up in the Bay Area."

"That's right," Elway said. "So you'd be coming home."

Home. Interesting word. He once would have considered this to be home, but now he wasn't so sure.

"I'm going to have to think about it," he said. "How soon would you need to know?"

"I can give you a few days," Elway said. "But after that I'm going to have to move on. I've got to get this job filled."

"I understand."

They shook hands, and Jackson went out to his truck, stunned at the memory of the dream kitchen and the figure written in black ink on a small, white piece of paper.

"So? How did it go?"

Jackson sat at the kitchen table of his childhood home with his mother. His father sat in a reclining chair in the living room, watching a baseball game and occasionally yelling at the screen.

Claire Graham, a woman in her fifties who, in earlier times, would have been described as handsome, had just come home from her shift at the hospital, and she looked dead tired as she sipped a cup of tea across from Jackson. Her reddish-brown hair was streaked with grey, and it was pinned up on top of her head to keep it out of her way. A large woman—fit, but with big bone structure—she'd come off as a formidable force when Jackson was younger. She still did.

"He's offering me a lot of money." Jackson, rather than drinking tea, held a squat glass with two fingers of Scotch on ice. He took a sip. The kitchen hadn't been updated since his childhood, and the vinyl flooring and Formica made him nostalgic for his youth.

"Takes a lot of money to live in San Francisco."

"It does." He looked into his glass, rattled the ice around a bit. "Beautiful restaurant. You should see the kitchen."

"I'll bet," she said.

After a while, he said, "Elway wants me to create a new menu."

"Having control over the menu in a place like that? It's the kind of thing you've always wanted to do."

"It is."

"THAT WAS A STRIKE, YOU WORTHLESS BAS-TARD!" Jackson's father yelled at the screen in the next room.

"Oh, for God's sake, Bill, quiet down. We're trying to talk!" Claire called to him. She turned to Jackson. "Sounds like an incredible opportunity."

He nodded. "It really does."

She reached out and put her hand on his arm. "Then why does it feel more like your dog died? What in the world is bothering you, Jackson?"

He looked at the hand on his arm, at the Scotch in his glass. He shrugged. "I'm not sure."

She put a hand under his chin and tipped his face up so he would look at her. "You're a poor liar, Jackson Graham. Always were."

He grinned. "Okay. There's this girl. Woman. In Cambria."

She scoffed. "Isn't there always a girl in Cambria?"

"OH, FOR ... GET SOME GODDAMN GLASSES IF YOU CAN'T SEE THE GODDAMN BALL!" Bill yelled.

"This one's different," Jackson told his mother.

"Uh oh," she said.

"Why? Is that a bad thing?"

She shook her head. "No. Not at all. But it's a new thing for you, and I'm wondering if you're ready for it."

"I am, too." He drank some more of the Scotch and felt its warmth seep into him. "If I take the job, I can be closer to you and Dad."

"Don't," she said. The vehemence in her voice startled him.

"Don't what?"

"Don't use me and your father as an excuse to run away from this woman in Cambria because you're scared you might be in love. We're not exactly in our dotage. We'll get along here on our own, just like we have for the last few years."

"I wasn't doing that."

"Like hell you weren't." She gave him the look he remembered from his childhood, the one that said she knew what he'd been up to, and she was having none of it. "The idea of a real relationship—the idea of love—might be frightening for you, Jackson, but it's time you faced that fear, don't you think?"

"RUN! RUN, YOU ... THAT'S IT, RUN!" Bill said. "AH, FOR THE ... HE WAS SAFE!"

"If I give this up, and she doesn't stay ... "

"Then at least you'll know you tried," Claire said. "You'll know you weren't the one to walk out."

"Yeah," he said, nodding. "Yeah."

Chapter Twenty-Three

Before Jackson had left for the Bay Area, he had talked to Ryan. Then, over beers at Ted's, Ryan talked to Daniel. And then, during a visit to the gallery to check on an installation, Daniel talked to Gen. Before Jackson even got into his truck to head back south to Cambria, knowledge of the real reason for his trip had filtered through town to just about everyone—except Kate.

On the phone with Kate on that Monday, toward the end of the workday, Gen had concern in her voice as she asked, "So, how are you doing?"

"I'm good," Kate said, upbeat and perky.

"Really?" Gen asked doubtfully.

"Sure. Why wouldn't I be?"

"Well, I thought you'd be worried about what Jackson's going to do."

"Do about what?"

And that's when the conversation took a turn. "Oh. Shit. Nothing," Gen said. "I ... Nothing."

"Genevieve," Kate said. "What the hell are you talking about?"

"Oh, Jesus," Gen said.

Kate's pulse started to thump as a feeling of dread spread through her. "What do you know that I don't? What is Jackson doing in the Bay Area? Is he even *in* the Bay Area? He said he was visiting his parents." She felt herself gripping the bookstore counter with her free hand until the pointed corner jabbed into her palm.

"Yeah, he really is up there."

"But he's not just visiting his parents."

"Um … no." Gen sounded miserable, as though she were near tears.

"I swear to God," Kate said, "if you don't tell me right now, I'll … "

"He's got a job interview. I'm so sorry. I thought you knew."

Kate's first reaction was relief, because she'd thought Gen was going to say he was up there with another woman. His past might have suggested such a thing. But when the reality of it hit—he was at a job interview, for a position more than two hundred miles away—the breath went out of her, and she had to sit down.

"What?" Her voice was barely more than a whisper.

"Oh God," Gen said. "Oh God. Listen. I'll get the girls. We need an intervention. Just stay there. Don't go anywhere. Okay?" She hung up, and Kate sat behind the counter in her little store, stunned.

She knew Jackson had a track record of short-term relationships. She knew he wasn't usually a guy who stayed. She just hadn't expected him to run quite so quickly. He wasn't even gone yet—not really—and already, it hurt like hell.

Kate didn't have any right to cry and wail and wallow in self-pity. That's what she told herself. After all, they'd only been on five dates. Five dates didn't make a commitment. Five dates didn't mean forever. She wasn't naïve enough to think that sex changed anything. She didn't want to be the cliché, a woman who believed if a man had sex with her, it meant he loved her.

But even as she was reminding herself of all of that, she also had to acknowledge that there'd been magic. Whatever that mysterious pixie dust was that made you know someone was right for you—that they were the one—it had been sprinkled over Kate in generous, heaping handfuls, and no amount of logic could change that.

She'd thought he felt the same way.

She felt like an idiot.

Gen, Rose, and Lacy scooped Kate out of her shop, whisked her off to Rose's house, took away her cell phone so that Jackson couldn't call from San Francisco and tell her painful lies, and did that thing women do when one of their own has been heart-broken.

They trashed him.

"What an asshole," Rose said, shaking her head. They were all drinking wine Rose had brought home from her shop, in the hope that if Kate got really, really drunk, it would numb the sorrow. "I've known him longest, so I feel like I can say that. He's just a big, puckered-up asshole."

"This is bullshit," Gen added. "I mean, a guy shouldn't be lounging around on your deck wearing nothing but a tablecloth one day, and then driving off to the Bay Area seeking escape routes the next."

"Wait," Lacy said. "I want to hear more about the table-cloth."

"The tablecloth is beside the point," Gen went on. "The point is, he did that, and now he's doing this. It's bullshit."

"And there's the sneaking. And the deception," Lacy said. She took a sizable slug of chardonnay. "If there was an opportunity he just couldn't pass up, why didn't he just *tell* you about it?"

"Well. Maybe he's not sure what he wants to do," Rose offered. "Maybe he doesn't know if he's going to take it, and why have a big, emotional conversation over something he might not even do?"

"We're not defending him," Gen said. "That's not why we're here. You're off-task."

Rose shrugged. "I'm just saying ... "

"Just a minute ago you said he was an asshole," Gen reminded her. "Let's get back to that."

"Well, just ... Maybe he's not an asshole so much as he just doesn't have any relationship skills," Rose said.

"This is stupid. This is stupid," Kate said. It was the first time she'd spoken up since they'd arrived. "We had five dates. Five. And I'm here acting like I've been left at the altar. Ugh. I'm the idiot. I'm the asshole in this scenario."

"Oh, honey," Gen said.

"What right do I have to think I have any claim on him?" Kate demanded. "After five dates? What right do I have to ... " She pressed a hand to her breastbone, the place where the hurt sat like a stack of hot rocks on her chest. " ... To *fall in love*?"

Rose, who was sitting next to Kate on the sofa, reached out and rubbed Kate's arm. "Oh, sweetie. The heart wants what it wants."

"This sucks," Kate said.

"Drink more," Gen said, refilling Kate's wine glass. "It'll help."

"What exactly did Daniel say?" Kate asked Gen.

She shrugged. "He said Jackson got a call out of the blue from a guy who owns this fancy-schmancy restaurant in San Francisco, saying he was interested in Jackson for an executive chef job. He said it was a big opportunity. Money, glory, yadda yadda."

actually *looking* for a job? The guy just called

heard."

that's something," Lacy said.

Rose said.

"Would you go with him?" Gen ventured. "To San Francisco?"

Kate closed her eyes. "If he asked? I feel like a stupid, idiot loser for saying this, but yeah, I probably would. I'd probably pick up my life and follow him like a puppy after five dates, because that's how ridiculously, stupidly in love I am. God, I suck."

Rose resumed the arm-rubbing. "You don't suck," she said in a soothing voice.

"I want my phone," Kate said.

"No!" Gen and Rose called out in unison as Lacy vehemently shook her head.

"Please?"

"No way," Gen said. "No, no, no. What if he called? What if he left some text or voice mail sticking with this charade that he's just visiting his parents? It's going to make you feel like shit. And if he didn't call, that'll be even worse."

"You'll have to give it back to me eventually," Kate reasoned. "What's the difference?"

"The difference is that we can't get you through the initial shock if he's texting and messaging and making it worse," Gen said. "Trust us."

"But what if … "

"*No*," Lacy said.

"I should have known better." Kate buried her face in her hands. "He's a leaver. He's not a … a stayer. We all knew that. I should have known."

Rose got up from the couch, went into the kitchen, rummaged around in a cabinet, and returned with a bottle of tequila and a stack of four shot glasses.

"Wine's not going to cut it," she said.

The drinking worked, but not in the way Kate would have expected. It wasn't the numbing effect of the alcohol that helped her get through her feelings about Jackson. It was the searing, grinding misery of the hangover. When you felt this bad, who could even sort out whether it was heartbreak or Jose Cuervo that had caused it?

She stumbled out of bed the next morning and made some strong, black coffee. She peeked at her cell phone—which had been returned to her, reluctantly, at the end of the night—and found two texts and a voice mail message from Jackson. In none of them did he mention a job interview.

Liar, liar, pants on fire.

She decided the best course of action was to do nothing. She erased the voice mail message and ignored the texts.

Kate fumbled around in the kitchen, found some Tylenol, and took a couple to combat her headache. Usually, she would drink her coffee out on the deck, but today, her eyes couldn't take the assault of sunlight. She kept the curtains drawn and huddled on her sofa with her coffee.

After a while, Gen came upstairs and knocked with merciful gentleness on the front door. Kate dragged herself over and opened it. Gen looked almost as bad as Kate felt.

"Coffee?" Gen said.

"Yeah," Kate answered, stepping back to let her in. "Tylenol?" she offered.

"Oh God, yes."

With the caffeine and the analgesic seeping into their systems, they sat side by side on the sofa, each of them still in pajamas, with mussed hair and bare feet, saying nothing.

"He called," Kate finally told Gen. "One voice mail, two texts."

"What are you going to do?"

"Nothing, I guess."

Gen nodded. "Yeah."

By the time Jackson got back into town on Tuesday afternoon, Kate still hadn't returned any of his calls or texts. He wondered if maybe her cell phone wasn't working. He tried her land line at home, and got no answer there, either. Finally, he called the store. Fury answered and said Kate wasn't available, though he would offer no more detail than that. The guy sounded kind of pissed.

Jackson got home, unpacked his overnight bag, flopped back on his sofa, and called Daniel.

"Hey, Jackson!" Daniel sounded cheerful. "How'd it go?"

"Good. He offered me the job."

"Wow. How does the place look? Did he make you a good offer?"

Jackson rubbed at the scruff of stubble on his chin. "The place is amazing. And the offer is almost too good to believe. He wants me to create a new menu. A new menu, for a top-tier restaurant like that? This is the show, man. It's what I've been waiting for."

"Well, congratulations. Really."

"Yeah. I guess. Thanks."

Daniel paused. "You don't sound quite as excited as you should be."

"I am. No, I am. It's just … Kate hasn't returned my calls."

"Ah."

Jackson sat up straighter. "What does 'ah' mean?"

"Well, it means I'm not all that surprised. She's got to be upset, right?"

Now Jackson stood. "What do you mean? Upset about what?"

"I'm just saying, you two seemed like you had something good starting up. And now you're looking to leave the area. She's got to be unhappy about it. You had to have expected that."

Jackson spoke slowly and deliberately. "Daniel. How does she know about the job interview? Ryan is the only person I told. I knew he told you, but that was supposed to be it."

Daniel was silent.

"Daniel?"

"Oh, shit."

"Daniel."

"I told Gen. I didn't know it was a secret. I had no idea you didn't tell Kate. Why didn't you tell Kate?"

"Ah, fuck."

"Listen … wow. I'm sorry, man."

Jackson rubbed at his face with his free hand. "Okay. Don't worry about it. I'll … I'll talk to her. I'll deal with it."

"And you're gonna tell her what? That you're leaving? That'll go over well."

"Ah … damn it."

"Good luck with that, man."

A few more phone calls went to voice mail, and he said screw it and headed over there. He walked into the bookstore, and she was behind the counter. When she started to look up, she had a professional look on her face. A *how may I help you* sort of look. But the moment she saw it was him, a flash of hurt crossed her face, and he felt it like a blow to the chest.

"Kate, can we talk?" He went to her, and she backed up and turned around, picked up a stack of papers, and fixed her eyes on them.

"I'm really busy right now."

"Look. I know you're upset … "

"Jackson." She tossed the papers down—they were just for show anyway—and looked at him. "I can't do this right now. I'm working. I need to work. I'd like you to leave."

He stepped back. "Can we talk later?"

"I don't really see the point," she said.

"You don't see the *point?* You don't see the fuckin' … ah, come on, Kate."

Kate called into the back room. "Fury, would you cover the front for a bit? I have some things to do in the back."

The kid with the eyebrow piercings came out, and Kate went into the back room and snapped the door shut behind her.

Fury looked at Jackson with at least some sympathy. "Dude, you fucked up," he said.

Jackson nodded. It was true. He had.

He turned around and walked out of the store.

Jackson's next stop was the wine shop. He'd known Rose for a few years now, had known her since before he'd gathered up the nerve to even talk to Kate. He would consider Rose a friend, or at least a friendly acquaintance. Maybe she could get through to Kate for him.

When he walked into the shop, Rose was pouring tasting portions for a trio of tourists seated at the bar. He took a seat a few stools down and waited. As she talked to her customers about the qualities and flavor notes of the wine she'd poured for them, she shot Jackson a look that was one part anger, one part pity.

"That stool is for customers," she said.

"What? Come on, Rose, I … "

She pointed at his stool. "Customers."

"Fine. I'll do the tasting. Five wines for ten dollars, right? And you'd goddamned well better give me my free souvenir wine glass."

She scowled at him, and the tourists down the bar looked at him curiously.

Jackson pointed to a chardonnay on the tasting list, and Rose splashed some into a glass and thrust it in front of him.

"Aren't you going to tell me about the oaky notes?" he said.

"Bite me," Rose said.

The tourists started to back timidly away from the bar, and Rose called them back. "I'm sorry," she told the grey-haired guy, probably in his sixties, and the two women of about the same age.

"See," Rose went on, "this guy over there, he was dating one of my best friends. Then, when he had her seeing babies and puppies and white picket fences, he went off to interview for a job in San Francisco. Without telling her. She had to find out through the grapevine." She looked at the wine bottle in her hand. "So to speak."

The tourists looked at Jackson with judgment in their eyes. One of the women muttered something and shook her head.

"She was seeing babies?" Jackson said. "And ... what's this about the puppies?"

"She's in love with you, you shithead," Rose said. She splashed wine into the tourists' glasses with some force.

"It sounds like you really hurt her," one of the women at the bar said.

"I ... ah, shit. I didn't mean to."

"Uh huh," Rose said. "You meant to run like hell. Like you usually do. And you thought that wouldn't hurt her?"

Jackson ran a hand through his hair. "Rose, Jesus. I ... Can you get her to talk to me? Just talk? She won't even answer my calls."

"No."

"What? Why not?"

"Because it'll hurt her friend even more to hear you try to justify yourself," one of the women at the bar said.

Rose pointed a finger at her. "Bingo. Here. Have some extra pinot." She poured more wine into the woman's glass. The woman looked pleased.

"I just want to talk to her."

Rose turned to him. "And say what? What are you planning to do? Are you staying or going?"

He didn't answer. He honestly didn't know.

"Right." Rose turned away from him and back toward the tourists. "Until you know, there's no point in talking."

Jackson put a ten dollar bill on the bar and started to slink away.

"You forgot your goddamned souvenir glass!" Rose called after him. "Asshole."

Chapter Twenty-Four

Jackson needed time to think. But with his schedule, there was no time. He was due back at Neptune that afternoon, and they were closing the restaurant to host a private wedding reception. He likely wouldn't have time to tie his shoes, let alone ponder his future.

Maybe that was good. Maybe that was what he needed—to immerse himself in work. He went home, showered, and went downstairs to start his shift. He put on his chef's coat and tied his apron. The dining room was already decorated and set up for the reception, which would start in a couple of hours. He reviewed the menu. A baby field greens salad with goat cheese and candied walnuts. An appetizer of seared scallops, or a vegetarian option of stuffed mushrooms. A choice of three entrees: salmon with wild rice, beef tenderloin with garlic mashed potatoes, or a vegan risotto. And, of course, the cake, which was being brought in from the bakery on the corner of Main and Burton.

It was all pretty basic, and Jackson found himself wishing for a culinary challenge to keep his mind busy. Was this what the happy couple really wanted to launch their lives together? Salmon? Beef goddamned tenderloin? If they didn't have any more imagination than that, how the hell did they expect to keep a marriage going?

He started banging his way around the kitchen, into and out of the walk-in refrigerator, slamming doors, scowling. He looked over the shoulders of two prep chefs and yelled at them for their uneven carrot julienne.

Goddamned amateurs.

He tasted the salad dressing, and it had too much goddamned vinegar. "What the hell did I tell you about the vinegar?" he said to the prep chef mixing the dressing. "Jesus. Get on your fucking game!"

Jose, who was preparing the marinade for the scallops at a counter about a foot to Jackson's right, looked up.

"You know, she probably just needs time. Let her cool down, then try talking to her."

Did *everybody* know about his troubles with Kate?

"What the hell are you talking about? How the hell do you know about my relationship problems?"

Jose raised his eyebrows. "Small town, chef. You know how it is."

And so did everyone else, apparently.

Jackson sighed. "I don't know. I don't think it's gonna be that easy."

Jose looked at him. "I didn't say it was gonna be easy. I said let her cool down, and then talk to her." He shook his head. "Truth is, you're probably fucked."

"Yeah, thanks, Jose. That's really helpful."

The rest of the evening, Jackson did some of the worst cooking of his career. He burned some of the fillets. He undercooked at least a few scallops. The risotto crunched. Risotto wasn't supposed to crunch.

Remarkably, though, he didn't hear any complaints from the dining room. Usually, the bridezilla—or the bridezilla's mother—was the first to bitch about every little thing, whether there was truly something wrong with the food or not. But tonight, he heard nothing except laughter, music, and happy conversation from outside the kitchen door.

He took a peek out there once the dinner rush was done, and saw the young bride in a white, silky, A-line dress dancing with her groom, a fairly geeky-looking guy in his twenties, who nevertheless looked like he couldn't believe his luck in landing this beauty, this goddess, this vision of contentment and joy.

Jackson felt a squeezing sensation in his chest and wondered if maybe he was having a heart attack. A Kate attack, more likely.

Gavin came over to stand by Jackson.

"Happy couple," Gavin said. "Sometimes they aren't. Sometimes you can just see the tension under everything, and you know they're not going to last. But these two ... who knows? Looks like they've got a shot."

Jackson couldn't breathe; he couldn't think.

"You okay?" Gavin asked him.

"No, man. I'm ... no."

"We're about done here. Just the cleanup. You want to head upstairs? We can do the rest without you."

"You sure?" Jackson asked.

"Yeah."

"Hey, Gavin."

Gavin looked at him. "Hmm?"

"You probably heard about where I was. Everybody else did. I just wanted to tell you ... "

"Don't worry about it." Gavin put a hand on Jackson's shoulder. "You'll do what you've gotta do. I don't know if I could say no to a chance like that. I can find another chef if I have to. I won't like it, but I can do it."

"Thanks, man."

"Sure. Now get out of here. You look like shit, and you've already terrorized the staff enough for one night."

"Yeah. I gotta go. I've gotta make a phone call."

He went up to his apartment and made the call.

❖

He showed up at Kate's house late—after ten p.m. He'd tried to call again, but it had gone to voice mail. He could see that there was a light on in the living room, so he was sure she had to be awake.

He knocked on the door and waited, his hands shaking.

She opened it a crack, saw that it was him, and started to close it again.

"Kate. Don't close the door. Wait. Let me in." He put a hand into the doorway to stop her from closing it, and she shut the door on it. "Ouch! Shit!" He quickly withdrew the hand, and she closed the door. He heard the dead bolt slide into place.

"Goddamn it, Kate," he yelled through the door. "Let me in! I want to talk to you!"

"I don't want to talk to you!" she yelled back.

He thought about what to do. They hadn't been together long enough for him to have a key. He could shout to her through the door. He could slide a note through the door frame. He could hire someone to dress like a monkey and do a singing telegram.

He walked down the stairs at the side of the house and onto the lawn that stretched out under the deck. "Kate!" he yelled up toward the sliding glass door that led to her living room. The living room light turned off—an unmistakable signal to him that it was time to shut up and leave.

But he wasn't going to give up that easily.

He looked around, picked up some pebbles from the ground, and started throwing them, one at a time, at her sliding glass door.

Ping!

Ping!

The door slid open slightly and Kate yelled out, "What are you doing? Stop throwing rocks at my window!"

The door slammed shut again.

Right in front of him, one floor below Kate's deck, was another sliding glass door, this one leading into Gen's apartment. The light inside had been off when he'd arrived, but now it came on. Inside, a curtain moved aside and Gen's face peered out through the window. Her door slid open.

"Jackson? What are you doing?"

"I need to talk to Kate."

"Aw, Jackson, I don't ... "

"Just hear me out," he said.

She let him inside, and they talked. When he was done, she went to her kitchen drawer, found the key that opened Kate's front door, and handed it to him.

"Don't screw this up," she said.

"I won't," he answered.

When Kate heard the front door unlocking and opening, she called out, "Gen. Hey, is Jackson gone yet? I ... " And then she looked up from where she sat in the darkness, and saw him.

She felt everything, all at once. Tenderness, excitement, pain.

"How did you get in?" she said.

He held up Gen's key.

Traitor. She was going to have words with Gen later. Or she might have to drown her in the bathtub.

"You shouldn't have come. You need to go." She stood and started walking toward the door, which she intended to hold open for him.

As she passed, he took hold of her arm and turned her toward him. "Please. Just let me talk to you. I shouldn't have gone up there for the interview without telling you. I'm sorry. I didn't know what to do."

She pulled her arm out of his grasp. "You didn't know what to *do?* It's fairly simple, Jackson. You should have just said, 'Kate, this has been fun, but now I'm ready to move on.' You should have *said* that, Jackson, instead of letting me hear it from someone else."

"But that's not the truth."

"Which part? The part where it's been fun, or the part where you're ready to move on?"

He closed his eyes and took a deep breath. "Both. Both parts. It hasn't been fun. It's been … Kate, it's been *everything*. Everything good. Everything I was missing before. Everything I want, but didn't know I wanted. And I *don't* want to move on."

As what he had said began to sink in, hummingbirds fluttered just beneath her breastbone. "You don't?"

"No."

"But what about the job? You don't want this to end—us—but if you're going to be in San Francisco … "

"I turned it down."

"You what?"

"Tonight. I called the guy and said no. Right before I came over here."

"Wait." She went to the sofa and sat down, hard. "You turned it down because of me?"

"Well, yeah. Or, partly because of you. Mostly because of you."

She held up both hands, palms out, trying to hold off this flood of feelings, of questions.

"But, Jackson. I can't be the reason you said no. I can't be the reason you turned down the opportunity of a lifetime. What if we don't work? What if we don't last? You're going to resent me, because you could have had this great job … "

"We'll work," he said, sitting down beside her. "We'll last."

"How do you know?"

"Because that job wasn't the opportunity of a lifetime. *You are.*"

She turned on the lamp on the side table and looked at him. What she saw in his face made her soft inside, made her feel unbearably fragile and raw. He was everything, too. Her everything.

"Please forgive me," he said.

"You can't run," she told him. "If it gets hard or you get scared. You can't just quit."

"I know. I won't." He reached out and touched her face.

"You have to trust me," she said.

"I do. I will."

He kissed her, and for Kate, it didn't feel difficult or emotionally painful or conflicting. It felt right. It felt like an irresistible force. And most of all, it felt like home.

The next day, when Kate showed up to open the shop, Jane Austen was waiting at the front door, scratching at the glass and meowing.

"Jane Austen!" Kate scooped her up and cuddled the cat into her arms. Jane Austen was purring the purr of the contented.

Jane Austen knew where she belonged, apparently.

So did Jackson.

Kate carried Jane Austen inside and went to find some kibble.

Acknowledgments

Writing a novel is never easy, for the author or for the people in that author's life. First and foremost, I would like to thank my husband, John, for his enthusiasm, for his belief in my ability to do this, and for his patience. Date nights spent hashing out the ups and downs of Kate and Jackson's love life might not have been what he had in mind, but he indulged me without fail. He also did more than his share to keep the household running while I was lost in the world of Neptune and Swept Away.

I would like to thank Gaetane Burkolter for volunteering to be my first reader. I greatly appreciate her generosity, her comments, and her encouragement.

Thank you to the Writer Unboxed community. They were always there to answer my questions, offer suggestions, and cheer my accomplishments. While the Writer Unboxed Un-Conference of 2014 wasn't directly involved in the production of this book, I think it's fair to say the novel would not exist without it. That wonderful, warm, giving group of writers gave me the inspiration I needed to keep writing at a time when I had almost given up.

I'd like to thank Cambria, California, for providing the setting for this book and for those to come in the Main Street Merchants series. I can't think of a prettier place to have a romance.

Finally, I'd like to thank my readers. In the words of John Cheever, "I can't write without a reader. It's precisely like a kiss— you can't do it alone."

About the Author

Linda Seed writes funny, sexy contemporary romances full of friendship and family. Her books are set in Cambria, a small town on Central California's rugged, breathtaking coastline. At a time when close personal relationships are increasingly hard to find, Linda aims to write a better world full of the kind of love, loyalty, and companionship that we all long for.

Join Linda Seed's Readers' Group

Visit Linda's website at www.lindaseed.com and sign up for her e-mail newsletter to get the latest information about new releases, events, giveaways, and more. When you join, you'll receive "Jacks Are Wild," a Main Street Merchants short story, at no cost. The story, featuring Kate and Jackson from *Moonstone Beach,* is only available to newsletter subscribers.

Stay in touch with Linda at the following places:

E-mail: linda@lindaseed.com
Facebook: www.facebook.com/LindaSeedAuthor/
Twitter: www.twitter.com/LindaSeedAuthor
Pinterest: www.pinterest.com/lindahseed/

Made in the USA
Columbia, SC
02 June 2021